Nine Pound Hammer

Michael Vernon Harding

Copyright © 2024 Michael Vernon Harding

No part of this book can be reproduced by any means without the written permission of the author.

All rights reserved.

ISBN# 9798327370968

Nine Pound Hammer
Written by
Michael Vernon Harding

Editors Lisa and David Webster

Publishing Assistance
By
Sue Breeding

Nine Pound Hammer

by

Michael Vernon Harding

Foreword

My father, a mining engineer, who worked on the atomic bomb in Oak Ridge, Tennessee where I was born, moved us to the coal mining town of Gary, West Virginia when I was four years old. Gary was a busy place as coal was king and in great demand because the country was recovering from the war. From Gary we moved to Lynch, Kentucky, in bloody Harlan County, where dad was Chief Mining Engineer.

Lynch was probably where the nine pound hammer was invented as it seemed like a land of giants to a young skinny sixth grader. Many of the miners were from places like Poland, Ukraine, and all the Slavic countries where the children looked twice as big as me, and their fathers were huge.

The mine owned everything and had full control over the lives of the miners. The housing was owned by the mining company, and the mining company issued its own currency called "scrip" that could only be spent in the company stores. If you lost your job, you had to move out of your house, and if you left the area your scrip didn't work anywhere else.

The mining camps were a tough place to live. I remember walking to school one morning after payday and seeing a dead man in the gutter. I told the school principal, and he said: "Not to worry it will be cleaned up before you go home today."

I got to know Mike when he set up the Flight of Discovery where we flew the route of Lewis and Clark in light aircraft and helicopters from the starting point near Louisville, Kentucky to the Pacific Ocean. It became one of the highlights of my life. I worked as an environmental engineer on a lot of mining and other environmental projects in the west.

Mike has captured the everyday life of the mining communities. His book is a great read and brings back a lot of memories for me, and it will for anyone who has worked in or around the mining industry.

John Egan MS, MPA

Acknowledgements

No one accomplishes anything in their life without the help of others. *Nine Pound Hammer* is a work of fiction, and the characters are, at best, composites of individuals that I had the privilege to work with, and learn from, during my seven years with Peabody Coal Company at the Dugger and Latta Mines in southwestern Indiana. If those people read this book, they will undoubtably seek to identify themselves or people that they knew in the narrative. But like a jigsaw puzzle, the pieces by themselves are colorfully separate; it's when they're all put together that one can see the entire picture. Still, I need to acknowledge a lot of people from then and now who contributed to the crafting of this yarn.

Primarily, my wife Gaile and our two children, Lee and Katie, who were with me during my time at the mines. Working five, then six, and eventually seven days a week, I left in the dark some mornings before the kids got up and often returned after they were in bed. I know I missed a lot of stories that I can never write. I hope that they understand that I worked for them and not for the Company.

I was employed by a great company, Peabody, the legendary coal operator that songs have been written about. It's still the best job I ever had. That's because of its people, too numerous to name, but I'm gonna try.

It starts with Joy Fitzgerald who hired me in 1979. Always supportive and encouraging, even when I left my comfortable corporate job with her to go to the mines and do the actual dirty work of learning and performing land reclamation. I remember Joy saying: "You'll be at the mercy of the Superintendent; he's God in the coalfields, and I won't be able to help you." Still, she somehow managed to get me the equipment that I needed to do my job: a new International 1086 tractor, complete with an eighteen-foot disc, a bushhog, grader blade; a mower conditioner, Brillion and Herd seeder, straw blower, and a 2-ton stake bed truck. Great tools that allowed me to *learn my job*. Her steadfast support at the Indiana Division was probably more important.

Then there's Dr. Virginia Leftwich, who helped guide not only my reclamation efforts and ideas, but she facilitated the education of all the Reclamation Managers within the company. She became a personal friend and mentor. A true coal miner's daughter and former English teacher, Ginny is the person who suggested that I write this book over thirty years ago. I hope that it meets her expectations.

There are the main players in this drama. If you worked at Peabody recognize a lot of their first names in this story, but their roles in *Hammer* don't correspond to their real jobs at the mine. Without them I would not have survived a week at my job. The farm crew included Randy Hennecke, Bob Camden, and Max Hicks, the survey crew, Harold Chaney and Marvin Goodman. The Jasonville engineering group was led by my good friend Don Wile and included Gib Tucker, Pat Tribby, and Mary Prindiville. At Dugger Mine, Andy Short oversaw the engineering group of Brian "Iggy" Hart, Dave Jobe, and a few others that with age, I find hard to remember.

And then there are the real miners, both Company and Union. They are as real to me now as my own children. I can see their faces and hear their voices, but their names, like the mine itself, have disappeared into immortality in my mind.

But one person does stand out: Superintendent, Larry Shepherd, who, by example, taught me more about dedication and responsibility than all of my other jobs before or since. That experience has served me well through the remaining forty years of my career. From pipelines in the Arctic, Russia, Australia, and West Virginia to mineral mining in New Guinea, Indonesia, and Madagascar, I have put into action what I learned at Dugger Mine, and it was not all technical.

I never understood fully the weight of responsibility that Larry had in his position as Superintendent at Sycamore Complex until

I was Field Supervisor for remediation of the Southern California Firestorm of 1993. That year there were twenty-two separate wildfires from Malibu to the Mexican border. I worked with dozens of engineers at URS Corporation, my wife's company, fifteen hydraulic seeding contractors, and hundreds of California Conservation Corps members. It didn't take long to realize how dependent I was on others to do my job and paradoxically, the weight of my accountability. I've worked on over one hundred incidents of wildfire and high-dollar litigations since then, and it doesn't get any easier.

Lastly, I would like to thank my dear friends John and Jeanette Egan, who reviewed various drafts of *Hammer,* my Editors, Lisa and David Webster, and my Agent, Sue Breeding. Without them none of my scribblings would have come to light.

Mike Harding
May 2024

For Gaile, Lee and Katie

Dark as a Dungeon

Words and music by Merle Travis

*Oh, come all you fellers so young and so fine
Seek not your fortune in the dark dreary mine
It'll form as a habit and seep in your soul
'Til the stream of your blood runs as black as the coal*

*Where it's dark as a dungeon, and damp as the dew
Where the danger is doubled, and the pleasures are few
Where the rain never falls, and the sun never shines
It's a dark as a dungeon way down in the mines*

Prologue

Old coal miners will reminisce about a time when the coal cropped out on the surface of the ground, and they picked up bucketsful without any digging. How much of the story reflects on their own experiences, and how much of it echoes stories told to them by their fathers or grandfathers cannot always be established. But regardless of the preacher's age, the words are always taken as gospel. Time has a way of circling back on itself in the coal region. Laid alongside the millions of years required to produce a line of thin black stoker, one man's life doesn't account for much, particularly if he toils in the subterranean recesses that form the dimensions of his own being.

Miners followed the pitched trace of the coal underground, shoring their passages with forests of living timber. Under the overhang of rocky millennia, they drilled the face of the coal, loaded the holes with powder, tamped, lit the slow fuse, and crawled to safety yelling, "Fire in the hole! Fire in the hole!" Every blast drove the shaft deeper. Each time the men clambered back by the light of their headlamps through the sooty, clinging air to load out their dark labor. The coal came to the surface first in buckets, then heaped on carts drawn along narrow iron rails by mules that bulged their great brown, blind eyes in the light of the portal.

Some men stayed underground to mine. Others began to remove the soil and rock from above the coal, stripping the living earth to its framework and exposing its black skeleton to the sun from which it was first formed. They ripped through the geologic detritus of ancient seas, transposing the vertical order of history, casting aside centuries of rock in brutal pursuit. The humped overburden of the steam shovel and the saw-toothed spoil of the dragline scarred and grayed the horizon, while the earth hemorrhaged iron-red water through the shattered stone.

The people of the coal are born; they work, and they die surrounded by this inverted land that they consider a monument to their lives. Each has inherited a kinship between himself and the coal, and it is the one thing they hold title to and receive a royalty from, for most do not own the land, not in the same sense that it possesses them. The rough-timbered, corduroy shale is home ground to the coal miners who hunt its dense forests, live beside blue-green spoil impoundments, and fish the deep, cold, final cut lakes. Seen through their eyes, it is not an exhausted, ravaged land; it is consecrated ground, a dominion set apart from the rest of the world by the toil and struggle of generations of coal miners.

After a night of labor, the dragline rested. The glare from its electric eyes dimmed by the morning light, a suspension of fugitive dust and cold fog shrouded the place where it crouched, revitalizing itself for the day's work ahead. From the darkened pit below came the metallic, skeletal sounds of lesser machines unlimbering their steely joints in the still morning air. At times, the muffled rhythm of their awakening was bracketed by men's voices, but the dragline squatting above kept its silence.

Already men were probing and testing the machine's weaknesses. The ground man crawled under its belly to check its electric umbilical, a three-pronged cord four inches in diameter that delivered animation. Two other miners climbed the ladder on its side, entering a whining belly to inspect the inner workings of the beast. Still another man welded a new tooth on its bench-rested bucket while a greaser checked and lubricated the slack cables and their fittings. The men moved with a familiar efficiency around the sleeping giant, their ease determined by collective years of experience.

One daring miner in grease-striped coveralls began a long ascent up the boom to adjust targets on the cross-members. As he climbed into the sun, the haze fell away below him until he finally wiped the cold sweat from his forehead, secured his safety belt, and rested at the catwalk's end, higher than the Statue of Liberty. He liked this part of his job a lot. It lasted for only a few minutes each month at the shift change, but while field engineers were setting up their transit on the bench far below and measuring the boom angle, he had what he considered to be one of the best views in the world all to himself.

Looking to the east, into the rising sun, he shaded his eyes and could almost see the White River. The courthouse of Bloomfield stood above the fog. The tops of seven church steeples were all that could be seen of Worthington, on the west bank of the river by the old iron bridge. Dugger sat on the uplands just east of the mine, above the floodplain of Busseron Creek. His eyes traced the highway as it emerged from the swamps to the west, crossed the bottomlands beneath him, and gradually wound and climbed its way out of the low mists into the town, its buildings sharp and clear in the early light. It was late Fall, and most of the leaves had fallen from the trees. The morning sun whetted the sharp angles of the old mine spoil that surrounded the entire town. The abandoned tipple lake shimmered, and like a flat stone, the growing daylight skipped across its surface.

From this height the pit seemed to lie directly beneath the boom, an open furrow ninety feet deep and twice as wide, slicing the earth for nearly a mile north to south. The climbing sun struck the western side of the pit and glazed the vertical high wall of rock that overlaid a thin, three-foot seam of undulating coal. Down at the far end of the pit, loading shovels were already bucking coal, anticipating the arrival of six one hundred twenty-ton trucks now hurtling down wide haul roads toward them.

On the bench, the ground man was pulling cable and moving junction boxes. A rainbow of water fountained from a broken coupling that connected a section of four inch hose to a sump in the pit. The rock in front of the dragline was fragmented from blasting and ready for the bucket, and the drill crew bumped down the bench over the uneven shale to begin a new pattern.

On the spoil side of the pit, to the east, dozers were already at work grinding and bullying the overburden. Earth movers – called "pans" by the miners - dropped dark gray streaks of shale on the haul road.

Turning his back to the sun, the man adjusted his thoughts from where the mine had been to where it was headed. West of the bench lay the low fields and swamps of Busseron Bottoms, continually wet and all but impenetrable, except to poachers and draglines. Swamp oak, river birch, and sycamores for miles interspersed with open water on which he saw a few migrating ducks lifting from their night's roost. Within a shot blast from the bench stood a grove of gigantic white oaks, still holding onto their brown leaves late into October, their slack-muscled branches ribboned with age. Among the low branches, the man could make out the broad tail and tufted ears of a great horned owl as it winged away from daylight into the failing darkness of the forest. *Time to move your nest*, he thought.

The man's escape to this peripheral world was ended by the drill rig's whistle blast. Making the final adjustments to the targets, he headed back down the rattling boom walkway.

I hope when I'm dead, and the ages shall roll
That my body will blacken and turn into coal
I will look from the door of my heavenly home
And pity the miner a' diggin' my bones

Where it's dark as a dungeon, and damp as the dew
Where the dangers are doubled, and the pleasures are few
Where the rain never falls, and the sun never shines
It's dark as a dungeon way down in the mines

Chapter One

The Dream of the Miner's Child
Traditional

A miner was leavin' his home for his work,
When he heard his little child scream,
He went to the side of his little girl's bed,
"Daddy, I had an awful dream!

Daddy, don't go to the mine today,
Dreams can so often come true,
Daddy, dear Daddy, Oh, don't go away,
I never could live without you."

"Your daddy was up before the crack of dawn when he worked in the mines," Rose Johnson said as she watched her daughter bustling around the kitchen, trying to get ready for work and prepare the older woman's breakfast at the same time. "My land, child, that coffee done yet?"

Katie stopped pressing the sleeve of her blouse and swept across the kitchen to the stove where the water had just started to boil. Measuring out the instant coffee into her mother's favorite cup, she poured the hot water, stirred, then set the cup on the table in front of Ruth, flipping the spoon into the sink on her way back to the ironing board.

Folding her hands across her lap, Rose looked at the cup. "Your daddy and the boys liked their coffee *strong*," she said, with emphasis. "Bacon and eggs every mornin', liked 'em both crispy. Biscuits 'n gravy on Sundays, put them in a pie plate, they would, and take 'em down the road when they went huntin'. Never seen a man able to drive and eat like your daddy. Peppered the hell out of that gravy, too."

Katie noticed a spot on the front of her blouse. Throwing it back with the dirty clothes, she rummaged through the laundry basket for a clean one to iron.

"Any sugar in this house?" Rose asked.

Katie went to the cabinet and took down the sugar bowl, pulled a new spoon from the drawer, placed them both in front of her mother, and returned to look for a clean blouse. *Wanted to wear this blue one anyway*, she thought, glancing up at the clock while beginning to iron.

She finished the blouse and rushed to the bathroom, buttoning on the way; she finished her makeup in the mirror and had just begun to brush out her long, auburn hair when she heard something fall, she ran into the kitchen to find her mother still sitting in her bathrobe staring at a widening coffee spill that spread across the yellow Formica tabletop and was dripping onto the floor. Katie grabbed a wet washcloth from the sink and began to clean up the mess.

With her hands folded in her lap, Rose looked at the sugar bowl, saw the steam rising from her coffee, then turned her head slightly to gaze out the window.

"I remember that mornin'. Had to batch for themselves, they did. Lordy, couldn't get out of bed. Fever knocked me weak as a calf." Her heavy eyes descended to the floor where Katie mopped up the last of the coffee. "I felt terrible sick. Felt a lot worse since."

"Mama, you want some toast?" Without waiting for a response, Katie put two pieces of white bread in the toaster and pushed down the lever.

Katie was barely eight years old when the eleven men were killed at the old Daggett Number Three underground. Methane gas, the families were told. Her father and oldest brother Billy were at the coal face loading shot when the narrow world surrounding them exploded. Part of the roof collapsed, killing all but four men who managed to be pulled to safety. The concentration of gas and the danger of new explosions kept rescuers from going back down into the shaft. Then - after five days and nights of vigil at the mine portal - the townsfolk watched as company engineers sealed the opening, entombing the ten missing men.

One of the four men pulled out was her brother Danny, younger of the two Johnson boys. He and an equally young Ernie Milts were bringing down the men's dinner buckets when the concussive wind rush knocked them off their feet. The mine rescue team found them unconscious. Conner Owen was saved by the frame of his roof bolter, which deflected the rock fall. He had crawled through the dust and darkness to where Ezra Jeffries lay half covered with rock beside his machine, called a continuous miner. Ezra's hardhat was on the ground beside him, its pitiful beam flickering on a wall of rock that compressed the end of his machine and sealed the fates of the men on the other side. By the time the rescuers got to them, Conner had managed to clear most of the rocks that covered Ezra. As the men hurriedly stretchered Ezra to the surface, the gas was already beginning to filter up from the lower rooms. Conner walked out of the shaft and retired from mining the same day.

Being the furthest away from the blast, the boys were not severely injured. Danny was sent home from the hospital in Terre Haute with a broken leg. Ernie was kept under observation for a mild concussion and stayed at the hospital to look after Ezra, who had always looked after him.

Ezra Jeffries died a few days later from his injuries. He was buried in the little cemetery south of the mine. Practically the whole town attended, including the widows and orphans of the men in Number Three. His tombstone was the cutting bar from an ancient continuous miner some of the men had retrieved from a shed full of old motors and other mining equipment that had been scrapped by the company. They cut three feet off the end of it - like you would the bill of a sawfish - and stood it upright, teeth and all, in the same ground Ezra Jeffries mined for forty years of his life.

Like Conner Owen, Danny never went back into the coal. Instead, he joined the service and got as far away as he could. Even now he was in Southeast Asia doing things he couldn't talk about in his letters home. Some years he made it back for Christmas. Sometimes, he would just show up in the kitchen and stay for a few days. Always, there was a present in the mail on Katie's birthday. When she turned twenty-one a few years back, the gift was a dozen yellow roses. Katie had a few memories of her father and oldest brother, Roger. They were mostly the smells and sounds of early mornings, shadow voices in her room, half-lit and half coal dust, murmuring kisses on her forehead while she slept. She loved the memory of Daddy and Billy, but she adored Danny.

"Who you goin' with to the homecomin'?" Rose asked. "They put me and Dolores Cooper in charge of the refreshments for the alumni dance. I'd like to see my girl on the arm of some good lookin' man this year instead of one of her cousins."

Katie buttered the toast and set it on a plate in front of her mother and turned to the refrigerator to get a jar of peach preserves.

"Hell, Mama, everybody in this town's practically kin. It'd be hard to find somebody not related."

"You stop that cussin' girl! Besides, Larry Miller ain't no relation; Larry Miller's a catch. It don't hurt none that his old man's superintendent, neither. Don't you like workin' for old Dutch?"

"What's that mean? That I should date Larry just because his father's my boss?" *God*, she thought, *I have enough trouble with people thinking that's the way I got my office job*. She was determined not to demonstrate in public what a lot of people at the mine thought went on in private. Besides, she detested Larry and thought he was a slob. Dutch was a good boss, perhaps a little overprotective of her, but she attributed that to the fact that he had known her father and maintained a territorial attitude, like most superintendents.

"Your daddy and I got hitched when I was a little more than half your age. You got to be thinkin' about getting married, havin' babies, settlin' down in a place of yer own!"

The one thing I'm thinking about right now, Katie sighed to herself, *is to get out of this town and away from the mines, like Danny*. She kissed her mother's offered cheek and turned for the door.

"What? And leave you here all by yourself, Mama?" she quipped, grabbing her hard hat and jacket from the hall tree as she opened the back door.

"I'd just like some grandbabies before I'm too old to see 'em!"

"Got to go!" Katie answered, gently pulling the door shut.

Chapter Two

Nine Pound Hammer
Words and Music by Merle Travis

*Oh, a nine-pound hammer,
Is a little too heavy,
For my size, buddy, for my size,
So, roll on, buddy,
Roll a load of coal,
How can I roll, when the wheels won't go?*

By five-thirty that morning he had packed the Bronco with everything that meant anything to him. He locked the front door of his parents' house and drove up Water Street, along the bluff and through the old section of Newburgh, Indiana until the street joined the river road just east of town. The low angle of the rising sun was somewhere between the truck's dash and the overhead visor, causing him to squint in the early light. *Pretty soon I'll head up north through Boonville,* he thought, *and the sun will be on my right shoulder and higher up in the sky. Hope the company's rental house is on the east side of the mine. I'd just as soon drive to and from work with the sun at my back.*

Donald Rodgers did like the consequence of an easterly bearing this morning, an open lane opposite the main flow of traffic that headed west. Most of the rolling stock from Warrick County was tracking into Evansville for the start of another week. He had decided to take the back roads up to his new job, partly to get a feel for the country, and because he wanted to see what the new Ford Bronco could do out of the range of highway radar. Now he glanced up periodically at the instructions for shifting that were glued on the back side of the visor, lifting himself slightly off the seat to avoid the glare from the clean, white hood. Loaded with everything he owned, the truck still smelled new. Pressing his stiff new steel-toed boot to the floor, he accelerated into the sun.

Above the Newburgh Locks, the Ohio River danced in the early morning sun. Barges were anchored in the wide water, great rust-covered islands which appeared to flutter on the river's sparkle. Each waited its turn to pass through the narrow, concrete turnstile of the lock that bottlenecked passage downriver. Lashed together in the swift water below the lock and dam, rafts of empty barges floated high and hollow, their bows pointed into the bank, the suppressed power of the tugboat engines rumbling against the current. Irregularly, the giant gates of the lock would open and disgorge a barge into the downstream channel. Its deckhands worked the forward section of the vessels, coiling line around the cleats before scrambling back down to the tug. Their movements along the deck seemed both deliberate and indifferent when compared to that of their iron iceberg, now caught in the current's sway and fighting to maintain steerage.

Across the water on the Kentucky side, bobbed flat-bottomed boats straining against the long ropes which fastened them to sycamore roots at the forest edge. Through the yellowed trees drifted the campfire smoke of a few fishermen who ran trotlines beneath the low dam of the locks. The imprint of boots up and down the steep, muddy bank indicated their progress, ferrying a daily catch of catfish, carp, and drum from boats to their trucks and eventually into town.

Don approached the signal at the river road's intersection with Highway 61, turning left just before the Yankeetown Docks, heading north through the bottoms of the Little Pigeon River.

On both sides of the road, farmers were out servicing their equipment, waiting for the dew to burn off the fields before harvesting the remainder of their corn. The Bronco paused at a railroad crossing as a coal train rhythmically clacked its way toward Yankeetown and a waiting barge.

North of Boonville, he followed the winding road through the most extensive strip-mined area of the state. On a map, there were no towns shown within the perimeter marked by Elberfield, Lynnville, Folsomville, and Boonville where, for more than half a century, companies had chased the coal deeper and deeper underground. The surface scars created by extinct draglines filed by Don's window in unending exactness, and the gray outline of irregular shovel spoil bulged through the dense forests of pine. Hillocks of slag and reddened shale rose like Indian mounds from the middle of cornfields, tombstoning ancient underground mines while, from subterranean ruptures, the earth bled an iron-stained extract.

Spurgeon, Coe, Winslow, to Petersburg, and all along the way, there was evidence of other violent, though smaller disturbances. Coal so close to the surface that any backhoe or dozer operator could strip back the soil to expose the black soul beneath. Bicknell, Edwardsport, and Don stopped in Westphalia. Spotted among the pines and spoil were the rusting hulks of antique engines and the hollow-eyed ruins of abandoned mine buildings, surrounded by the slurried black sweat of their exertions. The surface residue from energy extraction remains long after the light that burned from its output.

Don took the curve at Bucktown a little too fast and skirted the shoulder for some distance before being able to get back on to the elevated pavement. He turned onto the blacktop west of town, and now he was stair-stepping down from the uplands on a ribbon of asphalt, hopping one-lane bridges that arched narrow, brick-red creeks. He cranked down his window to the sound of locusts in the roadside weeds, dry reverberations that undulated above the low whine of his new lug tires on the pocked pavement. Rising beyond the tassels of unpicked corn to his right was a line of long black gob piles and the remains of an old tipple.

A sign on the roadside indicated that Linton was only ten miles ahead. Don turned left at the first stoplight in town, saw the sign for Daggett Mine, and drove westward.

Chapter Three

Wheel Hoss
From *The Hoss* by James Whitcomb Riley

The hoss he is a splendid beast:
    He is man's friend, as heaven designed,
And, search the world from west to east,
    No honester you'll ever find!
The hoss is strong, and knows his stren'th,-
    You hitch him up a time 'er two
And lash him, and he'll go his len'th
    And kick the dashboard out fer you!
But treat him allus good and kind,
    And never strike him with a stick,
Ner aggervate him and you'll find
    He'll never do a hostile trick.
Each hoss has his appointed place, -
    The heavy hoss should plow the soil; -
The blooded racer he must race,
    And win big wages fer his toil.
I love my God the first of all,
    Then Him that perished on the cross,
And next my wife, - and then I fall
    Down on my knees and love the hoss.

It must have gotten cold last night, Ray thought, as he turned the thermostat to eighty and listened for the blower to kick in; *this kitchen's the coldest place in the house early in the morning.* He recollected how, when he was a child, his mother would be in the kitchen before light, getting breakfast for the old man, fixing his dinner bucket while the fire in the coal stove gathered momentum and the coffee boiled. Her kitchen was warm; it was the early morning run to the outhouse that was cold. *Now, there's a definite advantage to modern living, he considered – indoor plumbing and warm toilet seats. Better living through science.*

Ray Kelso's eyeglasses steamed up as he rinsed out the coffeepot in the sink before filling it with cold water. *Should've figured that it might get cold last night,* he thought, *should've turned the furnace on.* Late October in Indiana is not very predictable. Peering over the tops of his glasses, he poured the water into the coffee maker and flipped the switch.

Leaning on the counter, he cleaned his glasses on his work shirt and looked out of the kitchen window, watching the frost on the grass melt to dew in the early sun except in places where long tree shadows from the woods held back the morning. The sun's low angle, filtering through the poplar and sycamore trees, gave the woods a warm, yellowish cast. Kindling maple leaves covered the ground beneath the trees, their orange iridescence blurring the focus of his eyes.

Out of the corner of his mind, he heard a hiss and knew the coffee was done. He took half a cup, then filled the long stainless-steel thermos. From a roll of waxed paper, he tore off two squares. Sprinkling a little salt and pepper into the middle of one, he neatly folded it and placed it beside the two hard-boiled eggs he had retrieved from the refrigerator, wrapping everything up in the second piece of paper. Two cold chicken legs and a banana later, the big aluminum lunch box was packed. He worked the cup end of the thermos through the hand-cut hole in the side of the lunch box lid and snapped the whole thing shut before he remembered the cupcakes. Picking up a half-cold cup of coffee, he went back to the window.

"Yer up awful early this mornin'. Fed the dogs yet?" Nancy asked through the bobby pins between her teeth. "Gonna have to get some straw for them dogs' boxes. Got pretty cold last night."

"No, just getting ready to," Ray replied, and without looking, knew that his wife was busy compacting her hair to fit up underneath her hard hat. "I'll see if I can get some straw off the farm crew. They're good for a couple of bales. Tolerable frost to drop persimmons, but not enough to kill a sick rabbit. We should load up on some twelve gauge, though."

Putting on his coat, he went out the back door to feed the beagles, already straining their chains in anticipation. When he got back inside the house, his wife had made another pot of coffee and was at the kitchen table with last night's paper.

"There's a sale on twelve-gauge shells at K-Mart. Better get some 'fore the weekend."

"Good idea," he said, as he emptied his old coffee into the sink and poured a new cup. He looked first at the clock then out the window. "The boys are a little late this morning, aren't they?"

"Safety meetin' today, too," Nancy sighed. "Learnin' about some revolutionary way to improve the cast blast from the company experts. I reckon everybody's lookin' forward to it. New shot, new patterns, the whole bit. Seen some film; man! They can launch some serious rock. Fills in the pit; supposed to save a lot of dragline time."

He'd already heard the mine superintendent and the pit boss talking about the procedure down in the supply room – angled drilling, differential shot loads, critical timing. Nancy was a driller's helper and a good one at that. Most of the miners called her Tommie, a name derived from her maiden name of Thompson. She worked with Ernie Milts and Me Evert who were two of the most experienced miners in the local, but he still worried. The doubts always came each morning just before the boys' old pickup rattled up the gravel road and into the drive. There were no small accidents when it came to strip mining.

He'd known Ernie Milts since they went to high school together. Ernie was a well-read, quiet traveler who had slipped through school relatively unnoticed in four years. Ernie had even avoided participation in sports, quite an accomplishment when you figured that a school with a total enrollment of just over one hundred students needed to field almost every male, athletic or not, in order to fill the team rosters. Ernie was big, but he was stubborn. No doubt he was smart enough to go on to college, but in the boom time that followed graduation he went to the mines and had been there ever since, twenty years and counting.

Me's real name was Maxwell Evert. At first glance, most people figured that he couldn't weigh ninety pounds dripping wet, and they were right. If they assumed that "Me" stood for his initials, M.E., they were wrong.

He had gotten his nickname after attaching himself to Ernie like a tick. For some reason, Ernie didn't seem to mind, and the two spent all their waking hours together – drilling, blasting, fishing, hunting, chewing, or spitting. Before dinner, Ernie would put a plug of Redman in one cheek, Union Workman in the other, a dip of Skoal in the bulge of his lower lip, and settle down to a lunch that always varied in composition but always included an apple at the end. Me, toothless, but in his best imitation of Ernie's style, had to settle for just the Skoal and two fried egg sandwiches, from which he removed and threw away the crusts. The same thing every day.

And no one ever saw Ernie without Me or Me without Ernie. Asked what they had been doing, the reply was always, "Well, me and Ernie went fishin'," or "me and Ernie are gonna fry us up some rabbit!" or, "Me and Ernie think it's gonna up 'n rain." That's how Me got his name. Just how old the old man was, nobody knew exactly, and anyone who would know was probably already dead.

Ray was sipping his coffee by the sink when he saw the dust plume above the corn as Ernie's GMC skirted the bottoms before turning up the gravel road and into the driveway.

"There they come," Nancy said, looking out the window past his shoulder. "Is my dinner ready?"

"All set. Dead chicken."

"Did you remember the cupcakes?"

"You bet."

"Frozen?"

"Of course."

"You're a sweetie!" She smiled, kissing him on his cheek before heading out the back door.

"Be careful and keep your hands to yourself," he laughed after her.

"Oh, Ray," she said, her shout punctuated by the slam of the outer screen door.

Ray waved through the window to Ernie, who returned the salute with half an apple core already in his left hand. *It was fortunate that Me is so thin*, he thought, as he watched Karen bounce up on the seat and slam the truck door.

"Me and Ernie saw a bunch a deer on the bottom road, Tommie!"

"Where 'bouts, Me?"

"In the field by the 'arn bridge."

"How many?"

"I saw six, Ernie says they's more. Can't see as sharp as ol' Ernie, picked 'em right out of the woods, he did. Reckon me and Ernie can hunt down there? You and Ray ain't huntin' down there, are you Tommie?"

"No, I don't think so, but I'll ask Ray. Mornin' Ernie."

"Mornin', Tommie."

Ray saw the gravel fly and heard the stones hit the mailbox as the truck backed out of the drive and accelerated down the road. For a few moments, Ray's heart began to race, and he felt a slight dizziness as cold drops of sweat beaded up on his forehead. Turning on the kitchen faucet, he splashed some water on his face, then patted himself dry with a kitchen towel. *What in the hell was that? Too much coffee*, he thought. *I've got to start cutting back or switch to decaf.*

Ernie's truck disappeared beyond the dust cloud that formed behind it. At that moment, Ray was overwhelmed with a dark anxiety that squeezed his chest, then slowly subsided, bruising his thoughts with a feeling of impending sadness. Turning away from the window, he set about assembling his own lunch.

Chapter Four

Through the Looking Glass
Lewis Carroll

*Come, harken then, ere voice of dread,
With bitter tidings laden,
Shall summon to unwelcome bed
A melancholy maiden!
We are but older children, dear,
Who fret to find our bedtime near.*

"Ain't no way they can lose. Not by twenty points."

"Says right here they're due for a twenty-point upset, Bobby."

"Ain't no way, I tell you. Besides, Dugger don't lose no homecomin' game," Bobby replied. "No way," he muttered and went back to mopping the floor of his mother's restaurant.

John half enjoyed seeing Bobby get worked up over next Saturday's homecoming basketball game between Dugger and Linton. It was too easy to get him riled, though. Basketball was the one thing Bobby still got excited about.

John and Roger had made their usual morning stop at Cooper's Gas, Grocery, and Cafe. It was a little after seven-thirty and the early morning crowd of miners had already left through the side door. It was quiet now, except for the shrill spooling of a cooler fan over in the grocery. At their table by the front window, John folded the paper and leaned his chair back, slowly nursing his coffee. Roger watched the road through the reverse-paint of the weekly specials on the front window and contemplated the intermittent four-wheel drive truck traffic. Beneath his Beech-Nut hat, with his dark hair and a heavy beard, Roger's face was emotionless; only his eyes seemed to let in the light.

Both men had been laid off a few months back when the third shift was reduced, and now they showed up at the corner store every morning, before the first shift passed through on its way to the mine. At first, they hoped to get information about when everyone would be called back to work; later on, it just got to be a habit. The front counter was as far as most of the miners would come into the restaurant, stopping only long enough to buy some chew or a pack of cigarettes. The sympathetic words which followed the layoffs ended after a few days. In the drought which followed, only an occasional nod of a hardhat acknowledged the men's attendance at the front table. Owing to lack of time or because each was afraid to look his own future in the eye, those still working avoided the gaze of the two bearded ghosts by the window. Out of respect for the living, the two men kept their own company.

John and Roger's conversations were usually one-sided and pertained to everything other than their present state of leisure. John would read the headlines from a paper someone had left on a table, interpreting the day's news for Roger. Sometimes he quoted a few lines verbatim for emphasis if he agreed with a particular point. Occasionally, John would dust off an old hunting or fishing story. With each retelling the deer became larger, or the fish got longer. Roger stared out of the windows and watched the days get shorter, nodding without changing his gaze. Only Bobby, working his mop over the black and white tile floor, showed an interest and seemed to be genuinely happy to have company.

John picked up his paper and unfolded it again. "They claim there's oil shale covering the whole southern third of the state. Says here, 'The potential size of the field has yet to be determined, but state officials were quick to admit that development of this new source of energy would provide a boost to the state's sagging economy and *provide needed jobs for most of the region's currently unemployed coal miners!*' John read that last line with emphasis, "How about that, Roger? Could mean some boom times, huh?"

"I 'magine," Roger mumbled.

Bobby Cooper had returned and was looking over John's shoulder. "Maybe it's their record," Bobby said. "The Bulldogs, I mean. Linton has a better record than Dugger; that's why they're favored. Hell, Linton don't play nobody, though. They don't play Sullivan; they don't play Terre Haute. Besides, it's homecoming." He borrowed on Roger's view out the window then droned in his most rhythmic and solemn voice: "When the goin' get tough, the tough gets goin'."

John looked over his shoulder at the tall man-boy leaning on the mop. *Jesus,* he thought, *I could use a decent conversation partner now and then.*

Bobby began to relive a crisp, October night six years before. "Remember that time we was twenty points underdogs back in Seventy-two? We was twenty-five down at the half, and we still come back and beat 'em. You remember, Roger, don't you?"

"I 'magine," Roger said.

John remembered. That's why he had concocted his story to Bobby, about the paper claiming Dugger would lose by twenty points. He knew that the paper allowed that Dugger would win by at least ten points. And he was there in 1972 when Bobby Cooper brought the Union Bulldogs back from twenty-five points down at the half. Most of the crowd left the game at halftime to get a start on the homecoming dance in the old gym. At the end of the third quarter, when word spread across the parking lot that the lead had been cut to ten points, everyone at the party surged back through the double doors and massed along the out-of-bounds line at the Union end of the court. John was part of the crowd that saw the big center drag his team into overtime, and he was knocked to the floor by the stampede when Bobby hit a turn-around jumper at the buzzer to beat Linton.

Dugger High School never won another game that year, but that night, with thirty-five points and a bushel basket full of future, Bobby Cooper was elevated to local legend and a stature eighteen-year-old boys in Indiana daydream about in history class. And that's where the dream would begin and end. For although Bobby's season was extraordinary, while he was named second team All-State, and every high school-aged girl in Dugger wanted him, no college would accept him. Everyone in town had assumed that he would make his way in the world with his bulk, not his brain, so Bobby's academic requirements had been foreshortened to accommodate his athletic growth. Bobby wasn't dumb, but he had gone unchallenged in certain areas. He could read a scoreboard; he just couldn't read the paper. It was just as well, John thought. Bobby got one of the cheerleaders pregnant his senior year. Patty dropped out of school; she and Bobby got married; and they moved into the apartment over the store. The baby was born nine months to the day after homecoming.

"Hey, easy money," Bobby said, as the front door opened, tickling the cowbell suspended above the jamb. "What's goin' on?"

"Not much, child labor," Larry Miller replied, walking across the wooden floor to pull a carton of Marlboros down from behind the cash register. "Where's your momma?"

"In the back, doin' the breakfast dishes."

Larry came into the restaurant and bumped a chair up beside Roger, still staring out of the window. "Howdy, boys, how's the coffee?"

Thank God, sighed John, *someone with conversational skills*.

"Tastes like crap," replied John. "Bobby, get Larry a cup, will you?"

"Sure thing, Mr. Hicks, comin' right up."

"Hey, Roger," Larry said, and grinned, "been gettin' any?"

Roger turned toward his tormentor, his smile coming as slow as his words. "You're one to talk. Ain't you got Katie to go to the homecomin' dance with you yet?"

"Hell, no, and don't expect it, neither. Miss Katherine Johnson don't go with just anybody," he smirked, shaking his head. "I'm beginnin' to wonder about that girl. You don't reckon she's, you know, funny or somethin', do you?"

"What do you mean?" John asked.

"Hell, she never goes out with anyone, never has."

"That's because you run 'em off," John said, laughing.

"Just because I dunked that Tucker guy don't mean I run everybody off. Hell, he wasn't even from around here."

"That's my point, man," replied John. "Nobody in their right mind, particularly if he lives in Sullivan County, is going to mess with you, let alone her. Everybody knows you got your eye on her. She might as well take up vows and be a nun."

"She'd be a good nun," Bobby said, setting a cup in front of Larry and pouring in the coffee. "She played a nun in the school musical. I remember. She was good."

"That was *Sound of Music,* and she ain't even Catholic, dammit," Roger said.

"She probably goes out," John said, "just not around here. Drives up to Terre Haute twice a week for some evening classes. I'll bet she meets somebody up there."

Larry slowly stirred his coffee, his eyes narrowing as his face reddened. He graduated from Union High School with Roger and John back in 1968. Larry was captain and quarterback of the football team and expected a certain amount of stroking, but it was not a good idea to get him angry, even if you were one of his best friends.

John decided it was time to change the subject. "Any word on when they'll add the third shift?"

"Maybe I should just take me some night classes," Larry said.

"Why would you want to do that, anyway?" said John, realizing that Larry had ignored a subject that for him and Roger was a very important question of livelihood. Larry always dangled opportunity in front of them, then pulled it back, just to keep them off-balance and needy. John felt the heat begin to burn his ears, but he backed it down and as usual, humbled his thoughts into words Larry would want to hear: "She ain't going nowhere for awhile. As long as her old lady's around, she'll stay put."

There was a studied silence while everyone sipped his coffee and contemplated John's assessment. *Once again,* John thought, *an astute observation turned to good use. Now let's talk about getting back to work.*

"Lucky for you old Danny ran off to the service," Roger said.

"Dammit," John sighed.

"What the hell do you mean? Think she's queer for her brother, or something?" Larry said and scowled.

Roger took a deep breath. "No, but if he were around, she'd probably be off to college somewhere, and there'd go your chances. Danny wouldn't put up with you, neither. He always could whip you."

The room got quiet except for the cooler fan. Roger returned to his window watching. He was one of the few people who could talk tough to Larry Miller. The words angered, but Larry let the annoyance settle.

"Yeah, we'll I'd 'a been your daddy if a dog hadn't beat me over the fence," Larry laughed as he stood up and slapped the bill of Roger's hat down to his nose.

"Kiss my ass," Roger replied, repositioning his hat.

"Y'all are just pissed because you'd like to spark her," Larry said and chuckled.

"Too young for us," replied John. "We ain't no cradle robbers."

"Hell, you're the same age as me," Larry stopped mid-sentence as he realized what John had said. He pushed his chair back away from the table and stood up. "I'd best not catch you sniffin' around."

"Don't need to fret about us none," said John. "Headin' out?"

"Yeah, new man in from corporate. Got a meetin' with the Dutchman on new company policy," Larry said, picking up his carton of cigarettes from the counter. Tell your momma to put this and the boys' coffee on my bill, okay, Bobby?"

"Yes, sir, Mr. Miller," Bobby said.

"See you boys at the game Saturday?" Larry asked.

"Of course," replied John.

"Goin' to the dance, Roger?" Larry asked.

"I 'magine."

"Well, then, I'll see you around," Larry said through the tinkling of the bell as he slammed the door shut.

"Thanks for the coffee," John yelled after him.

The outside bell rang as someone pulled up to the pumps for gas.

"Boy, if you don't get out there and get that man his gas, I'll snatch you bald-headed," Dolores Cooper said as she ambled to the counter from the kitchen, drying her hands on a dish towel.

Bobby propped the mop against the window and headed out the door to where the white Ford Bronco waited by the pumps, its driver still inside, checking a road map.

"What can I do fer ya?"

"Fill 'er up, unleaded," the driver said as he climbed out. "You got coffee inside?"

"Restaurant on your right, restrooms on your left."

"Thanks," the man said.

Roger and John watched the stranger dodge the oily puddles in the concrete and scrape his new boots on the rubber mat before bumping across the floor to the counter.

"Can I get a cup of coffee, ma'am?" Don Rogers asked Dolores.

"Sit yourself down right over there, and I'll bring you one and a menu," she replied with a smile.

Don chose a table by the corner window, nodding to John and Roger as he passed.

"That must be the new Company man," said John, as Dolores poured the stranger's coffee and handed him a paper menu.

"I 'magine."

Dolores pointed out the breakfast specials. Then she shuffled over to their table to give the man time to look over the menu.

"Nice-looking fellow. You boys gonna do any work today or just sit around here drinkin' coffee?" she asked as she filled their cups.

"As a matter of fact," replied John, "we're presently in the firewood business. Larry had the dozers push over some fence rows for us to cut up. You wouldn't be needing any wood, now would you, Mrs. Cooper?"

"Let me see. Is it seasoned and split?"

"Been down all summer. We'll split it for you," John said.

"What kind of wood?"

"Ash, oak with some locust thrown in."

"We won't split the locust," Roger said. "Ain't very big around, anyway."

"How much a load?"

"For you, here today, and today only, fifty bucks a truckload," John replied.

"Forty bucks, delivered and stacked, and I'll take three out back by the shed and deliver two more to the Bedwell's, and put it on their porch," she said.

"Deal," John said.

"Now, drink yer coffee and get to work," she said with a laugh.

"Drives a hard bargain, she does," Roger said.

"I 'magine," John said.

Dolores sidled over to Don's table and eased into a chair. She took out a damp towel from her apron pocket and wiped off the tabletop before setting the coffeepot down. *Oh, what a handsome boy*, she said to herself. *And well kept, too. I wonder if his wife ironed that shirt or creased them pants?*

"Let me get you a clean menu," Dolores said, pulling the paper menu away from Don's grasp. A quick glance verified the absence of a ring on his left hand. *Oh ho*, she thought, *he ain't hitched, neither. His momma must take good care of him.* She took a laminated menu from her apron and replaced it carefully in the young man's hands. "That there's the full menu," she said, slightly flushed.

Don glanced up and smiled at her, then seriously considered the menu choices.

"See anything you like?" Dolores asked.

"What would you recommend?"

"The biscuits and gravy are pretty good, especially on Mondays which is when the cook bakes the biscuits."

"And you're the cook."

"The one and only. My name's Dolores Cooper. I own the place."

"Pleased to meet you, ma'am. My name's Donald Rodgers. I think I'll have the biscuits and gravy."

"Good choice if I do say so myself. Bobby!" Dolores yelled at her son as he came through the screen door from pumping Don's gas. "Get Mr. Rodgers here a plate of biscuits with lots of gravy, and while yer at it, bring me a clean cup for my coffee." Then as an afterthought she added: "And wash yer hands before ya do."

"That boy," she confided to Don. "He'd lose his head if it weren't screwed on." She shot a glance toward John and Roger. "What're you two gawkin' at? Get outa here an' get me some wood."

The two men got up from their table and silently but quickly left the café, the slam of the screen door punctuating their dismissal.

"They's good boys. Just a little hard up on their luck here recently."

"They work at the mine?" Don asked.

"Not for a few months now. They been laid off for a while."

Bobby brought in Don's breakfast and set it in the middle of the table along with his mother's empty coffee cup then walked back to the kitchen. Don began to dust the gravy with a heavy dose of pepper but stopped abruptly.

"Sorry, ma'am. Guess I should've given it a taste before seasoning it, huh?"

Dolores laughed, and her eyes softened.

"Don't you pay it no never mind, son. You'll probably find it needs a little salt, too." She watched him begin to eat, then added: "I prefer a man that likes a little spice in his life." *Oh my god*, she thought. *Am I flirting with this boy?* She checked Don's expression, but his eyes were on the plate of gravy as he tried to cut up the thick biscuits with his fork. Thankfully, he hadn't noticed. *My, my! He is a handsome boy,* she sighed. *I'd put him about thirty years old.*

"So, you must be that new company man."

"What do you mean?" Don asked, swallowing a mouthful of food before he was ready. It lumped in his throat, and he swigged some coffee to wash it down.

"We heard there was somebody from the corporate office comin' up to cause some problems. That you?"

Don put down his fork and took a sip of coffee. "You're pretty direct, aren't you, Mrs. Cooper," he said.

"Oh, don't mind me," Dolores said, leaning back in her chair and crossing her arms. "Ask anyone, it's just the way I am; I don't mean anything by it, just a mite curious."

"I'm not here to cause any problems. I just have a job to do."

"And what would that be?"

"The State of Indiana is requiring that all the coal operators get new permits to mine. I'm here to help that process along."

"Why do we need permits to do what we been doin' all our lives?"

"It's a new law. I didn't write it, but it's my job to make sure Daggett Number 7 meets the new regulations. I think that's good for everybody."

"How you figure that?"

"No permit, no mine," Don replied. "It's as simple as that."

"So, yer actually here to help us? That would be a first, most people ain't gonna believe that."

Don had been told that there could be some resistance, perhaps even outright hostility to his presence at the mine. *I wonder what they're saying about me already,* he thought. *This lady seems nice enough, but I'll bet everyone won't be as direct or as nice.*

"There seems to be a lot of speculation around, huh?"

"Let's just say they were expecting someone from outside. You ain't exactly the Second Coming."

"Now, I'm curious. What exactly is the local gossip?"

Dolores looked around her empty store and café, uncrossed her arms and smoothed out the apron in her lap.

"Well, you know these towns are generally divided in opinion anyway. If you live around here, you're either with the union or yer company. Me, I'm union, so was my father and his father and my late husband, rest their souls. Times are changin' though. Some families got both company and union folks in 'em. Most company men that live around here started out union."

"Is that considered disloyal?" Don asked. "Taking a company job, I mean."

"You do what ya have to do to survive. Take you, for instance. People's just curious, waitin' to see what yer up to. Because yer company, people associate you with the rumors about mine closures. Some people figured you were one of them accountants sent here to write us up and put us out of business."

"But I'm not."

"What do you do - exactly, I mean?"

"I'm a little ashamed to say it, 'cause it doesn't seem much like work to some people, especially miners, but nowadays what I do is necessary in order to keep mining coal in this state." *Jeez,* Don thought, *I hope that doesn't appear to be bragging. I didn't mean it to sound so crucial.*

Dolores laughed. "Go on. If you can make a livin' at something that don't break your back, I say good fer you."

"Well, to get the permits to mine, we – and I mean the miners and the company – have to know what's out in front of the mine so we can put it back pretty much the same way after we finish mining. A sort of inventory of things, I guess you'd say."

"You one of them tree huggers?"

Why is it, he wondered, *that if you show an interest in the environment, it gets you immediately branded as an extremist? Those kinds of activists actually piss me off.*

"Nope," Don laughed. "What I do is identify the soils, plants, and animals that exist in an area prior to mining so that when we start to reclaim the land, we can aim toward a future target that resembles what was there before it was mined. Where there are woods now, we'll plant trees later; where there are corn fields, we'll put them back, too."

"That don't sound so bad."

"It just makes sense, and here's the real good part. Instead of just piling up the spoil, it's gonna have to be graded down, then covered with topsoil. That's gonna take a lot of work, so some people that are idle right now – like those two guys who were in here earlier - are probably gonna be back at the mine in the future."

Dolores considered Don's words for a few minutes while he finished off the biscuits and gravy. She refilled his coffee cup, then her own. *If what he said was true,* she thought, *then this good-looking young man isn't half the demon everyone in town is making him out to be.*

"So, how'd you get in the minin' business."

"I like working outdoors. I've always had an interest in environmental things."

"Where you from, anyway?"

"Newburgh, right down on the Ohio River, near Evansville."

"What does your momma think about you goin' to work in the mines?"

Don hesitated. "My parents are both gone," he said. "Killed in a car accident when I was in high school."

"I'm so sorry."

"My brother's gone, too," Don offered. "Just two months ago."

"Sweet Jesus," Dolores said, reaching out to touch Don's forearm. "If you don't mind me askin', you got any kin back in Newburgh?"

"No, just our house on Water Street."

"Where are you livin' now?"

"I'm supposed to pick up some keys today for a little house the company owns south of the mine." Don looked at his watch. "I'd better get going. I'm not late, but you probably know the mine superintendent, Mr. Miller. I think the earlier I show up, the better."

"Don't you worry about ol' Dutch," Dolores laughed. "He's tough, but fair-minded. His son Larry, now that's another subject."

"It was a pleasure meeting you Mrs. Cooper," Don said as he stood to leave, offering a handshake. "I'll probably be taking my meals here for a while, that's if you don't mind."

Dolores clasped his hand with both of hers. Then, inexplicably, she kissed him on the cheek. Don blushed and reached for his wallet.

"Shush!" Dolores scolded. "First batch is on the house. You just watch out for yourself at the mine for a while, Mr. Donald Rodgers. And don't you worry 'bout folks around here. I think you'll get along just fine."

"Thanks a lot. The biscuits were great. Maybe I'll see you tomorrow?"

"I ain't goin' nowhere soon," she laughed. Don opened the screen door and headed for his truck. Dolores stood in the doorway holding the screen open and waved to Don as he drove away.

"Oh, if I was younger, I'd chase him all day if he never caught me," she said to herself. She smiled slowly, raising a conspiratorial eyebrow. *He's just the guy for Katie Johnson*, she thought, *oh my lord, yes*. Without being aware of it, she began to nod her head in agreement with herself. *But what about Larry*

Miller? Her smile faded. There'd be some fireworks there, for sure, but her money would be on the company man. There was something special about him. *Talked about his loss,* she thought. *That poor boy. Showed a lot of strength when he did. And he definitely looks strong, hard and lean. Damn! I gotta quit thinkin' like this!*

"Bobby!" she barked, slamming the screen door behind her as she made her way back to the kitchen. "Finish sweepin' up. I'm goin' over ta Rose's for a while."

Chapter Five

Sixteen Tons
Words and music by Merle Travis

Some people say a man is made out of mud,
A poor man's made outa muscle and blood,
Muscle and blood, and skin and bone,
With a mind that's weak, and a back that's strong, I said

Sixteen tons, whadya get?
Another day older and deeper in debt,
Saint Peter don't you call me 'cause I can't go,
I owe my soul to the Company store ...

It was mid-morning, and the first shift crew was lined out by their bosses and started for the pit. Twelve bossmen sat in molded plastic and tubular chrome chairs against the walls of Dutch Miller's office like gray, hard-hatted jurists. Most of them didn't like what they were hearing, and in truth, Dutch didn't much agree with what he had to tell them either. They were all company men, and it was Dutch's responsibility as mine superintendent to implement company policy. He framed his words with a familiar edge of sarcasm which they knew meant, "This is the new company procedure, but you'd damn well better remember who's in charge at this mine and who signs your paychecks."

Dutch got up from his desk which was the signal for quiet. All eyes followed him as he leaned back against the Formica front, casually picked up his cigar, and rolled the ash off in his coffee saucer. A few men seized the moment to shake out a cigarette.

"Get that pump fixed, Shag?" he asked.

"Got 'er this mornin', Dutch."

"How we doin' on grease?"

"We'll need some by the end of the month; truck's due in 'fore then," someone said.

"How's work on the bucket shed comin'?"

"She'll be done long before the snow flies. Just some insulation left to do," a man from the back of the room said.

"Good, good," Dutch said, squinting from the cigar smoke. Turning to tip the ash, he asked back over his shoulder, "Any other problems?"

There was no reply, and Dutch didn't expect one. If a man had a problem that Dutch didn't already know about, he'd bring it to him privately, maybe pulling up alongside the superintendent's pickup on the haul road. No one was willing to court embarrassment or ridicule at these meetings, even though Dutch seldom jumped on anyone in front of the group except, of course, when he felt the need to demonstrate his absolute authority which could be as unpredictable as a tornado, and just as terrible.

Even in those moments, Dutch usually addressed the situation peripherally, and not the individual. There was never any question about the guilty party, but the procedure saved many a personal embarrassment and earned him the men's admiration. He respected the experience and knowledge of his subordinates and knew that only with their loyalty and collaboration could he run his mine efficiently. At Daggett Number Seven Mine there was a fine line between co-operation and intimidation, and Dutch Miller could work both sides of that road with equal ease.

"Boys, it's like this. We all know it's been comin' for some time, but now we're gonna have to abide by these new minin' regulations. The company's decided to quit fighting a losing battle in court and just bite the bullet and comply."

"What's it mean to us, Dutch?" Jim, the blasting foreman asked.

"I've got a copy of what they call the Federal Register here on my desk, and I've got copies on order for all of you; should be in next week. I've got the people from Corporate outlining sections that deal specifically with each of your jobs. Read them."

"What's it say? In general, I mean," Emory, the dragline operator asked.

"It says we're gonna have to mine more responsibly and treat the land with more respect," Dutch replied, on the edge of sarcasm.

"Damn!" someone said. "Whose land is this anyway? It sure ain't the federal government's!" There was a rumbling of agreement.

"Well, it's the company's damned land," Dutch said a little loudly as the men's voices died back, "and we'll do what we're told."

"You got an example, Dutch?" someone asked.

"Well, to start with, before we strip, we gotta remove all the dirt and stack it in piles. Then after we mine, we gotta knock down the spoil to what's called the *approximate original contour* and put the dirt back." The men were silent, slowly absorbing what this meant in terms of increased costs to mine.

Dutch leaned over and thumbed the button on the intercom. "Get my boy on the radio and tell him I said ta get his ass in my office, pronto!" Dutch turned back to his men. "All the water from the pit," he continued, "has to be put through a pond and treated if it's bad, no more hoses in the creek. The haul roads'll have to be watered more often to keep down the dust, and you better pray that we don't find some endangered snake or some such critter out in front of the drag."

"How'll we know if it's endangered?" a miner asked.

"Don't worry about that," a man said. "If Luke here sees a snake, it'll have Goodyear on its back."

"All snakes are endangered around me," Luke offered sheepishly.

Everyone broke into laughter and turned toward the reclamation foreman who smiled slightly and extended the middle finger of his right hand.

"Corporate's sendin' an expert up here to help us understand our new environmental responsibilities. He'll be gatherin' information to get our new permit and that, gentlemen, is very important, so I expect complete cooperation from each of you. He'll be out on the bench and ahead of the drag collecting samples, counting birds or some such thing, so keep an eye on him. I don't want him goin' up with the shot."

There was a low undercurrent of laughter. To reach the Number 7 coal vein at Daggett, the crews drilled nearly one hundred feet through solid rock. The holes were then loaded with ammonium nitrate - commonly called *fertilize* by the men – followed by fuel oil. The deadly mixture was known as ANFO. Blasting caps were used to electrically ignite the ANFO at millisecond intervals so that solid rock undulated and fractured into bite-sized pieces that the dragline could remove to get to the coal. In recent times, the blasting crew at Daggett had won an award from the corporate office by innovating a new method called *cast-blasting*. The technique called for drilling the shot holes at an angle, loading the ANFO at varying rates depending on the depth of the bore, and carefully coordinating the blast timing.

The result was that instead of just fracturing the rock and leaving it in place vertically, cast-blasting threw the rock out into the open pit where it was more easily and economically removed. However, one problem with cast-blasting was that it required greater charges of ANFO that resulted in houses being shaken for some distances away from the mine. At times, large chunks of rock and debris were launched back toward the reclaimed side of the pit, sending up small geysers of gray water in the impoundments behind the spoil. Blasting was usually conducted at the shift change - when there were fewer workers near the pit - to reduce the possibility of injury. Still, a lot of folks stopped at a respectable distance to watch the blast ripple the landscape.

Half the men in Dutch's office visualized what would happen to a human body caught in the blast. Even Dutch, who had had a lunchbox-sized piece of frozen mud catapulted through his windshield last winter by an especially potent effort on New Year's Eve, gave in to the fleeting thought. He leaned over to pick up a memo from his desk.

"Name's Donald Rodgers. Says here he's an environmental engineer."

"Damned company EPA," someone whispered.

"That's our endangered snake," someone said and laughed low.

Sitting at her desk, Katie Johnson rotated her chair around to the mine radio and clicked the button on the microphone:

"Daggett Mine to car eleven, Daggett Mine to car eleven."

"Car eleven, go ahead," Larry answered.

"Dutch wants you in his office right away."

"I'm pullin' up right now, darlin'!"

A few seconds later Larry came through the front door with an embarrassed grin and settled into the chair by her desk.

"Who's all here?"

"First and second shift pit bosses, blastin' foremen, gradin' foremen, everybody really," she responded without looking up from her paperwork.

"How long they been in there?"

She turned to look at the time clock. "About fifteen minutes."

"I'll go 'round to the side door," he said, standing up and moving slowly toward the front entrance. "Is that new guy here from Corporate?"

"No. Dutch told me he's due anytime. Where have you been?"

"Cooper's."

So that's where he's been, she thought. *No wonder Dutch couldn't get him on the radio. He's been down at Cooper's Cafe having coffee with the boys.*

Attempting to look unhurried, Larry leaned against the doorframe. "So, you gonna go to the homecomin'?"

"I suspect. My mama's in charge of the refreshments with Dolores Cooper." She did not want to be rude, but Katie had learned, where most men were concerned, that to respond with anything other than the facts would give the wrong impression. With Larry, it made no difference.

"Yeah but are you gonna go to the dance with anybody?"

"Like I said, I'm gonna help my mama with the refreshments."

"That ain't what I asked. Anybody takin' you to the dance?"

She hesitated. No, she thought, but that's none of your business. She resisted being maneuvered into a position where she would have to give a simple yes or no. She shuffled her paperwork.

"Nobody you'd know."

"What do ya mean, nobody I'd know?"

"Just what I said."

"Local talent not good enough for you? One of your college pukes from Terre Haute?"

She flushed at the thought that he might be shadowing her weekly trips to the city. The intercom on her desk answered for her; it was Dutch.

"Has Larry come in yet?"

She pressed the intercom button without looking up from her desk. "He's on his way back now."

Larry turned around as he opened the front door to leave. "We're gonna talk about this later," he said in a low, almost whispering voice. Then he slammed the metal door and stalked past the window on his way to his father's office.

Chapter Six

Endangered Species

Don followed the arrow on the sign for the Daggett Coal Company, jumping the truck off the asphalt and onto a loose gravel road. Almost immediately he had to slide to a stop at a railroad spur while the empty cars of the mine's unit train slowly backed into the loading yard. While he waited for the locomotive to clear the road, he adjusted the plastic band of his new white hardhat. He put it on his head, returned the wave of the engineer leaning out from the cab and the smile of the black-faced fireman who stood at the switch. Then he bumped across the tracks and within a few minutes pulled into the mine office parking lot.

Don parked in front of the building and got out. Locking the doors, he began to walk across the newly watered expanse of the lot, its dust now turned to a gray glue which weighed down his new boots.

The lot was a confusion of four-wheel drive trucks, most of them jacked up high off their axles, muddy stalactites dripping from their rocker panels and fenders. The office itself looked like a large corrugated, sheet metal warehouse with a few holes punched in it for windows and doors. An attached shop area had four large bays with doors thirty feet tall and wide, one into which a haul truck had thrust its huge head. From his research, Don knew it was one of nine diesel-electric Euclids in use at Daggett Mine; each was an example of the largest rubber-tired vehicles ever built. The haul trucks stood over twenty feet tall and wide with fifty foot long beds, each capable of carrying 120 tons of coal from the pit to the tipple. Black clouds of exhaust preceded the sound of a starter as men climbed over the truck's massive engine, probing and testing. A miner wearing dirty blue coveralls and an ancient metal hardhat steered a mower over a small grass patch in front of the office. The lawn seemed to be the only green and living thing within sight. He bumped and rattled circles around the flagpole in the center, and each revolution caused the circles to become larger, like ripples on a pond.

Don tried to kick the mud off his boots before entering the office. He used the big bristle brushes bolted to the walkway outside the door but ended up with scratched boots and mud crumbs all over his pant legs.

He opened the door and stepped into a dark hallway, hesitating for a moment while his eyes adjusted to the light. The heavy metal door slammed shut behind him as he walked tentatively into the first doorway on his left.

He had not expected to see many women at the mine, particularly one as young and pretty. The receptionist returned his surprised look with an easy smile. He introduced himself to her, saying that he had an appointment with the superintendent.

"Have a seat. I'll let Dutch know you're here."

Don sat down in the chair by the front door as the receptionist left through a side door. He followed the sound of her footsteps on the tile floor until they stopped some distance down the hallway. He heard a door close and stood up at the sound of her footsteps coming back toward the front office.

Don turned to look out the office window and tried to appear reserved. His heart was beating faster than normal, and he could feel the pulsing of it in his ears. *Damn,* he thought, recalling rumors he had heard about this superintendent: *Am I nervous about meeting this guy, or is it the caffeine? Or is it this girl?*

Katie stood in the doorway of her office and leaning against the doorframe, sized up the engineer. *This could prove very interesting*, she thought, remembering some of Dutch's past encounters with people from the main office. She enjoyed the occasional drama; it broke up the tedium that was the day-to-day mine fare, and it usually ended with a corporate man slinking out through her office like a whipped dog. *Maybe this one will be different*, she thought. She saw Don take a deep breath and exhale slowly, his shoulders slackening with the effort. *Nope, same as always,* she thought, and began to laugh to herself. But the laughter that started in her head got caught as it passed through her heart. She saw the engineer grit his teeth and narrow his gaze out the window as if he were concentrating on an object in the distance. Her stomach flipped.

"Would you like some coffee?" she heard herself say, words that seemed to come from outside her body.

Don had drunk so much coffee already that he felt that his teeth were floating, but eagerly accepted what he thought was her offer to wait on him.

"Sure. And I take cream and sugar."

"Right through that door," Katie said, her smile softening a bit. She pointed to a room down the hall he couldn't yet see. "Cups are down below in the cabinet."

A little flustered, Don shuffled out of the door as Katie went back to her desk. Halfway down the hall he turned and walked back to the office.

"Would you like a cup?" he said.

Her eyes brightened, and she almost laughed.

"Sure, my cup's the one with the pink flamingo on the handle. Just a little cream, please."

When Don returned to the office, the woman was gone, so he set her cup down on the desk and began to inspect the large number of certificates and photos which covered the dark paneled walls. Most, he decided, were related to safety meetings or awards. Slick-haired, leisure-suited men smiling awkwardly at the camera, hands crossed below their belts, while one of their number accepted a plaque, or in some cases, a trophy from a man with a white, flattop haircut. He noticed that although the supporting cast of miners might change, the same man appeared to be presenting the award in each of the pictures. *The awards must have taken place over a span of many years*, he thought, noting changes in the clothes and hairstyles of the men in the pictures. The only exception was the white-haired man who seemed to remain ageless, with perhaps only his belt line increasing slightly as the wall chronicled the passing years. *That must be Dutch Miller, the superintendent.*

In the corner stood an ancient bronze torch on a pedestal. The trophy stood about three feet tall, and its base was engraved with the names of mines and superintendents. Shielding the curved band of brass from the glare, he could make out the names of recipients going back to 1954. On the wall above the trophy hung a framed photo of Dutch Miller receiving the award and shaking hands with a man who had a similar smile.

He heard the roll and clack of file drawers behind him and realized the woman had returned. Picking up a company magazine from the wall rack, he sat down in the chair across from her desk. He'd already read the issue, so he leafed through the glossy pages and tried to find renewed interest in one of the articles.

"Long drive up from the river?" she asked.

"Yes, but not too bad. Took the back roads." His anxiety at starting a new job combined with the hours alone in the cab of his truck eagered his conversation, and he began to describe his windshield Indian summer.

"I see they just watered the parking lot," she said, smiling at the mud on his pant legs. "Don't worry, it'll come out in the wash. The boots? Well, they'll just get worse."

He uncrossed his leg to look at his boots, leaving a broad smear of gray across the right knee of his tan work pants. Slightly embarrassed, he looked up as she turned away, nearly spilling her coffee as she fluttered a hand up to her lips, concealing a giggle. She smiled, and his heart laughed with her.

The moment was broken by a scratchy voice on the intercom.

"He'll see you now, down the hall," she said. "Good luck."

Good luck? He wondered, rising reluctantly from the chair. At the doorway he paused. "Sorry about the coffee, You know, assuming that it was your job to wait on me."

Her eyes softened with her voice, and she smiled. "My name's Katie. Thanks for bringing me a cup," she said, then turned back to try to focus on her work.

The scrape of many chair legs across the floor funneled down the hallway as Don headed for Dutch's office. The superintendent's morning meeting had concluded, and the men were leaving by the side door. Some lingered in the room, hoping to catch the opening act of the next show they knew was about to begin. A sidelong glance from Dutch, and they high tailed it out the door with only a few remaining.

Don entered the room and waited by the doorway. The man in the photos, still somewhat ageless, was sitting on the edge of his desk, engaged in conversation with a small group of men. Without breaking the stride of his discourse, Dutch motioned for the engineer to enter. The rest of the men, intent on whatever it was the superintendent was saying, never turned a head, except for one large, round-faced miner. His eyes cut through the hum of the discussion as he inspected the new man from floor to ceiling. Feeling exposed and a little uncomfortable, Don turned away from his stare and scrutinized some aerial photos of the mine along the wall. When he looked back toward the group after a few moments, the man was still looking at him but was now grinning broadly, as if some secret had passed among the men during the brief time Don had his back turned.

After a few minutes, two of the men withdrew through the side door while the superintendent and a smaller, bespectacled man in a flannel shirt continued a low-keyed discussion. The smiling one also stayed behind.

"Donald Rodgers, isn't it?" Dutch said from across the room. "I'm Dutch Miller. Pleasure to meet you, son," he said, extending his hand as Don walked toward him.

"This here's Ray Kelso, our supply clerk and this is Larry Miller, first shift pit boss," Dutch said, grasping the engineer's hand firmly while indicating each man in turn with a nod of his head. When Don relaxed his fingers and attempted to withdraw his hand, Dutch tightened his grip and his smile. Don felt a slight prickle on the back of his neck and tightened his own grip, wondering how long the arm wrestling would last. *One of those*, he thought. After a few teasing seconds, Dutch let go and walked behind his desk, easing down into the high-backed chair.

"Says here you're an en-vi-ro-men-tal engineer," Dutch said, pretending to read from the papers on his desk. "What does that mean?" he said, leaning back in the big chair and putting his hands behind his head. Don looked for a chair, but since one wasn't close by, he remained standing.

"It means I've been hired by the company to help you get your mining permit."

"Well, we need the help, that's for sure, especially from the experts at corporate. You one of them experts?"

"I don't think so."

"Good, 'cause an "ex" is a has-been, and a "spurt" is a drip under pressure, and we don't have time for neither at this mine," Dutch said, as he rose from his chair, quieting Larry's snicker with a quick, frowning glance. He leaned forward on his knuckles, balancing by his enormous thumbs. Dutch glared at Don from beneath the short bill of his hardhat, his thumbnails whitening from the pressure of his weight. "Let's get one thing straight. Nothing, I mean nothing goes on at this mine, unless I know about it first. Whatever it is you're here to do, you run it by me first; not your boss or somebody else's boss. Period. Got that?"

Don felt a little weak in the knees but managed to nod.

"The last thing we need around here is company people acting like the federal Environmental Protection Agency," Larry said.

"We don't need to be informing on ourselves," Dutch said, flashing a look of hot disapproval toward his son, then returning his attention to Don. "Anything that gets sent out of here, I want to see it first."

Don looked to the two men beside him, but they only stared blankly at the floor. *I can't count on much help around here*, he thought.

"And another thing. Those steel-toed boots you got on?" Dutch said.

"Yes sir."

"Hard to tell under all that mud," he chuckled, then continued sternly. "This is a safety conscious mine. You'll wear steel-toed boots, safety glasses, and your hat, no exceptions. Tomorrow morning you see my secretary about safety training. Ray here will get you some glasses and some maps, so you'll know where not to be. Learn all the blasting signals and schedules. Always give haultrucks the right of way, and don't follow them up the incline."

Dutch stood upright, appearing a little larger to Don than he had before the one-sided conversation began.

"Ray, get him a radio in his truck and a key to the gas pumps. Anything I'm forgetting?" Dutch asked.

"Don't think so, Dutch," replied Ray.

"Okay. I want an itinerary every Monday and a report on my desk by Friday at noon," Dutch dismissed them with a wave of his hand and settled back into his chair. "I want to talk to you," Dutch said to Larry as the men turned to leave. Ray followed Don into the hallway and closed the office door behind them.

"I'll go in the back and get your safety glasses and the gas keys," Ray said to Don, as they walked from the safety room toward the mine office. "You go see Katie about that safety training."

They stopped at the doorway to Katie's office. Ray peered past the engineer to the woman working at the desk.

"Don here needs some safety schooling, Katie. Take good care of him, okay?"

"Got the papers right here."

"I'll be back up in a bit," Ray said, shaking Don's hand earnestly while offering a knowing smile. "Welcome to Daggett Mine. Don't worry, it gets better." Then he turned and walked back to the shop.

"You need to read these papers and sign the third one at the bottom," Katie said as he came into the room. "You look a little piqued. You all right?"

"Oh, yeah," Don said distractedly, picking up the forms and falling into a chair.

She noticed the beads of sweat on his forehead and temples and felt a little ashamed. *It's always the same*, she thought; *the old man drops the hammer on them right off the bat; lets them know who's boss. I've seen it too many times.*

After a few minutes, Don signed the papers and laid them back on her desk, then sat down to wait for Ray.

She was quiet for a few moments. "I hear you're gonna be staying in the old Goodman place off the red shale road."

"I guess that's the place," he replied, his eyes questioning. *It seems like everyone knows what I'm doing but me*, he thought.

"Don't worry, everybody knows everybody's business around here," she said and laughed. "They left me the keys to give to you."

He smiled and began to relax. "Is it very far from here?"

"No, just southwest of the mine about a mile. It sets back in the woods, real pretty little place. Ray'll show you how to get there."

"He seems like a nice guy."

"Ray? Yeah, everybody likes him. Most people around here had him for science in high school."

"You mean he used to be a teacher?"

"Yep, at Dugger Union. I got straight A's from him my senior year."

"Why's he working at the mine?"

She looked at him and smiled. "The pay's a lot better. It's the only reason any of us work here. What about you?"

"What about me?"

"Yeah, why did you decide to come to work at the mines?"

"Believe me, I have a lot of friends who think it was a major sellout of my principles to come to work for a mining company," Don said, recalling his conversation with Dolores Cooper. "I've always had an interest in the outdoors, nature, you know, the environment. With all the new regulations, somebody needs to be responsible for putting things back the way they were. I always thought that even one person can make a difference sometimes, but I'm beginning to wonder," he said while looking toward the hallway.

"Depends on who that one person is, I suppose. Don't worry about old Dutch. He'll treat you fair."

"What about Larry? Isn't he Dutch's son?"

"Yeah," she sighed. "And he does have a temper. Inherited it from Dutch's first wife. She was from Kentucky. Larry's a good example of why some mothers eat their young."

"He's a pretty big boy."

"Yeah, and likes to shove it around too. Just stay outa his way and try not to piss him off."

Don remembered the undisguised, churlish glare Larry had shot his way in Dutch's office and felt an answering irritation he had not experienced before. Only now did he recognize the provocation, and he felt a latent humiliation. Larry's sinister smile cheshired in his mind's eye, causing Don's voice to come out a little hard-edged.

"Well, I've got to be up here for awhile, and I'd like to get along with people. But I do have a job to do. If some people feel a little threatened, I can't help that."

"It just takes time," Katie said, trying not to appear too soothing.

"I'm not here to put anybody out of work. There seems to be a rumor going around about that."

"Rumors around coal are like fleas on a dog's back. Numerous and unavoidable. Folks around here are friendly once they get to know you."

"I hope you're right," Don said, backing down a little bit. "This area's real pretty, and I wouldn't mind sticking around." He got out of his chair and walked over to the window.

Don looked out the dust crazed window, his eyes focused on nothing. He recalled a conversation with the mine safety director at headquarters. "Keep your eyes open," the man had said, "and watch your back. For the last few months someone at Daggett mine has been sabotaging equipment, probably with the idea that slowing down production might extend the life of the operation. That mine's not scheduled to be closed for quite a few years, but there's a rumor going around that we'll be shutting it down soon. I'm not asking you to be a detective, but if you see or hear of anything suspicious, let me know."

Katie watched him for a few moments, studying his silhouette against the bright glare outside. *He's a little weak from the effort*, she thought, *but he must have held his ground with Dutch one way or another; that much was obvious from Ray's attitude. That makes him different from a lot of men around here; and I like that.* Then she remembered her lie to Larry, that she was going to the dance with someone, someone Larry didn't know. *Oh, what the hell*, she thought.

"Look," she said, "there's a big get together over at the high school this Saturday night. It's homecoming. There's a basketball game and the alumni dance afterwards. I'm helpin' my mama and Dolores Cooper with the refreshments. Want to come along? I mean, you bein' new and everything, maybe you could meet some people there."

He turned around, smiling awkwardly. "Sure, thanks. That'd be great. You don't have any other plans, do you?"

"If I did, would I ask you to go?"

"No, I guess not. I'll have to get directions to your place. What time do I pick you up?"

She opened the drawer to the desk just as Ray came back into the room. "Ray can show you how to get to my mama's house from your place, won't you, Ray? Here's the keys to the front and back doors of your house. Six o'clock will be fine."

"Safety glasses and pump keys," Ray said, handing the items to Don. "Run on out and make sure they fit in number twenty-eight. I'll be out in a minute to take you over to your place."

"I'll see you later," Don said, touching the brim of his hard hat for Katie before walking out the door.

"Well, well!" Ray said, shaking his head and smiling. "Seems like a pretty nice fellow. Kept his cool with the Dutchman, he did."

"He's going to homecoming with me, Mr. Kelso."

"So, I gathered," Ray said while smiling more broadly.

Chapter Seven

The Big Rock Candy Mountain
Words and music by Harry McClintock

One evening as the sun went down, and the jungle fire was burnin',
Down the track came a hobo hiking, and he said: "Boys, I'm not turnin',
I'm heading for a land that's far away, beside the crystal fountain,
Come along with me and we'll go see the Big Rock Candy Mountains."

In the Big Rock Candy Mountains everything is fair and bright,
The handouts grow on bushes, and you sleep out every night,
The boxcars all are empty, and the sun shines every day,
On the buzzin' of the bees in the cigarette trees,
By the lemonade springs where the bluebird sings,
In the Big Rock Candy Mountains.

"Me and Ernie's thinkin' about goin' elk huntin' out in Colorado. Ain't it right, Ernie? 'Cept 'n I ain't got no days off comin', and Ernie says the truck won't make it."

Maxwell Evert began his conversations to no one in particular, casting at anyone within hearing radius and eventually directing his words toward the first to show an interest. Ernie and Tommie knew the trick, so they busied themselves unpacking their dinner buckets and avoided any verbal response or direct eye contact; acquiring a comfortable position for dinner was the overriding concern. Each tried to find a truck tire to lean against or a little patch of shade to exhaust. It was noon, and the midday sun allowed only a few tight shadows on the rocky bench above the pit.

Me fished out one of the two fried egg sandwiches from his box and unwrapped it, letting the waxed paper blow away. The paper cartwheeled the short distance to where Ernie sat with his legs extended, his back against the drill rig's tire. The wind flattened the paper against the bottom of the big man's boot, and Ernie leaned forward as far as he could, pulled his foot in carefully, and grabbed the paper before it could blow away again.

Very slowly and deliberately he wadded it up and placed it in his dinner bucket. Tommie, sitting next to him, threw a little glare toward Me, who was flinging the crusts from the edge of his sandwich into the weeds. *It wasn't so much his littering*, she thought, *it's those damned egg sandwiches; you can smell them a mile away.*

"You ever gonna eat anythin' besides them rotten damn eggs?" she said exaggerating her disgust.

Me had just gummed off a mouthful. "They's the perfect food, I read," he said, swallowing heavily in a rolling motion that distended his neck and threw his chin forward. *He looks just like an unborn chicken sometimes*, Tommie thought.

The grease truck bumped down the cable route toward them, dusting to a stop in front of the drill rig. Its fenders and running boards carried a lumpy veneer of mud and gravel, and it smelled like a refinery. So, the driver deliberately parked it downwind of the group. Sputtering to a stop, the engine backfired as it was turned off, and the springs wheezed rhythmically before the truck settled down on tired shocks.

"Howdy, boys! Why don't you join us for some dinner?" Me called to the driver.

"Don't mind if we do," came the reply.

"Looks like you boys customized that door there, Harold." Tommie said, laughing.

The driver leaned out of the door and looked at a horizontal crease that started at the front fender and extended back across the door to the rear of the cab.

"Oh, that," Harold said, and he chuckled. "Slid sideways along the cable route on the way here. Damn near swapped ends. Nailed a stump pretty good." He tried to open the door as he spoke, but the dent on the hinged side caught the door. "Randy," he said, turning to his companion, "get out the rubber mallet and go talk to this here fender so's I can get out of this truck, will you?"

The passenger door squeaked sharply as it was opened. Around the back side of the truck rolled a huge man in dirty blue denim coveralls, his face nearly hidden by a confusion of beard and dark, greasy stains. In his right fist, he held a large rubber mallet.

"Need some help?" Me said, out of courtesy but with no intent to get in the way of a man three times his size.

"Nope," Harold said. "Old Randy here likes to beat on things. Smack her right there," he said to Randy, pointing to an area just ahead of the door.

The big man braced himself against the fender with his left hand, drew his weight back, and brought the hammer head down with a dull, bouncing thud against the metal. Some of the mud fell from the fender and a deep semicircular dent appeared in the door frame.

"That ought to do it," Harold said. "Stand back and let's see."

The door opened stiffly; Harold worked it back and forth a few times to make sure, then grinned at the group.

"I always said that boy was a born mechanic," he said as he got down from the cab.

Randy walked back toward the rear of the truck, tapping the fender as he went, watching the mud flake off and fall to the ground. He replaced the mallet in the toolbox then took out the hand cleaner. He rubbed his hands together, squeezing the cream around through his fingers until most of the grease was loosened, then took a red rag from his back pocket and carefully wiped his hands clean. Retrieving a platoon-sized, plastic cooler from the front seat, he lumbered back around the truck and joined the miners who had already started eating.

"Me and Ernie might do us some elk huntin' in Colorado this year," Me said.

"Don't you kill enough deer around here already, Me?" Harold said.

"Just one a year; it's all the law allows. That ain't near enough."

"Damn, Me," Randy said. "Everybody knows you're the poachingest son of a bitch in the bottoms. One deer, why!"

"That ain't true, and you know'd it. Me and Ernie abide by the law; we're born conversationists, ain't it right, Ernie?" He looked quickly toward Ernie for help and received a smile and twinkled eye in response.

"They claim them elks come down when the snow gets bad up in the mountains," Me continued. "Right into people's front yard. They eat their flowers and plants. Makes some folks mad as hell. They's glad to have you shoot 'em."

"Where you gonna stay?" Randy asked. "On somebody's front porch?"

"No, dammit, we mean to camp," Me said.

"You'll freeze your toes off, old man. It gets cold in the mountains, I know. Hell, when it gets a little chilly around here you go to shakin' like a dog passin' peach seeds. You ain't got enough meat on your bones."

"We can dress for it," Me replied, "you big, dumb chicken eater!"

"Yeah? Wait till it snows waist deep to an Indian. Ernie'll have to pack you out like he was a damned mule."

As severe as the conversation sounded, everyone was familiar with the verbal sparring and enjoyed it up to a point. Even Me and Randy seemed to understand the limits to which they could go at each other. Besides, there was too much difference in size and age between the two men for anything serious to develop.

"Maybe you can loan him some beef, Randy, " Tommie said. "You look like you might have some to spare."

"Not on this crap my wife keeps sendin' me for dinner," the big man replied, pulling two packages of waxed paper from his cooler. "Celery and carrot sticks. How's a man supposed to work on this?"

"Reckon you got enough room in that cooler for all that there food?" Harold asked, laughing.

"She's just concerned for your health, that's all," Tommie said.

"Yeah, well, she don't care if I starve to death; that's for damn sure."

"You want one of my sammiches?" Me said.

Randy looked up from the void in his cooler and studied the little man's face. "No thanks," he replied, a little ashamed. "Thanks anyway. I'll just stick to my rabbit food."

"Really, you can have it. I ain't gonna eat it anyway."

Randy could smell the repulsive egg sandwich through the waxed paper, but the honest, almost begging look in Me's eyes brought out a weak smile on the big man's face.

"Throw it over here. I'll eat it later this afternoon. Thanks."

The sandwich passed around the circle through everyone's hands before Randy placed it in the bottom of his empty cooler.

Ernie had been listening to the conversation with his customary detachment. It was hard enough to eat with two cheeks full of tobacco and snuff in your lower lip, let alone try to talk at the same time.

Everything about Ernie seemed slow and deliberate. Even changes in his mood were subject to the same rhythms that ruled his physical movements. He seldom vocalized his thoughts, but his face and eyes were the barometer by which those who knew him could read his mind. Watching Ernie's expressions change was like watching grass grow, but a slow darkening of the brow gave a person time to reconsider his words or to change the subject. On the other hand, a good humor would spread across Ernie's face like ripples on a pond. Me read Ernie's moods better than anyone else, and to his credit, could adjust them like a thermostat with the same banter most miners found simply annoying.

Within the shelter of his outward lethargy, Ernie had a secret. He had been in love with Tommie longer than he could remember. It was a secret that he picked up in the morning, carried through the workday, took home at the end of the shift, and was the touchstone of his dreams. His secret imparted an impassioned eloquence to his thoughts and peopled an inner world with images and smells and touches, creating secret, sensual images that played on his heart and mind like words to an old song. Only Ernie knew how dependent he was on the abstraction, and he shared its confidence with no one, for in doing so, he knew that his secret would be at the very least degraded, and at the most, lost.

Just now, Ernie was inside this universe when the real world abruptly intruded. A hand touched his forearm, and he turned to confront his secret face to face.

"Did you hear what I said?" Tommie asked.

Ernie looked around. Most of the others were looking at him apparently awaiting a response to some important question. He felt their eyes intruding on his thoughts. For a moment his face flushed, and he shivered a little in transition. He imagined a strained silence. Then he leaned over and spit out his chew.

"Nope. What did you say?" he said, looking at her intently.

"I said that all them chicken legs hangin' in the trees 'round the old tipple is just kids playin' around, nothin' else. Me's just imaginin' things."

"Am not," Me replied. "Them's satanic symbols, voodoo, and the like. I read about that somewheres, ain't it right, Ernie?"

For as far back as people could remember, there had been strange goings-on in a small, wooded section of abandoned mine land along the county line road between Linton and Dugger. There was a legend, still enunciated as fact, that in the 1930s a Dugger miner's wife tracked down her husband to an illicit rendezvous with a Linton miner's wife somewhere in these woods. Slipping two buckshot shells into the breech of her husband's double-barreled 12-gauge shotgun, the wronged woman declared to her friends one night: "When I find that sonofabitch and his whore, first I'll shoot her in the head, and then I'm a gonna blow his privates off."

Legend had it that the next morning, the county sheriff - from physical evidence at the scene of the crime - deduced that the wife had caught up with the lovers in the shadowed remains of an old log cabin and accomplished her double goal with one shot.

"Old man, you ain't read squat about that; you just hear things," Randy said.

"Did not. Me and Ernie come down the backroad one night past that old cemetery and they was lights in the woods, all weird like, hangin' in the trees. And peoples was dancin'. You could see the shadows against the walls of that ol' whore's cabin. They had a fire inside, too. Leapin' the flame, I bet! I heard they do that at certain times of the year and every full moon, too."

"That right, Ernie?" Tommie asked.

"Saw the lights," Ernie said. "Didn't stop."

"Strange noises, too," Me said. "Sounded like they was sacrificin' somethin', or somebody. Lots of yellin' and whoopin'. Made the hair on my head stand up."

"You're confusin' hair with cooties, old man," Randy said, and laughed. "I got more hair on my ass than you got on your head."

"Damn, you chicken eater! One of these days, you'll see! I dare you to go down there!" Me said. "They'd split you like a hog and slow roast you to boot, with a, with an apple in your mouth!"

"Listen," Harold said. "I'd say it's just a bunch of local kids blowin' off some steam. What you think is screamin' is probably just some kind of music."

"What about all the dead chickens in the trees he says he saw?" Tommie asked.

"Seems to me that whoever's back there's pretty smart at scarin' off old farts; don't ya think?" Harold said, looking at Me.

"There, old man," Randy said, laughing. "Makes perfect sense to me."

"Maybe so," Me said. "But me and Ernie ain't gonna drive that road when there's a full moon. Ain't that right Ernie?"

Ernie smiled and nodded. He'd already settled back into his half-world and was watching Tommie out of the corner of his eye. She had left the circle of men and was standing away from the vehicles, looking into the woods from the edge of the bench. She held her hard hat between her knees and took the pins out of her black hair so that it fell freely about her shoulders. The shifting breeze revealed a slender and graceful neck. Tucking her hardhat under her arm, she walked toward the woods and into the wind, her head tilted slightly upward as if attracted by some diffuse scent.

Tommie knew about Ernie. Ray was considerably older than she was but was happy to have married him last year. With all her heart, she wished that Ernie could find someone to make him happy, too. *He needed to realize that it wasn't going to be her*, she thought. Every day on the job, she struggled between thoughts of pity and acts of kindness toward the big man. Mostly she just tried to do her job and hoped that Ernie's infatuation would fade in time.

Exhausting their arguments, the men settled down to steal a few short naps. Ernie turned his back on the group and leaned against the rear wheel, watching Tommie from the shadow of the drill rig. *She is the most beautiful creature I have ever seen,* he thought, his imagination looking past the slate gray coveralls and work boots. Mirrored in the frame of his inner world, she was both perfection and unattainable. He had been in love with her since the first day she came to work at the mine. Even when she married Ray, his love remained constant. He considered his feelings to be eternal and above temporal boundaries. In those brief moments when he descended to think of her in a physical way, he was overwhelmed by a sense of guilt and perversity, and later mentally flogged himself for degrading her innocence. Ernie's idea of platonic love had given him the opportunity to wander life in a self-imposed tragedy, and he was content to live that way. And he knew this course spared him from not only the pain of possible rejection but also from the physical experience of sex, which had always scared the hell out of him.

"Hey, Tommie," Harold called out. "Lookin' for a fire hydrant?"

"Screw you," Tommie said. "Easy for you to say."

"Y'all throw your trash in the pickup," Me said. "We'll take it down to the pit after work."

"Thanks, boys," said Randy. "We got a sack full in the cab."

One after another, the miners rose to their feet, some stretching, others slapping dust from their backsides. Tommie put her hard hat on and headed back to the truck.

"Time to get back to work," Harold said, popping open the door of the grease truck. "Somebody's gotta save this company."

Chapter Eight

Big Bad John
Words and music by Jimmy Dean

Every morning at the mine you could see him arrive,
He stood six-foot-six, weighed two forty-five,
Kinda broad at the shoulder and narrow at the hip,
And everybody knew you didn't give no lip to Big John.

Nobody seemed to know where John called home
He just drifted into town and stayed all alone
He didn't say much, kinda quiet and shy
And if you spoke at all, he just said, "Hi" to Big John

Somebody said he came from New Orleans
Where he got in a fight over a Cajun Queen,
And a crashin' blow from a huge right hand
Sent a Louisiana fella to the Promised Land, Big John.

Big John, Big John, Big bad John.

Ray wheeled the pickup down the parking lot to where the young engineer was studying the bank of locks by the gas pumps. Sliding to a stop, he leaned over the seat and rolled down the passenger window.

"Jump on in. Let's go for a ride."

"You think I should just follow you in my truck, so I can unload my stuff?" Don asked.

"Not right now. We'll send some of the farm crew over at the end of the shift to help you. Sound okay?"

"Great," Don replied, opening the door while attempting to kick the gray slag from his boots before getting into the cab.

"Don't worry about that," Ray said with a grin. "I flush this thing out every night. Hop in."

Don swung up onto the seat just as Ray gunned the engine, slipped the clutch, and headed out of the lot. Caught slightly off-guard and unbalanced, Don grabbed the doorframe and used the forward momentum of the truck to swing the door shut.

They headed out past the railroad spur, across the blacktop, and jumped onto a rust-red road, washboarded and so badly in need of grading that Ray had to slow his speed to maintain control of the steering.

"This here's Red Dog Road," Ray said and laughed, his words corrugating with the shock as his head jackhammered from the rough ride. "We'll have to send a grader out to blade this off some time this week."

"Damn!" Don laughed, grabbing for his hardhat, which was bouncing around between his head and the roof of the cab. He welcomed the jostling and humor of the moment. It seemed to shake away most of the tension that had enveloped him since the meeting in the superintendent's office. It introduced an informality and a shared exuberance with the older man at the wheel. As the rhythmic bumps evened out into an occasional jolt, he began to relax and notice the countryside along the road.

To the right, a string of tired, gray-boarded shacks mushroomed among the locust and cottonwood trees. The trunks seemed to grow out of each house's foundation with branches buttressing slanting walls and shouldering, green-mossed roofs. The clapboard sides were tattered with a calico of torn black tar paper and asphalt shingles, horizontal roofing put to vertical use. Behind one house, the rusty remains of household appliances were scattered at the edge of the woods. Overgrown by vines and briars, old bedsprings, broken chairs, and wringer-type washing machines chronicled two generations of purchases from the Sears catalog.

"Yep, there's people that still live in those houses," said Ray, answering Don's unspoken question. "Tried to buy that old Chevy truck off Milo a few years back, but he wouldn't sell. See it back there in the weeds? Now it's gone to hell like everything else. Rats have torn out the upholstery, and there's a tree growing through the radiator. Still won't sell it."

"Why not?"

"Reminds him of something, I guess. Doesn't want to part with his memories."

"Maybe they're the only thing he's got," Don said, reproaching himself as soon as the words came out of his mouth.

"Maybe so, but don't feel too sorry for the old boy. Fact is, there's a lot of people like him around here. You'll see. Old Milo's like most; sold off his land to the company years ago. Got what he thought was a passel of money at the time, probably less than a hundred dollars an acre."

"That's it?"

"No. He also got a job at the mine sweeping out the warehouse, and one of his boys still works for the company. Fact is, old Milo took the money for the land and went to Florida for the winter that year. Never been out of the state before that, hasn't been since. Now that he's too old to work, he just sits around, tends his garden, and waits for the company to mine his ground so's he can get the royalty checks. That's why his place looks like a wreck. He doesn't want to put any money into something that'll eventually be torn down."

"Well, at least he's got that coming. I've heard some people sold their mineral rights along with their ground, lock, stock, and barrel."

"Yeah, but he'll never live to see it. The dragline's two miles west of his property and heading away. The mine plan doesn't call for stripping this area any time soon."

"Does he know that?"

"I suspect he does. But things can change."

"What if they do?"

"Then he has to move. We'd start the box cut right about where his outhouse sets," Ray said with a chuckle.

They turned off the red shale onto a narrow gravel road, high-crowned in the middle with deeply incised ditches along each edge. Soybeans yellowed in fields on both sides of the road. Diving down into wooded hollows at the fields' edges, the truck crossed numerous streams spanned by small concrete bridges. In some places, the crossing was merely two culverts covered with gravel. At one ford, the creek ran over the road, instead of the other way around.

"That's Barren Fork," Ray said, as they crossed a bridge with a sizable amount of red water running beneath it. "Been that way since I was a kid. Never did have any fish in it. Redder'n a spanked baby's butt."

Just amazing, Don thought, *that for generations these people can live and accept this type of environmental degradation. It's like the earth's bleeding.*

"Iron," Don said.

"Yeah, bubbles up from the old Star Mine."

"Did you live around here?"

"In Dugger, but my grandparents owned a farm down this road. It's their house you're going to live in."

"Are they still around?"

"No. My grandma passed on almost ten years ago. It was Palm Sunday. No sooner got her buried then Grandpa died. Buried him on Easter. Guess he didn't want to live without Grandma."

"That's too bad."

"Not really. They were both in their eighties and very religious. Married sixty-five years. Here's their place."

Ray slowed down as they approached a stretch of woods. Up ahead on the right was a trail that ran back into the trees, wheel-rutted, with grass growing high in the center. Turning right, Ray bumped across the culvert in the side ditch, stopped a few yards into the woods, and turned the engine off.

"Hear that?"

Don rolled down his window, cocking his head. After a few seconds of strained anticipation, he replied.

"No."

"That's right!" Ray said, laughing. "Not a damn thing. That's what I like about this place, nice and quiet. Used to live here myself before I got married. Come on. Let's look around and get you situated."

The men got out of the truck and walked up the separate wheel paths, scattering the blanket of orange and yellow leaves as they went. The house was set back into the woods, partially hidden by the deep shade and a veneer of new fallen leaves that blanketed the roof.

"What a fantastic place! I sure didn't expect anything this nice. It's made from logs. I'll be damned."

"How about that? My father, my uncles, and I built this about thirty years ago for my grandparents. Cut the poplar right off the ridge out back. I chalked and scored every log, and my uncles broad axed them square. Done my share of chinking mortar to keep it up since then. Real sound, though. Look at these dove-tailed joints in the corner. Real craftsmanship."

Don went to one corner of the building and measured the joints with an engineer's eye. "I'd say they're damn near perfect!"

Pleased by Don's admiration of his family's handiwork, Ray grinned, grabbed Don's elbow, and headed for the front steps.

"Been awhile since anybody's lived here, though," Ray said, opening the screen door to the front porch. "Tommie and I came over last week and straightened it up a bit but didn't do much dusting. Got the water going and moved in some furniture. Not much, though, just a bed, dresser, a couch, and a kitchen table with some chairs."

"I really appreciate that, thanks. Who's Tommie?"

"She's my wife. Works here at the mine as a driller's helper, first shift. Her real name's Nancy, but everybody calls her Tommie because of her father. Big union man years ago, last name was Thompson. We'll have you over to supper some night. Works the same for the front and back," Ray said with a smile, fitting the skeleton key into a simple lock on the front door. "I don't think you can find keys like this anymore. Probably the safest locks around."

The square windowpane rattled as Ray shook the wooden door slightly to force it open.

"Just a little warped," Ray said as they stepped inside. "Got to work it a little bit. The fuse box is on the back porch. I'll get the lights. Make yourself at home."

Don took a few steps across a hardwood floor dappled with patches of sunlight sifting through the dirty windows. Particles of suspended dust angeled down the beams into the still interior of the house. There were at least two windows in every wall. Even without the electricity on, the whole interior of the house seemed illuminated. A few threadbare curtains framed a few windows, and yellowed blinds were pulled partially down over others.

Ray came back into the room and flicked on the light switch next to the door. A large brass chandelier in the center of the room chased the shadows from the corners, revealing the open nature of the cabin. At one end of the room, a fieldstone fireplace replaced the wall of logs, its chimney reaching up through the gable. To the side of the hearth stood a large chrome Florence Hot-Blast wood stove, an umbilical of rusty pipe connecting it to the flue. At the other end of the room were stacked the pieces of furniture Ray and Tommie had brought over earlier in the week.

"We figured you'd want to do the arranging of the furniture yourself. I'll give you a hand now if you'd like."

"No, that's all right. I'll wait until I get all my stuff in. Thanks anyway."

"Well, there are really only three rooms in the house, counting this one," Ray said with a chuckle. He pointed to a door in the log wall across the room. "That's the bedroom, and the bathroom is off it. There are electric baseboard heaters in both for when you're gone, but that old wood stove will keep the place real toasty for quite awhile. Plenty of wood out back. You can cut some at the mine if you want, or I can have John and Roger bring some by when you run low. Just let me know."

Ray walked across the floor to a broad opening in the log wall behind the wood stove. From the sound of Ray's boot heels on the wooden floor, Don could tell the cabin was probably as solid as the day it was built.

"This here's the kitchen," he said, flipping on a switch for the overhead light. "Pretty modern kitchen. Plenty of cabinets, but no disposal or dishwasher. The stove is propane, and the tanks are out back. I had them filled last week. That door leads to a side porch where you can bring wood in for the stove."

"Look like you've done about everything. I sure appreciate it. Anything else I need to know?"

"Well, it's probably a good idea to leave the water running a little bit when it gets below freezing. That way the pipes won't freeze up. You might stuff some insulation around the windows on the west side. It can get drafty in a wind. Oh, yeah, close the damper to the fireplace when you're not using it. There's a little room off the back porch with some old furniture in it you might be able to use. It's the small key," he said, handing the keys over to Don.

"Any neighbors?"

"Right across the ravine. Come on, let's go out the back, and I'll introduce you."

The two men walked out the kitchen door and across the wooden planked back porch. Don followed Ray along a path of uneven fieldstone that led to a wooden bridge straddling a ravine.

"Built this for Grandpa myself. He and Conner were buddies. Just two telephone poles and a bunch of two-by-sixes, but it works. That's his house back in the trees. Looks kind of like my grandparents' house, huh? Built them both about the same time."

The men clomped across the bridge and followed a similar stone path on the other side of the ravine.

"You can always tell when the old man's home. See the black smoke from the chimney? He's always got a fire going, especially this time of year. Burns a lot of coal. Gets it free from the mine."

Ray stepped up on the porch and knocked loudly on the door. "Hey, old man! You home? It's me, Ray!"

A chair squeaked from somewhere inside the house. After a few seconds, the door opened and out onto the porch stepped Conner Owen.

Don nearly jumped. *He must be six foot five and every bit of two hundred fifty pounds*, he thought to himself.

"Conner Owen," Ray said with a slight formality, "this is Don Rodgers, your new neighbor."

Conner wore a pair of denim coveralls over a blue work shirt and stood with a slight hunch to his shoulders, his arms loosely at his sides, like he'd answered a bell and was ready to wrestle. His piercing green eyes regarded Don with naked curiosity. He raised one eyebrow then a smile which eventually broke into a warm, friendly laugh. Don relaxed.

"Where ya been, boy?" Conner said, throwing a vise around Ray's neck with his left arm, knocking his hardhat to the ground. He rubbed his huge knuckles briskly across the crown of Ray's short hair while the smaller man tried without success to break his grip. "When you going to bring that pretty wife of yours by so's we can talk?" He loosened his hold and Ray, looking only slightly sheepish, adjusted his glasses and retrieved his hardhat.

"Don't get within arm's length of this old man." Ray laughed. "He ain't too fast on his feet anymore but he can still grab. Conner, Don here's an engineer at the mine, just came up from Evansville."

"Pleased to meet you, son," said Conner, offering his hand to Don. For an instant, Don regarded the huge hand worriedly, its black creases and gnarled nails reminding him of Dutch's earlier display of dominance. But when his hand disappeared inside Conner's fist, the grasp was firm but friendly, and Don took a deep breath and exhaled.

"Met the Dutchman already, did you?" Conner laughed, smiling knowingly. "I've seen him pull that stunt on everybody. You'd think it was some secret handshake or something, but then we'd all be Masons, wouldn't we?"

"Everyone but you, old man," Ray said. "I've never seen him try it on you."

Conner smiled at both, then winked at Don.

"Why don't you boys come on in for a bite? I've got some stew on the stove, plenty to go around. Ain't in a hurry, are you?"

"Actually, we need to get out to the pit. I want to get Don up on the dragline at the shift change so's he can get his bearings. We'll stop by after that. He has to unload his stuff and get settled in the house. We'd better get going. We're a little late already."

"Well, plan on eating supper here tonight, same stew, different plates. And bring that pretty wife of yours by. We need to talk."

"See you later," Ray called back over his shoulder as the men walked back down the path to the bridge. After they got in the truck, Ray waited a while before starting the engine.

"I think that I'm gonna like living here," Don said, breaking the silence.

"Yeah, that old man's all right," Ray said, hesitating before continuing.

"As a safety officer, I'm responsible for the well-being of every person that sets foot on the mine property. Like everyone else, you'll get the usual training and company policy stuff, but I've got to clue you in on a couple of unofficial things."

"Like what?"

"Like Katie Johnson."

"The receptionist?"

"Yep. Sweet girl ain't she?"

"Yeah. She asked me to a dance this Friday at the high school. Said it was homecoming."

"Don't get me wrong, I think that's great. Just be aware that Larry Miller has been after her for years; considers her to be his property in some way. She's never been interested in him, though, and that's meant trouble for any man that's tried to get to know her." There were a few moments of uncomfortable silence until Ray started up the truck. Don remembered the leering smile Larry cast his way in the office and pictured Katie sitting at her desk. *How many years has that poor girl had to endure that big sonofabitch?* he wondered.

"Just one thing. How do you think this will translate into my working relationship with Dutch Miller?"

"That's not going to be a problem, as long as you act professional at your job and you're respectful of Katie, which I'm sure you will be. She works for the Dutchman because her father and brother died in a mine accident when she was very young. He's always felt protective of her, as have a few of us, I guess.

He don't cotton with his son's behavior, but Larry don't listen to no one, least of all his old man."

"Then it won't be a problem. I'll keep an eye out for him, but I'm not going to be overly concerned about Larry."

"Just remember, you're new here, and Larry does have friends, such as they are."

"Thanks for the heads-up. What's the second item on my unofficial safety lecture?" They pulled out onto the red shale road and headed toward the pit.

"This one's a lot more serious. Someone, and I'm pretty sure it's an individual, has been sabotaging some of the equipment at the mine. Every couple of days a pump's shorted out, the oil plugs are removed from a generator, anything to slow down production and cost the company time and money. The mechanics are keeping pretty busy with repairs, so I don't think it's any of them."

There it is, Don thought. *That's what the safety director in Evansville was talking about.* For a moment he wondered if Ray had some hidden motive for sharing this information with him, a relative stranger, but the thought dissipated as they drove down the road.

"Have you reported any of this to Corporate? You know they have safety investigators that can come out to help."

"Not yet. Right now, it's little triflin' things, but I've a feeling it's gonna get ratcheted up pretty soon. The incidents tend to ebb and flow depending upon the mood of the person who commits them."

"So, you do have an idea who's doing this stuff? It's not some covert union action?"

"The UMWA ain't involved. Everybody's happy to be working right now. Shutting down the mine for safety violations is the last thing anybody wants, so we're trying to deal with it locally, if you know what I mean. That's why I haven't called Corporate for help."

It's his eyes, Don thought. *They have a weary, almost sad kind of look. He seems resigned that's something's going to happen, and he doesn't know when. He's being honest as far as the incidents are concerned. He's hoping to get it stopped while incidents are just minor irritations, but I think the problems will accelerate to where they can't be dealt with locally. Too much interconnection around these mines. I wonder if he knows that Corporate is onto the issue already.* "Are you gonna tell me who you think it is?"

"I have a feeling you'll figure it out."

Chapter Nine

The Wreck of the Number Nine
Tradition Folk Song

'Twas a cold winter's night, not a star was in sight,
As the North wind came howlin' down the line,
Stood a brave engineer and his sweetheart so dear,
His orders to pull Old Number Nine.
He kissed her goodbye with a tear in his eye,
The sorrow in his heart he could not hide,
Then the whole world seemed bright when she told him that night,
That tomorrow, she'd be his blushing bride.

Oh, the wheel's hummed a song as the train rolled along,
The black smoke came pourin' from the stack,
His headlight a-gleam seemed to brighten his dream,
Of tomorrow; when he'd be comin' back
He spun 'round the hill and his brave heart stood still,
His headlight was shinin' in his face,
He whispered a prayer as he threw on the air,
For he knew it would be his final race…

The back-up alarm beat a shrill cadence as the miner jack-knifed the haul truck out of the garage and into the lot, the huge tires compressing and spitting out an uneven gravel percussion. Sitting high above, gripping the vibrating steering wheel, the man alternately switched his attention from the right-side view mirror, then back to the left. Between these margins, at the lower boundary of his vision, two mechanics receded from beneath the front of the cab. One wiped his oily hands with a faded red rag; the other cleaned the grease from a wrench with a similar piece of cloth, but neither took their skilled eyes away from an area behind the front wheels of the truck.

This morning, the Master Mechanic had ordered that each haul truck be inspected at the beginning of each shift. Every man at the mine had heard and passed on the rumor about someone sabotaging the equipment. The shop superintendent had decided that absolutely none of the rolling stock was going to fall victim, particularly since uncontrollable heavy metal on the move could prove disastrous to not only the operator, but especially to anything in its path. The driver of this truck, probably spooked by the rumors, had reported some imagined problems in the hydraulic steering system.

"Reckon Linton'll beat Dugger this Saturday?" one mechanic asked distractedly, his mind indexing the endless number of possibilities for failure.

"Not a chance," replied the other, attempting to see through the creature's metal skin to discover cause and effect.

"You goin'?" asked the first. Inspecting for possible sabotage was not his usual line of work.

"'Course. The old lady's making pies for the dance," replied the other. *Still can't figure out if there's a real hydraulic problem or if it's just this driver's imagination*, he thought.

The brakes squealed, then stopped. The alarm cut out in mid-scream as the driver reversed direction. The engine's roar pitched higher as the truck gathered forward momentum, the iron-jawed doors closing slowly beneath the trailing hopper. Two blasts of the air horn, a wave to the mechanics, and the driver rode the monster out of the lot, wheeling it toward the pit.

"Reckon that'll do her for awhile?" the first man asked.

"I 'magine. Let's go home."

"Now, when you see that red light up on the side, it means the operator has seen you, and you're clear to come on up," Ray said to Don as they walked across the bench toward the dragline. "I flashed him as we drove up. See that ladder? When he drops the bucket into the rock, we'll climb on."

Don got out of the truck trying not to take his eyes off the huge machine that towered in front of him. The dragline alternately peeled back the rock from in front of itself, then swung a bucket load of overburden up and out over the yawning pit, dropping it in growing, graying slopes on the other side.

"It's so quiet," Don said. "I expected there to be a lot of noise."

"Yep. Only thing you hear is the fans on the backside," Ray said as he pointed up the side of the housing. "Hard to believe something so powerful can be so silent, huh?"

Even the rock dropping out of the bucket sounds like distant thunder, Don thought. "How big's the bucket?"

"Ninety-three cubic yards. We always tell people who take tours of the place that you can drive two school buses into it. Everybody always wants to have their picture taken in the bucket, too, especially Japanese businessmen. We seem to get a big group of them once a year. Got some one year on December seventh. Can you imagine? Wrong time to be around this place. Old Emory up there fought in the South Pacific, too."

Ray waved to the operator who sat in a small glass protrusion on the face of the machine, just to the right of the boom. Then he turned toward Don and smiled.

"He sees us now. There's the light. You go first. Grab the handles, not the steps. I'll follow."

Don's heart pounded inside his ears as one of the shoes, a giant barge-like structure, appeared from the front of the machine and swung around toward them. Ray had moved them forward, just outside the radius of the shoe's rotation.

"Go," Ray said, "now."

Don grabbed the handrails on each side of the steps, then made what he thought was a long leap onto the first step, about three feet above the ground. Anticipating that the drag would start moving at any moment, he scrambled up the remaining steps until he stood on top of the shoe. Still grasping one of the rails, he turned, expecting to see Ray right behind him. Instead, the miner looked up from the ground and grinned.

"I'll catch a ride on the next go 'round. Hang on."

Don felt a lurch, then heard the gears spooling up from somewhere inside the machine. Looking forward of the shoe, he watched as the bucket was lifted from the bench, trailing a fine rain of dust and rock. In almost the same moment, the boom began to swing out to the right, trolling the hoist cables and bucket beyond the boom point, first the pit, with its black ribboned bottom, rotated into view. Then, as the other side of the pit approached, the operator ran out the hoist ropes, rolling an even spread of rock across the cascading gray spoil banks. With the bucket swinging its predetermined arc beneath the boom, the operator reversed the drag's rotation and swung back toward the bench for another load.

"Fascinating, huh?" Ray grinned from beside him.

Don had been so intent on watching the business end of the dragline that he hadn't noticed when Ray had climbed up and onto the shoe.

"Unbelievable! Everything is done in one motion. Very smooth." *There's something paradoxical about how quiet this thing is compared to the destruction it is capable of,* Don thought. He looked down the length of the bench and across the far end of the pit to the spoil banks. *It just doesn't seem possible that one machine can move so much ground. I guess you'd just have to stand here and watch it over time.*

"No wasted motion," Ray replied. "How'd you like the view of the pit?" he asked, as the machine began to rotate outward once more.

"What do you mean?"

"One hundred ten feet straight down." Ray laughed, pointing down as the shoe cambered over the side of the high wall.

Don had been following the bucket on the first swing. Now he nearly jumped out of his boots.

"Nice white knuckles! Let's go inside."

"About time we called it a day. What do you say, gentlemen?" Tommie asked.

"Let's knock off now," replied Me. "It'll be time to go once we get back to the shop. Me and Ernie's gotta run up to Terre Haute tonight and get some shotgun shells."

Me slid across the seat of the old truck until he was almost touching Ernie. Tommie squeezed in beside him and slammed the door.

"We got a bunch of trash in the back, Ernie," she said. "Let's run down into the pit and dump it before we head back, okay?"

"Okay, Tommie."

The three bumped down the bench and onto the cable route, passing the dragline as they drove around the end of the pit.

"There's ol' Ray's truck," Me said. "You wanna stop?"

"Naw, looks like he's up in the machine," Tommie replied. "I'll beat him home tonight for sure. You say you're headin' up to town tonight?"

"Yep," replied Me. "Me and Ernie's gonna stock up on some shells for duck huntin'. You want us ta getcha some while we're out?"

"Thanks, but I think Ray and I are gonna go up there ourselves later in the week. We'll get some then," Tommie said.

"Don't wait too long. The ad was in the paper today, and there'll be a run on 'em."

Ernie drove around the south end of the pit and out onto the haul road which ran parallel to the pit for some distance before it turned directly into the spoil banks and dived down to the coal, a point where it is called an "incline" by strip miners. The ride along the haul road was smooth compared to the bench and the cable route. In building the road, tons of shale and gravel were spread by the graders and routinely packed smooth by the giant haul trucks. Before turning down the incline, Ernie hesitated, looking to his right up the intersecting haul road that led to the shop. There were no haul trucks in sight.

Tommie leaned forward to look the opposite direction down the incline and across to the bench.

"Ray's out by the bucket with Emory and the groundman. That's probably that new company man's with 'em," Tommie said to Ernie.

Me squinted past Tommie into the distance up the haul road. "All clear this way."

Ernie gunned the engine, angled left, and descended the incline toward the pit. Emerging from between the spoil banks, he made a sharp right-hand turn down the steeply sloping final grade to the bottom.

Halfway down the grade, Me spotted something in the spoil.

"Hey Ernie. Somebody's lost a gas can. Stop so's Tommie can get it."

"Oh, Me," Tommie said, shaking her head. "It's probably no good."

"It don't hurt none to check. Me and Ernie could use one for the chainsaw. Jump out and get it, will ya?"

Ernie stopped the truck in front of the can, and Tommie got out to retrieve it. Walking back to the open door, she flipped the can upside down to show Me the bottom.

"See here? The whole bottom's rusted out. Just more junk," she said, throwing it on the heap of trash growing in the bed of the truck. Climbing back into the truck, she slammed the door.

"Look here. Ray's probably gonna be awhile with that company man. Mind if I ride with you fellas up to town to get some shells? I'll probably still beat him home."

"Sure," Me replied. "Maybe Me and Ernie'll buy your supper, too. Ain't it right, Ernie?"

Ernie put the truck in gear and started down the incline again. He looked ahead toward the end of the pit less than five hundred feet in front of his truck, then down at the black seam of coal seventy feet below his elbow. He smiled.

Partly from the vibrations of the haul truck, but mostly from experience, the driver knew it was time to slow the monster down as he swung from the haul road onto the incline. He tapped the brake pedal expecting a familiar resistance, but this time there was none. *Hell*, he thought, *I must have imagined that*. He tentatively depressed the pedal further, then still further until his heel hit the floorboards. *This can't be happening*, he thought. *They just checked this rig out at the shop*. Desperately pumping the pedal twice more, his knee hit the underside of the steering wheel. The miner's mind raced with options, but the alternatives passed slower than the distance between the truck and the pit. He tried crabbing the wheels into the spoil beside the road, but the big truck merely plowed through the loose rock at the toe of the slopes. He thought about taking the truck over the side of the pit; he had heard of someone doing this before and surviving. He knew that if he tried to shift to a lower gear at his present speed, he might not be able to get out of neutral and would have no control at all over his speed.

Finally, in the short span of a few seconds, the driver made his choice. Crabbing into the spoil didn't work, and to go over the edge might not only be fatal to him but to the loader crews at the bottom of the pit. He would try to slow the truck by downshifting before the incline dropped into the pit. The loader was somewhere near the middle of the pit, so there wouldn't be anybody or anything in front of him at the end of the road. A hundred feet before the turn, he depressed the clutch slowly and attempted to feather the gear exchange, but the lower gear spun wildly and bucked against him. He held the clutch to the floor, dropped off the throttle, and jammed the stick into any gear that would take it, but the stick floundered in neutral. Tightening his grip on the wheel he swung wide at the final turn expecting to see an open road down to the bottom of the pit, but what he saw was Ernie's small, rusted truck fifty yards in front of him. He blasted two long prayers on the air horn. In the end, there was just a scared man riding down a hundred-ton piece of rolling death.

Across the pit, the dragline operator rested the bucket on the bench while the groundman and oiler inspected the teeth and lubricated the critical points. The men by the bucket heard the haul truck's air horn from across the pit and glanced up in time to see the truck barely make its turn onto the descending ramp, its trailer fishtailing out and over the road's edge. Ray and Don heard the horn as well, although only Ray and the other miners on the bench fully understood what the cry meant. They all saw Ernie's truck, pitifully trying to gain speed but losing distance with every second.

Don turned a desperate look to Ray. The older man glared across the pit, determined to will Ernie the speed that he desperately needed. Ray began what seemed to be a low chant that crescendoed into a wail.

"Drive, goddammit! Drive, goddammit! Drive, goddammit!" Ray cried. "Oh, Christ! Drive, goddammit!"

Ernie heard the blast of the horn and looked up to see the grill of the haul truck in his rearview mirror. He floored the accelerator, knocking Me and Tommie hard against the back window. Within seconds he knew that this was a race he wouldn't win. He turned to Me and Tommie, their eyes now riveted on the rolling scythe behind them.

"Jump," Ernie shouted.

Tommie looked at him wildly through the tangle of her blowing hair, her mouth partially open.

"Jump! Now!"

Tommie pulled back on the door handle. Ernie swerved to the right then back left again, throwing her out the door and against the bank and away from the roadbed. She disappeared in the dust.

Ernie watched the image grow in his rearview mirror. "Jump, Me!"

"But, but," Me stammered, frozen to the seat.

Ernie grabbed the little man by the back of his belt, lifted him off the seat, and threw him out the swinging door. Had Me not been so stiff with fear, it might have been like trying to throw a garden hose from one end. As it was, Me hit the bank and rolled back onto the road, feet first, in the path of the haul truck. Raising his battered head, Me saw the truck bearing down on him and mercifully fainted. Death passed over him, its iron jaws only a few inches from his body.

Two hundred feet from safety, with the haul truck ten feet behind him, Ernie knew the race was over. He decided to jump the truck over the embankment and take his chances in a wild ride down the slope. But it was too late. As he jerked the wheel to the left, he looked up into the cold eyes of the beast as its front wheels rolled over him, his scream welded to the shriek and tear of metal.

Along with the others on the bench, Don saw the terrible coupling of the two trucks, the final moments obscured by dust and distance as the fused metal mass ground to a stop at the bottom of the ramp.

"Come on," he said, grabbing Ray by the arm.

Ray looked at him, the shock evident in his face.

"Let's go, Ray! Does somebody have a radio?"

"There's one in Ray's truck," the groundman said. "Just get on the horn and call the office. Tell them to send ambulances. We'll follow you down."

The men ran for their trucks. Even slightly dazed, Ray reached his truck first.

"Slide over," Don said. "I'll drive. You don't look so good."

Don started the truck and headed down the bench. "Daggett office, Daggett office. Come in!" he yelled into the mike.

"This is Daggett office," replied a calm, female voice. "Go ahead."

"We've had a bad accident out here at the pit. We need ambulances!"

"Just a minute," replied the voice, this time with a slight edge.

A few seconds later, a male voice came over the speaker. Don recognized that it was Dutch.

"This is Daggett office. Whereabouts?"

"On the incline. A haul truck."

"Okay, We're on the phone. Who's this?"

"Don Rodgers."

"You with Ray?" Dutch asked.

"He's here with me in his truck. We're headed there now."

"On my way. Out."

Don made the turn at the end of the pit and hit the haul road in third gear. He clipped the mike onto the dash and turned his attention to Ray. *He's nearly as white as this truck,* Don thought.

"Are you okay? You gonna be all right Ray?"

"I think my wife was in that truck," Ray said quietly.

"Oh, Jesus," Don whispered to himself.

"Turn here," Ray said, motioning to Don with his left arm. "They're down there around the corner."

Don sped down the incline between the upraised spoil banks and into the glare of the afternoon sun. A few hundred yards from the right angle turn into the pit, he unconsciously took his foot from the accelerator.

"What's wrong?" Ray said.

"Nothing, nothing," he replied, downshifting his emotions with the truck. In his mind's eye he remembered the twisted wreckage of his parents' car accident. He took a deep breath and held it tight. *I can do this,* he thought; *I must do this.*

As they rounded the corner, the first thing Ray saw was Tommie crumpled in the spoil on the side of the incline.

"Oh my God," Ray said. "Pull over, quick!"

Before Don could get the truck completely stopped, Ray had jumped out and was clambering over the rocks to where his wife lay. Dazed, she smiled weakly at him as he approached.

"I think my leg's broke," Tommie said. "And my back's banged up good. You better not move me." Her teeth were tightly clinched, and Ray noticed a tear tracking through the dust on her cheek. "Me and Ernie's on down the road. Better check on them first."

Don and the men in the truck behind him were out of their vehicles and looking at Tommie in amazement. One of the miners spotted Me stretched out in the middle of the road, fifty yards ahead.

"Look," the man said. "There's another one. Bring the truck." The oiler ran down the road while the groundman raced back to his truck.

"Go help them," Ray called to Don. "I'll stay here until the ambulance comes."

"Okay," Don replied, running to his truck.

"Oh, Ray," Tommie sobbed, "I don't think Ernie made it. It all happened so fast."

"It's all right," Ray said. "The boys'll get him. You just take it easy."

"You look awful pale. Are you okay?"

"Yeah, I'm fine. You scared the hell out of me."

Don drove down the incline and eased around the groundman's truck. The miner had parked it halfway across the incline to avoid getting run over while he and the oiler ministered to Me, who was still lying half conscious in the middle of the road.

"Hey, Me! Hey, old man! You okay?" the oiler asked.

"Don't shake him," the groundman said. "He might have a head or neck injury. His feet's uphill, anyway, and that's good to do for shock. Give me your jacket."

"He don't look too hurt to me," the oiler said, covering Me's thin torso with his denim coat. "He's breathin' okay."

"Might be internal injuries," replied the groundman. "God, he's a skinny little guy!"

Me's eyes fluttered open. "Howdy, fellas. Is dinner over already? I tol' Ernie not ta let me sleep too long. Where's Ernie? I'll kick his butt."

"Old man, you just lay here for awhile and don't move," said the oiler.

"Yeah," said the ground man, looking across Me's prone body to the oiler. "You just take it easy. We'll find Ernie for you."

The dust still hovered around the tangled wreckage when Don pulled up behind the rear of the haul truck. It was apparent that the driver, in a last attempt to avoid the collision, had pushed the right front wheel into the slope. The left front wheel had rolled over the pick-up just behind the cab, crushing the bed and jamming the rear two-thirds of the old GMC between the jack-knifed tractor and the front portion of the haul truck's trailer. The whole rig had run up slope on the right side and even now looked ready to roll over onto its back. The cab of the GMC was twisted and upside down. Don got out of his truck and ran around the left side of the haul truck. Near the front, he found its driver sitting on a large rock holding his head in his hands. He sat up when Don approached. Covered in blood from the top of his head to his knees, his hands shook uncontrollably.

"Somebody's gotta get Ernie out. He's still in the cab!" the man cried.

Don looked quickly toward the crumpled pickup. "In there?"

"I think so. I been calling him, but he don't answer," the man said. "I'd give you a hand, but I can't see."

Don leaned over to quickly check on the miner. Both men flinched as Don pulled back the miner's hair to reveal the long gash just above the man's eyebrows.

"What's your name," Don asked.

"Goodman," the man said. "Who are you?"

"Name's Rodgers."

"Well, it's just a cut, ain't it, Roger?"

"Yeah, nasty-looking, but superficial."

"Good. Now go help Ernie. I can't see so good."

"Okay, but don't move."

"I ain't goin' nowhere for awhile."

Don walked over to where the pickup was pinned under the haul truck. The driver's side of the cab was smashed against the ground, so he crawled over the upturned frame. Bracing himself for what he might see, he looked in through where the passenger door had been.

The big man was crushed between the dash and the rear wall of the cab. The steering wheel was half-imbedded in his chest, and his right leg was bent up so that his knee nearly touched his ear. Blood from a nearly severed lower leg strained through his pant leg and dripped onto the back of the seat. Don reached through the tangle to grasp Ernie's right arm. The miner stirred at Don's touch, slightly opening his right eye. His pulse was weak and his breathing shallow. He moaned as Don withdrew his hand, bloodied and sticky, from the leg wound.

"Ernie?" Don said as calmly as he could. "Ernie, we're going to get you out of here, so hang on. You hear me?"

Ernie looked at Don, then closed his eyes and shivered as his body was racked by a spasm of pain. Don thought he was losing the miner and began to scream at him.

"Ernie, Ernie! Damn it, don't die on me!"

Ernie opened his one eye and looked straight at Don's face a few inches away. He drew a labored breath and whispered, "Tommie." It was a statement, not a question.

"Tommie is up the road a piece. She's okay. Maybe a broken leg, that's all. We've got to stop this bleeding, Ernie. I'm gonna put pressure on the inside of your leg, okay, Ernie? You just hang in there. More help's on the way!"

Don maneuvered himself inside the cab until he could wedge his elbow against the steering column and put pressure from his hand against the artery on the inside of Ernie's thigh. He felt the pulse of the big blood vessel through the man's skin and kept leveraging his arm until the spurting of blood from the open leg wound stopped. *Okay, hang in there, Ernie, until we can get some help*, he thought. *Where's that damned ambulance?*

In the dark dust of the wrecked cab, the two men waited, time marked by the ticks of Ernie's fading pulse. Don sensed that the man's lifeblood had found another rupture through which it could pass unchecked. He felt the throbbing of the miner's pulse ebb, then disappear altogether. A few minutes after Don had first crawled into the truck, Ernie took one final, shuddering breath and lay still. With his arm still wedged into the dead man's leg, Don looked up through the shattered doorframe at the failing light and started to cry.

In the wreck he was found, lying there on the ground,
He asked them to raise his weary head,
Though his breath slowly went, a message he sent
To a maiden, that thought she would be wed:

"Now there's a little white home that I built for my own,
I knew we would be happy bye-and-bye,
But I know you'll be true, so I leave that to you,
'Til we meet at the Golden Gate, goodbye."

Chapter Ten

Before the Scythe

"Look son," Dutch said. "There ain't nothing you can do for him now. The doc says he probably bled to death internally. Now head on back. We'll get Ernie out and take him home."

"I'd just as soon stay," Don said.

"In a few minutes, the sheriff'll be here, the coroner, and a bunch of other folks. You go back to the office in Ray's truck. Park it in the lot and drive over to your house and clean up. I'll be by later this evening. We'll probably need a statement. Don't talk to anyone back at the shop; just go home."

The Dutchman's eyes offered no options, so Don climbed into Ray's truck and drove back up the incline. Ray approached when Don edged the truck past the ambulances and stopped.

"How's your wife?" Don asked.

"She'll be all right. They're putting a splint on her leg now. She's pretty banged up, though. You're a mess."

Don looked down at his arms and shirt and for the first time noticed the shale caked to his skin with Ernie's blood. He almost started to cry.

"I've got to go clean up. How's the other guy?"

"You mean old Evert? We call him Me. He's bruised, got a concussion most likely. He's in the ambulance right now. Skinny little guys like him live forever."

"I'd better go, Dutch says - "

"Look, I heard what you tried to do for Ernie. That was real good. There's nothing you could have done."

"Maybe, but - "

"Maybe, nothin'. You got us here faster than greased lightning. I want you to know I'm grateful. My wife, too,"

"I don't know what to say."

"You'd better go now. They're getting ready to move the ambulances. I'm riding into the hospital with Tommie. See you tomorrow."

On the drive back to the mine office, Don pulled to the side of the haul road. He left the truck engine running and walked into the weeds, a strange, marionette-like feeling developed in his arms and legs. He went only a short distance before he crouched near the ground and vomited. As he stood up, a weak, electric tingle started behind his knees and spread up his spine. He bent over again and rested his shaking hands on his knees.

Through watery eyes he saw the dust plume of a vehicle coming up the road from the pit. Ashamed, he moved stiffly back to the truck. The man-trip carrying the second shift crew had been turned around at the pit entrance. Both the first and second shift crews sat squeezed inside the beat-up Chevrolet Suburban. The driver pulled over to the side of the road and let the following dust pass before he rolled his window down and spat out his chew. "You okay?" he called.

"Yeah, I'm fine." Reaching into the truck he found Ray's half-full coffee thermos on the seat. He poured out a cupful and swirled the cold black bitters around in his mouth before spitting it out and wiping his mouth on his shirt sleeve.

The driver of the man-trip turned his head and said something to somebody inside the truck. The back door opened, and a miner got out carrying his lunch pail.

"Ya mind givin' Jerry here a ride back to the garage?" he asked. It's a might crowded in here."

"No, I mean, sure. Jump on in the truck."

"Thankee," the driver said and pulled away.

Don and Jerry got into Ray's truck and followed the man-trip's dust down the haul road. After a few minutes, Jerry looked at Don through the rear-view mirror and broke the silence.

"I heard you was the first ta get to Ernie."

"Yeah, Ray and I managed to get there pretty quick, but it didn't make much difference."

"Yes, it did," the miner replied, then remained silent the rest of the way to the office.

Yeah, I guess it did, Don thought, remembering how he had ached to be with his brother, if just for a few minutes before he died. *In his last moments, the miner went peacefully enough,* Don thought; *I wonder if my parents felt any pain when they died.* As they drove toward the office, with a coldness that surprised him, Don began to overlay the details of both accidents in his mind until the facts of each event merged and nothing was left but twisted metal and a blurred, hollow ache in his stomach.

Don pulled the truck into the parking space marked *Ray Kelso, SUPPLY.* The nameplate was welded to a piece of steel rebar that rusted in the ground like a metal cross. Already a small crowd had gathered outside the mine office. Katie stood with a group of five men, some holding lunch pails. They all regarded Don expectantly, assured that he would have to pass by them on his way into the office.

"This is my stop," Jerry said. "Much obliged, mister. Them boys can be pretty ripe after a day in the pit."

Don managed a smile and held out his hand. "Don Rodgers."

"Jerry Neal, pumper," the miner replied, squeezing Don's hand. "Take care of yerself."

"Thanks, I'll see you around."

As Don started to get out of the truck, an ambulance flashed by the entrance to the parking lot, the wail of its siren trailing with the dust. A few moments later, a second ambulance passed by unhurried, its dome light flashing but its siren silent. The group's attention was drawn to the ambulance and away from

Don as he climbed out of the cab. He quickly walked across the lot to his own truck, a little more stiffly than he had hoped to appear, trying to carry his body at an angle where no one could see the dried blood that cracked like scales up his arms and stained the front of his shirt.

Standing by the door of the truck, fumbling through his pockets for the keys in what seemed like an eternity, he felt a soft voice emerge from behind him.

"Don? Don, are you all right?" Katie asked.

He tried not to rotate his entire body toward the voice, and instead, attempted only to turn his head. He felt a pinch in his shoulder and winced.

"Oh, Lord! You're a mess!"

"No, no, I'm okay. It's not my blood."

The woman's eyes widened, but she said nothing.

"Look, Dutch told me not to talk to anybody. I've got to get to my house and clean up. I'm sorry. I'll talk to you later."

He tried to put the key into the door, but his hand shook uncontrollably. Katie covered his hand with both of hers and unlocked the door for him, then held the keys at her side.

"Maybe I should drive you to the house."

"Oh, I really don't think that'd be a good idea. I'll be all right," he said, extending his dirty, blood-covered hand for the keys.

"Are you sure?"

"Yeah. Thanks anyway. I've got to go now."

He pulled out of the lot and headed down the red shale road. Halfway to the house he started shaking again, so he eased off the road until the spasm stopped.

Don pulled back onto the road and after a few minutes, found the rusted culvert in the side ditch and turned onto the path to the old house. He backed up to the porch so that he could unload the Bronco later. He didn't expect to get the promised help from the farm crew now. It was starting to get dark anyway.

He turned the key in the ancient lock, remembering to shake the door, working it open through the warped frame. Without turning any lights on, he walked through the house to the bathroom. Pulling the long chain that hung down from the shell globe light above the medicine cabinet, he turned on the hot water and looked up into the mirror, squinting at a face he hardly recognized through the dirt.

After showering and changing his clothes and shoes, he rolled the stained shirt and pants into a bundle and set them out on the back porch. Salvaging his favorite web belt, he put it in the kitchen sink to soak in cold water. He found a washtub under the back steps. Filling it ankle deep with water, he set his boots in to soak; they had looked so new yesterday; now they were caked with mud, and who knew what else. He sat down on the back steps by the porch light and began to pry away the mud, scrubbing at the leather with a rough bristle brush. It was hard to tell whether the dampened leather was also blood-stained; he hoped not.

Don thought that, *except for a traffic jam caused by the accident, he would have been with his parents when they died.* Now, based on today's experience, he was certain that coming onto that wreckage a few minutes after they were taken away in the ambulance had been a blessing. *I've had to deal with death before*, he thought, *but never so intimately.* Once again, he saw Ernie inside the crushed cab, and a white fog seemed to pass behind his eyes as he relived the tactile memory of the dying man's pulse. He bicycled his shoulders to dispel a shiver that was caught in a hollow space beneath his ribs.

Don traced his fear of death to a time when he and Mickey were young enough to still share a bed in the house on Water Street. The boys' parents slept in a room at the other end of a dark hallway. To walk that distance during the night, Don had to pass the door to the basement. Shadowy creatures under the house were kept at bay by a skeleton key that rattled loosely in its keyhole each time the blower to the coal furnace kicked on. It was a slight, almost imperceptible vibration, but the sound fueled the imagination of the four-year old boy, especially if the furnace groaned as Don passed the door on his way to his parents' bedroom, which was usually once every night.

The old man snored. Not particularly loud, but with enough volume that his nasal vibrations provided a comforting buffer against the metallic noises coming up from the basement through the heating duct in the boy's bedroom. Sometime during the night, the snoring would stop abruptly, and the little boy would awaken to the silent alarm. Climbing down from his bed, Don would stand on the cast-iron heat register in the floor, warming his feet before starting down the long hallway to his parents' bedroom. Eyeing the dull gray key to make sure it wasn't turning in the lock, he tiptoed on the balls of his feet across the cold, polished wood floors; past the line of coats and jackets that ghosted above his head, suspended from headless wall hooks. The bedroom door was always open. After Don waited for a few anxious moments at the edge of the dark room, his father's snoring always restarted. Reassured, the boy would run back down the hallway to his warm bed.

Looking back over his life, Don recognized that the fear of his parents' death, or more specifically his concern at not being around when his parents died, guided many of the decisions in his life. Rather than accept a full scholarship to a school in New York, he had chosen to study engineering at an in-state school. He came home on weekends and during summer vacations. After graduation, his parents allowed him to set up office space in one of the unused bedrooms in their house.

As his parents grew older, Don prepared himself for the day when he would step in to take care of them. He saw it not so much as an obligation but an accepted responsibility, a son's duty. His father had established the example by moving Grandma Rodgers into the house when she became too feeble to care for herself. She had died in the room that was now Don's office, surrounded by her family. His grandmother was the first close relative through which he had experienced the mystery and rituals associated with death. It was also the first time he had seen his father cry.

Over time, beginning with his nocturnal vigils at the doorway to his parents' bedroom, Don had developed a fantasy that eventually evolved into a desperate hope: that he might have the special ability to delay or altogether stop death's descent on his family. At age fourteen, with his grandmother's passing, he discovered that there was no special charm. With his parents' deaths shortly after he turned thirty, he understood that life's transition cannot be scheduled so that one can be there at the confluence. If you want to make Death laugh, he had heard, tell him what you're doing tomorrow.

Don had just finished cleaning the first boot when Conner came across the pole bridge with his lantern swinging at knee level. Don started working on the second boot while the old man held the lantern low, almost touching the tub.

"You might as well come over and have some supper," the voice said through the hiss and flare of the gas lantern.

"Ray won't be coming tonight," Don replied without looking up, taking a few hard scrapes at the boot.

"I know."

"How'd you hear so soon?" Don asked, astonishment overcoming his reserve.

Conner set the lantern in the grass and eased down on the steps next to the young man. "News travels fast in the coal fields. Besides, Katherine called me."

"Katherine?"

"Works at the mine. You met her today."

"Oh, you mean Katie! She looks more like a Katie than a Katherine."

"That's just what I told her mother when she was born." The old man chuckled. "Anyway, she asked me to check in on you, thought you might need some company."

"Thanks, it has been some kind of a day," Don said wearily.

The burning propane from the lantern smelled hot and metallic like the fused remains at the accident site, and the hiss of the gas reminded him of the sound the haul truck's ruptured radiator made as Ernie lay crushed beneath it. He heard his own voice, as if from some distance down a darkened hallway say: *"I don't know that I'm cut out for this line of work."*

"A man can't make decent conversation, let alone make decisions on an empty stomach," Conner said, as if reading his mind. Then the big man picked up the lantern and held it up high, illuminating the entire porch. "Come on, son. Let's go have something to eat."

"I need to finish this boot first."

"If you brush that boot any more, you'll take the hide right off it and be down to the steel toe. Come on, you can wash up at my place."

Don put the boot down on the step and followed Conner over the bridge, trailing the yellow light. Once inside the cabin, Conner hooked the lantern over a metal hook fastened to a roof beam above the kitchen table. "Sit down, sit down. I'll warm up the grub, and you relax."

In the swaying arc of the lantern light, the old miner moved to the kitchen stove. Taking a box of matches down from the warming shelf, he lit a burner underneath a blackened pot, adjusting the blue-orange flame until it danced along the pot's edge, alternating light and shadow on the ceiling overhead. Reaching toward the wall, he flipped a hidden switch, and a bank of fluorescent lights illuminated the kitchen.

"Thought I didn't have electricity, didn't you?" he laughed. "Blew a fuse this morning; that's all. Got to get another one before the front half of the house'll work. Go to town tomorrow."

Don suppressed a laugh, smiling instead. Looking around, he noticed that structurally, Conner's house was not far different than his own. A few inner walls had adjusted the space to the old man's tastes, but the basic form was the same. In the kitchen, instead of cabinets, there were open shelves on which cans of beans, corn, peaches, and pears rallied, sometimes four deep and slope-stacked against the wall. A few dishes and cups were filed in a metal drainer on the counter with a short-handled pump perched by the edge of the sink. The green and white linoleum was spotless.

"I like to know what I've got to eat," Conner said. "All those cans are in alphabetical order, too. Sometimes I have a letter day; that is, I eat peaches and potatoes. Sometimes I go for just consonants, like cornbread and beans. Vowels once a week."

"Like what, for instance?"

"Eggs and ice cream," Conner said, laughing.

"What's today?"

"Leftovers. You can consider it alphabet stew," and the old man chuckled.

In the front room, the end of the house had the same familiar fireplace, but the walls on each side were lined to the gable with tired shelves, burdened with books of every size and description. Don glanced at Conner who was busy agitating whatever was to be dinner in the big pot with a wooden spoon. *Now here's a renaissance man,* he thought. *I'll bet he's read every book on these shelves, too. Not something you expect to find a coal miner doing. Probably comes from living alone.*

"Mind if I look at your library?"

"Go ahead! Now, those books aren't in alphabetical order. I file them by subject matter. Novels are up overhead on the left; magazines stacked by the window. I don't put them on shelves, except for the *National Geographics*. All the others stack better than they stand." And indeed, the bottom shelves soldiered with the yellow magazine, enough volumes to go back at least twenty years.

"You've read all these books?"

"Cover to cover. It's about all I do anymore; the only way a man can travel when he doesn't have the money or gets too old to go anywhere."

"Some of these books look pretty old."

Conner placed the big pot on the table and joined the young man in the living room. Putting his hands on his hips, the old man squinted and craned his neck toward the darkened shelves, high on the wall.

"Yep, I used to go to book sales at libraries and such. Bought only hardbacks, classics mostly. Somewhere up there's an old copy of *Pilgrim's Progress* and an original *Roughing It* by Mark Twain. Got a second printing of *Grant's Memoirs*, too. Ain't been up there for awhile, so I don't know where. Getting kind of dusty, I suspect."

"They say you can tell a lot about a person by what he reads."

"That's why I bought all the classics." The old man chuckled. "I only read the magazines anymore. Time to eat."

"I'm not sure I feel like eating very much."

"Nothing like a little potluck to unknot the ol' stomach, I always say. Sit yourself down."

The two men took their places at the table. Conner ladled a browned pile of meat, potatoes, carrots, and gravy onto Don's plate. The aroma steamed across the table, reminding the young man that he hadn't eaten since breakfast.

"Boy, that does smell good," Don said reaching for the offered plate.

"There's bread and butter to go with it." Conner smiled, obviously pleased. "Iced tea in the pitcher. You like it sweet?"

"Yes, thank you."

"Good, that's how I make it."

Both men began to eat in a silence punctuated only by the scraping of forks and knives across their plates. A motion of the fork or a nod of the head indicated "pass the salt" or "I'll have some more stew, please." For all their differences in age and backgrounds, in their eating habits, the two were joined at the hip.

Using a piece of bread to sop up the last bit of gravy from his second plate of stew, Don wearily pushed himself back from the table, shook his head, and sighed.

"Damn, that was good. I wouldn't have thought I could put anything away; after today; you know what I mean."

"My pleasure," Conner nodded, picking up his plate and moving to the sink. "I'll put some coffee on. You take it easy."

Don watched the old man fill a kettle with water from the pump and rekindle the burner on the stove.

"Got regular running water, but this old well water makes the best coffee. Must be the iron in it. Dug that well before we built the house."

Feeling satisfied and more than a little obligated to his host for both the food and the company, Don ventured a conversation.

"You know, Ray's wife wasn't hurt too badly. A broken leg, I think."

"That's what I heard. Maybe a few bruised ribs," Conner said.

"And the old guy?"

"Maxwell Evert?" Conner asked.

"Yeah. Did you hear anything about him?"

"Busted wrist and a concussion. He'll be just fine. He's wiry."

Don stopped there. Conner sat down and continued.

"I've known Ernest since the day he was born. Worked with him from his first day at the mine. That's back when we were still working the old Daggett Number Three."

Conner slid a glance toward the engineer to determine if the name of the mine meant anything to him. The young man only stared at the table.

"It's hard work at the mines, even with all the equipment and dozers and scrapers. Easier with the machines, tougher on the men. There just ain't no 'little' accidents, never have been. Men are going to die. You just hope it ain't on your shift."

"But on your first real day?"

"A bad start, I'll give you that. But I heard you done a brave thing out there today."

Brave? That's not exactly what I would have called my actions, Don thought. *More like desperate.* Again, he thought about the similarities between today's tragedy and his brother Mickey's accident. He only did today what he wished he could have done for his brother.

"It made no difference," Don said, almost to himself.

"Yes, it did. Ernie had someone with him at the end. Most of us won't be able to say that."

"Yeah, but he didn't even know me," Don said, his eyes beginning to water. "And I didn't know him."

"And there's where you're wrong, son. Anybody who has the guts to go out and dig through the rock for a lump of coal is kin to a miner, whether it's your first day on the job or when they hand you the gold watch and chain."

"I'm no miner."

"Maybe you don't see it yet, but you will. Union, company, wives, kids. We're all related, some more than others. We're a clan of miners," Conner said.

"I thought the union hated the company."

"They get whipped up occasionally by the bosses, but most of the company men I know were union to begin with."

"Really?"

"Where do you think they come from? We're all mostly neighbors. Don't get me wrong. Years ago, a strong union was needed. There was a lot of unfairness in the mines and safety problems. I could make you a list you wouldn't believe: poor ventilation so's that gas seeped into the shafts and exploded;

companies tryin' to save money on timbers at the expense of roofs cavin' in on the men; hell, years ago there was no dust suppression; no rockin' of the shafts with gypsum to keep the coal outa your lungs. Ever heard of black lung? And the wages they used ta pay? Slave wages and sometimes not even real money at that; ever heard of scrip? Company funny money and not enough at the end of the month to pay your rent or settle accounts at the company store."

"But there are differences, I mean between being company or union, right?" Don asked.

"I guess you'd think so," Conner answered. "Even today there are differences. Maybe it's because I'm older that I can see it now like I didn't before. It always seems that both the company and union bosses sort things out at the top, using the working man to shore them up. Put them all in a room - the bosses I mean - and I'd bet you couldn't tell the difference between a company and union man. Anyway, all the same, the working man still has his job to do."

Don picked up his fork and began to make small circles in the residual gravy on his plate, his mind absent of thought. Then after a few moments, he remembered that his mother said it was an irritating habit, so he stopped.

"Likely somebody's going to try and blame somebody else for the accident today, but it don't do no good," Conner continued. "Things sometimes just happen, for no good reason."

Don considered his previous conversation with the corporate safety man and Ray concerning someone sabotaging the mine operations. *Maybe Conner doesn't know,* he thought. *I'd better keep those thoughts to myself.*

"Isn't it somebody's fault?" Don asked.

"Maybe, but it don't make any difference to Ernie, does it?"

"No."

"I'll tell you, most times it's not something big that brings about a tragedy, it's a combination of little things - a turn here, lost time there - the wrong decision at the wrong time. It all adds up to what a lot of people call fate."

"So, you think it was Ernie's time to go?"

"It was the end of his shift. It was Ernie's time to punch out."

"How'd you figure that?"

"A man only gets one chance to walk away from death, and Ernie was carried out of it years ago. I spent most of my life working right under it, and now it don't scare me none at all. I'll recognize it when it comes for me. I know Ernie did."

Jesus, I don't know if I'm cut out for this, Don thought and shivered. Visions of Ernie compressed inside the truck cab began to merge with memories of his brother's mangled car alongside the highway. He was having trouble separating the two images again.

"You might not think you're cut out for this kind of work now, but I'll venture to say you'll know in the morning. Nobody's got a gun to your head. You can walk away from it any time you want. Believe me, I know."

Don looked up as Conner got out of his chair to get the kettle of water for the coffee. The room seemed a little darker and the miner a little older.

"It's not as easy for me to walk away from all this as you might imagine," Don said softly. "I've got nowhere else to go. My brother was killed in an accident not unlike this a few months ago. I mean, it wasn't a haultruck, and the bastard that did it was drunk. Son of a bitch is out on bail even now with a suspended driver's license."

Conner came back with the kettle and the cups.

"Like I said, you done a brave thing today, nothing to be ashamed of. But don't expect to hear a lot from these here folks. That's out of respect for Ernie, and you."

Chapter Eleven

Bury Me Beneath the Willow

Don awoke from the couch Ray and Tommie had left clustered with other furniture in the cabin's living room. Too tired to unload his truck or set up the bed, he slept in his clothes rather than fire up the wood stove. He was warm enough in his sleeping bag. As he struggled with its zipper, he realized that the whole place was barely above freezing, and he needed a shower.

He rushed across the cold wooden floors to the bathroom, shut the door, and flipped on the baseboard heater. Turning on the hot water in the shower, he remembered that he'd need some clean and warm clothes. Running back across the living room and out the front door, he retrieved a suitcase and his heavy jacket from the Bronco. The cinders from the drive stuck to the bottom of his feet and hurt even more as he hopped across the porch, picking first at one foot, then the other. Noticing a yellow piece of paper stuck behind the porch light, he stuck it in his shirt pocket, struggled to close the warped front door, then ran back in the bathroom.

The room steamed hot from the shower water, and the baseboard heater began to click as it warmed up. He put on his jacket, sat on the toilet breathing in the wet heat, and unfolded the note. It read simply: "Meeting in Superintendent's Office. Tomorrow, 7:00 a.m.", and was signed by the Dutchman. Don rubbed the fog from his watch. It was already six thirty-five; he had to hurry.

His hair was still wet, but he had five minutes to spare when he pulled into the office lot. The sun was just coming up over the spoil banks east of the mine, and a large group of miners were leaving the washhouse next to the safety building. Another assemblage of men stood by one of the open bays of the shop drinking coffee. They regarded him without expression as he entered the side door. Coming up the hallway from the garage, he passed the kitchen area where Katie was making a fresh pot of coffee. She motioned him in.

"How about some coffee? I just made a new pot."

"Thanks, do I have time?"

"Sure, Dutch isn't here yet. All the others are outside. When you see them tramping to his office, you'll know it's time to go in. You sleep okay? I was over to Conner's shortly after you left. He said you seemed mighty upset."

"Well, I'm better this morning," Don said, wondering why she might have been at Conner's so late. "What's going on anyway?"

"Dutch always calls a meeting after an accident, and this being a fatality, well, I reckon there'll be an internal investigation by the company safety people."

"Why would they want me here? I don't know how it happened."

"You and Ray were the only company men that saw it, and," she hesitated, lowering her eyes, "you were there when Ernie died."

He turned away toward the wall.

"I'm sorry," she whispered. "I've known Ernie a long time, but it must have been hard on you, too. Here, the coffee's done. Cream and sugar, right?"

"Yes, thanks," he said smiling weakly. "You remembered."

"Well, it's only been a day."

"One hell of a day," he answered quietly.

The side door slammed, and, in a few seconds, Dutch appeared in the kitchen.

"Morning," he said gruffly.

Dutch looked toward Don with one eyebrow upraised. *Oh, Jesus,* Don thought, *I was supposed to meet him at the house last night. I must have been next door at Conner's when he came by. He's going to chew my ass.*

"I came by the house late. I take it you got the note on the door?"

"Yes, sir, that's why I'm here."

"Have you talked to anyone here about the accident?" he asked, glancing to Katie.

"No, sir, I just came in."

"Good." he said loudly, glancing toward the open door. "Now this morning we're going to have a meeting with all the bosses, company only. Later this afternoon you'll need to meet with the safety people from corporate. Just answer their questions and tell them what you saw. A labor relations man will talk to the union representatives. No statements to the papers, you understand?"

"Yes, sir."

"Believe me, it's better for everybody. Be in my office in five minutes. Katie, here's the funeral information for Milts. Type it up and bring me about twenty copies. See you in five minutes, son."

Dutch hurried out the door and down the hall. He was followed after a few seconds by the gang of men outside the door. After they passed, Katie looked at the piece of paper Dutch had given her.

"They're showing Ernie tomorrow night and the funeral's Thursday," she said softly. Looking up, she saw Don's face begin to cloud over. "Listen to me," she said sternly. "You can't go into a meeting in front of the men like that. I'm sorry, but you've got to get a hold of yourself."

"You're right," he replied, shamed into a half smile. "I'll be okay. Thanks."

"After work, I'm going up to Terre Haute to see Tommie and Me. You want to go along?"

Don thought for a moment.

"Ray'll be there; he'd be glad to see you."

"Sure, that would be fine."

"We'll go in my Jeep. Be here at four thirty. You had better get to Dutch's office now. I'll see you after work."

"Okay. Thanks for the coffee," he said as he hurried out the door and down the hall.

The sun was dusking the cornfields by the time the two turned north on Highway 41, heading for the hospital in Terre Haute. Answering the investigators' questions earlier in the afternoon proved somewhat analytical and easier than Don expected. Now the ride with Katie was turning downright therapeutic. The two had to practically shout their conversation. On the radio, Lester Flatt was trying to overcome the roaring engine and whining tires, a Jeep's way of protesting its use on a paved road:

Listen to the jingle, the rumble and the roar,
As she glides along the woodland,
through the hills and by the shore,
Hear the mighty rush of the engine
and the lonesome hobo squall,
You're travelin' through the jungle on the Wabash Cannonball.

Don scanned the inside of the jeep. The loose canvas top contributed to the general cacophony as the wind snapped it against the doorframe and the overhead roll bar. Two empty beer bottles lay parallel to each other on the back seat, lightly tinkling with each jolt from the road. A strange knocking came from the floorboards behind Katie's seat. He leaned back and saw a wooden bat.

"Hey," Don said, smiling. "What's the Louisville Slugger for behind your seat? You a softball player?"

Without taking her eyes from the road, she reached back between the seats until she felt the handle of the baseball bat, then glanced quickly at Don and laughed before returning her eyes to the road ahead.

"That's my persuader!"

"You don't mean?"

"Used to carry a .38, but it's against company policy now. Besides, a bat's enough to scare most guys off."

"Present company included?"

"Present company excluded!" She laughed, placing both hands at the top of the steering wheel, then weaving the Jeep slightly back and forth within the lane.

For a great deal of the way, the conversation was very one-sided. She carried most of the exchange, her hands leaving the wheel if a point needed emphasis. Don leaned back against the door on the passenger side and strained to hear the high points above the whistling wind and an engine that seemed set to explode at any minute. Occasionally, he would see her lips move but hear nothing, not even the engine. Sometimes she would look toward him expecting acknowledgment, and his only response was a smile. She laughed, knowing he couldn't hear much of what she said, and neither of them minded.

Don positioned himself so she was silhouetted against the low sun. His intent was to cut the glare, but the effect overwhelmed him. An aurora of burnished gold weaved through her hair and outlined her profile. When she turned toward him to speak, her face, eclipsed by the sunlight, disappeared into shadow. Caught on the lee side of a magic he'd underestimated his heart took over the function of his head. He tried to subdue the growing excitement by rationalizing away his emotions. She was different, very different than any woman he had met before. She was competent and confident, but not in an aggressive way. *If she were a man,* he thought, *I'd say she was cocky.* As it was, she just seemed damned smart. And beautiful.

Later that night, back at his cabin, he lay awake for hours. Not thinking about the accident, but about Katie. How strange it was, how guilty he felt, how easily she invaded his thoughts and pushed that awful accident to the back of his mind. He mentally chastised himself for downgrading Ernie's death to a secondary issue, and as he fell asleep, he rationalized that his attraction to Katie was just the result of the previous day's concentrated emotions; *it will pass*, he thought. But when he woke the next morning and she was the first thing on his mind, Don knew there was more to it than that.

A continuous stream of miners filed into the small funeral home during visitation hours on Wednesday evening. Their wives signed the register at the entrance to the chapel and clustered near Ernie's parents at the front, where Ernie reposed in a new suit. Most of the men, having escorted their wives past the coffin and spent a respectful length of time looking for their names on the flower cards, retired outside to the parking lot to smoke. Those who chewed or took a pinch from the communal can of Skoal that was being passed around spit into paper cups rather than on the ground, respecting the solemnity of the occasion.

"Don't remember ever seein' Ernie in a suit," one of them commented.

"I suspicion it was provided by old man Reed, the undertaker, just for the occasion," came a reply.

"Even so, don't he look natural?"

"There ain't nothing natural about being dead."

Most of the men nodded their heads and mumbled in assent; others shook their heads in disbelief; but they all agreed. None of them mentioned their common suspicion: that the failure of the haul truck's brakes was the reason Ernie Milts was dead. When they had the proof, somebody was going to pay.

On Thursday afternoon, Ernie Milts' body was buried in the little cemetery south of town, in the family plot, not too far from old man Jeffries. His pallbearers were his fellow miners and the president of the local union, who walked at the head of the coffin. Several company people took a long lunch to attend the short graveside service, including Don, who escorted Katie. Men from the second shift and men who had recently been laid off also heard the young minister litanize the usual dust to dust.

The preacher might have said much more on this occasion: things about a man in the mines: about how generations of miners have spent their lives underground inevitably and metaphorically digging their own graves; he might have called Ernie by name and suggested that the greatest gift one can bestow is to lay down his own life for someone else. But the preacher didn't know Ernie, and he was also new to his congregation and the town. Besides, the two people who knew of Ernie's selfless acts in the final moments of his life - Tommy and Me - were still in the hospital and couldn't attend his funeral.

After the service, and before they laid Ernie to rest, the mourners paid their final respects to Mr. Milts, who stood wide-eyed by Ernie's mother, seated in the only chair brought to the cemetery. As Don waited in line with Katie, he was surprised how small and frail Ernie's parents seemed when compared to the big man laid out in the coffin. He shook old man Milts' hand as Katie leaned over to offer a few whispered words to Mrs. Milts. Then turning toward Ernie's mother, Don vaguely remembered somebody saying that the greatest tragedy in life was to outlive your children, and he saw it in her eyes.

"We heard what you done for our boy," she said softly. "We want you to know that we're grateful."

"I'm sorry for your loss," Don said, taking her offered hand between both of his.

"Stop by and see us when you can," the old man said in a strained voice.

Don nodded because he didn't know what else to say. Rooted to the ground, he seemed unable to move, overwhelmed by a collage of memories – Ernie, his parents, his brother. Katie placed her arm around his elbow and lightly squeezed his wrist. The two turned away, walking back to the Jeep through the tall, dying grass.

"He was their only child," she said.

The wind winnowed and gentled the sound of slamming car doors and starting engines. The second shift was going back to work, leaving Ernie with his parents, under the bending willows, in the soft afternoon sun.

My heart is sad, and I am lonely,
Weeping for the one I love,
When shall I see her, no not never,
'Til we meet in heaven above,

So, bury me beneath the willow,
Under the weeping willow tree,
So she will know where I am sleeping,
And perhaps she'll weep for me.

Bury Me Beneath the Willow
Traditional Folk Song

Chapter Twelve

Muleskinner Blues
Words and Music by Jimmie Rodgers

Good Mornin', Captain,
Good Mornin', Shine!
Do you need another muleskinner,
Out on your new road line?

I like to work,
I'm a movin' all the time,
I can carve my initials,
In any ol' mule's behind!

Roger and John had been the last to arrive at the cemetery and so, after the short service, were the first to reach their truck which John had pole-positioned in front of the hearse on the roadside. They made the decision to show up at the last minute when Roger locked up the tailgate of the old pickup, springs busting with a load of newly cut firewood. Besides, it was on the way to Cooper's store, they agreed. In flannel shirts and coveralls, they stood in the road a respectful distance from the dark-dressed mourners, withdrawing their sweat-stained hats at the final invocation, honestly sharing in the sorrow, and for a moment recognizing their own mortality. Now John eased the overloaded truck out of the shoulder weeds and down the road to Dolores Cooper's. *For such a fine load of wood, she just might throw in lunch to boot,* he thought.

Once at Cooper's, the two men settled into their customary seats by the window. Bobby brought them the day's special and, today being Thursday, that meant cornbread and beans.

"My god, your momma knows how to cook, Bobby," John said, stirring the steam out of the thick bowl of beans in front of him. "Reckon we can have some chopped onions on the side? The beans don't need 'em, but Roger's a little partial to some raw onion, if you got some."

"Yes sir, Mr. Hicks," Bobby replied. "I'll bring some back with the cornbread."

Both men vigorously peppered the soup, Roger turning the surface nearly black before carefully folding it in with his spoon. Out of the corner of his eye, John saw Dolores approaching from the kitchen with a tray of cornbread and the bowl of diced-up onions.

"Now these are what I call beans," he said loudly to Roger who was bent over his bowl, testing the broth, sucking it loudly from his spoon. "She don't use no fatty pork, just real ham. Cooks it for a long time, too, and gets it nice and stringy-like. I ought to do the decent thing and marry that woman."

"What makes you think I'm looking ta marry!" Dolores said and laughed, setting the tray down on the table. "Besides, you ain't near feisty enough. I need a younger man who can keep up with me," she added, placing a saucer with two large pieces of cornbread in front of each man and a cereal bowl of onions between them.

"And this, Roger," John said, "is the sweetest cornbread this side of heaven." He cut one piece in two, buttered half of it, then crumbled the other portion on top of his beans. "What do you put in this to make it so sweet, Mrs. Cooper?"

"That's my secret," Dolores replied, raising her chin to appraise the situation through the bottom lenses of her bifocals. Cocking one eyebrow, she accepted half of John's words as a compliment while her eyes regarded both men suspiciously. Under his Beechnut hat, Roger avoided her prying eyes and continued to slurp at his beans.

"Just what have you boys been up to lately?"

"Take a gander out front," John said, starting in on his beans. She angled to the front window behind where Roger was sitting.

"Well, I'll swan. That's a nice load, boys."

"We'll put her out back and go get another, ma'am, soon as we finish these beans," John said. "Worked us up a powerful appetite. Been up since early this morning. Got some more cut up, and just need to load it out."

"And I suppose you expect me to throw in the beans, too!"

John puppy dogged a look her way.

"Don't I know it." She scowled, shaking her head. "All right, but just this once."

She looked back out the window beyond the cord of wood weighing down the old truck and spied the hearse pulling into the mortuary down the street. A few cars rounded into the lot behind it while a group of trucks continued toward the store, eventually filing in beside the boys' truck.

The miners got out of their trucks and huddled in small groups before breaking toward the front door.

"Oh, dear," she said sadly, "they must be comin' from that poor boy's funeral. Bobby! Bobby!"

"Yeah, Ma?" came a muffled response from the kitchen.

"Get up here, boy," she said, shuffling back to the kitchen while shooting a quick glance at the men occupying the window table. "We got payin' customers comin'."

The cowbell above the jamb banged as the men came through the screen door, some sidling up to the front counter to restock their supply of various forms of tobacco, others rustling into the restaurant for a quick cup of coffee before heading to the mine. Roger looked up from his beans just as Larry Miller pulled a chair over to their table by the window. He turned the chair around so that he could rest his elbows on its back and glared out the front window without saying anything to his hosts. In a few minutes, Katie's Jeep went by the window on its way to the mine office.

"Ain't that a bitch," Larry said.

"Yeah," John replied. "Old Ernie's passing sure was a shock." Roger ate in studied silence.

"Not that," Larry continued. "She's hangin' out with that new guy!"

Roger's face darkened beneath the brim of his ball cap. He glanced toward John with an undisguised look of disdain. Ernie's death seemed to mean nothing to Larry.

John turned away from Roger's glare. "Who would that be?" John said, feigning ignorance.

"Katie, dammit! Didn't you see her arm-in-arm with that son of a bitch as they left the cemetery?"

"Oh," John said. "*That* new guy. Reckon he's the one she threw you off for taking her to the dance?"

"Can't be," Larry said, slowly shaking his head. "She hadn't even seen him yet when I asked her to go on Monday. You know," he said with a low voice and narrowing eyes, "that means she - "

"Traded you for a player to be named later," Roger said, snickering. "Ain't that something!"

"Screw you," Larry exclaimed. A strained silence dangled between the men as Larry stared at Roger waiting for him to make eye contact; Roger demurred.

"No disrespect intended for the dead and injured," John said, breaking the uncomfortable silence, "but won't y'all be needing some drillers out at the mine?"

"Reckon we might," Larry said without taking his eyes off Roger, who continued to eat his beans, apparently unconcerned. "You and Roger figure to have a leg up?" he asked John.

"If I'm not mistaken, Roger and me's the next on the panel."

"So, why're you talking to me?"

"Between you and your old man, you being first shift pit boss and all, and depending on how you might move the men around, me and Roger might get called back."

"That so, Roger?" Larry said, gritting a smile as his mind reaffirmed the control he had over the two men. Larry had tolerated Roger's silent arrogance for years, and now his hate distilled into a malevolence that concentrated on his face. He seemed coiled and ready to pounce.

"Roger don't mean nothing by it, Larry, you know that," John whined to Larry, then turned to Roger. "Roger, dammit, clear back in third grade I warned you not to piss him off."

"To hell with him if he can't take a joke. We don't need him to say when we work and when we don't. I been down to the hall; we start work Tuesday."

Larry glared out the window for a minute, his thoughts shifting gears. Looking first at John's expectant face and then the top of Roger's hat, he stood up, turned his chair around, and slid it roughly under the table, bumping it against Roger's knee.

"Be out at the office Saturday evening about five o'clock. We'll look over the situation then."

"But the game starts at six," John said, a little whine in his voice. "Are we, I mean, are you planning to miss homecoming?"

"I ain't planning to miss nothing," Larry said, nodding at Roger. "And bring this piece of dirt with you. We'll go to the game together after we're done."

"Done doing what?" John asked.

"Just show up by five. I'll be waiting in the garage."

The big man clopped across the wooden floor, brushing past Bobby who had just come through the front door.

"Hey, easy money," Bobby said when he saw Larry.

The miner stalked past Bobby without response, the screen door slamming behind him.

"What's up with him?" Bobby said, taking a seat in the empty chair between John and Roger.

"Female problems," John said.

"I 'magine," Roger added.

Larry came up the hallway from the garage and stormed past the open door to Katie's office where she was settling down to an afternoon of typing memoranda and collecting time sheets. In the last few feet before Dutch's door, he slowed down, then stopped when he heard his father speaking over the telephone. As soon as Dutch hung up the phone, he stepped inside the office and closed the door.

"You got a minute?" Larry asked.

"Sure, sit down. What can I do for you?"

"You've been saying for a week that we're going to get new maps of the permit area, aerial photos, and topographic, right?"

"That's right. The new guy, Don Rodgers, is supposed to have them to me by Friday."

"That's tomorrow," Larry asked.

"I know what damn day it is."

"Is he going to have them done?" Larry asked with a sneer, refusing to back down.

"That's between him and me. But I expect that he will."

"Maybe he'll have to work Saturday to catch up."

"I'll decide when and who works around this mine. Anything else?"

"We need to replace the first shift drill crew."

"I'm aware of that. What else?"

"What's the word on Tommie and the old man?"

Dutch sighed. "Well, Tommie's out for at least eight weeks. Ray went to bring her home from the hospital today. The old man? That's a whole different story. He took a pretty bad whack on the head, so they gave him a good going over, a complete physical. In the course of giving him some tests, they found some things that are going to keep him from ever working again. I'm not at liberty to say what, but you keep your mouth shut about this. That was the corporate safety man on the phone. I think they're going to retire him early with some decent benefits. This way he might live longer."

Larry turned a questioning look at his father, who had already shifted his attention to a pile of papers on his desk.

Rising out of the metal folding chair, he walked to the closed door. Before he could turn the handle to open it, he heard his father's voice behind him.

"Son, don't let personal interests interfere with doing your job."

"What do you mean?"

"You know exactly what I mean. If the girl ain't interested, she ain't interested."

"I need those maps by Saturday night," Larry replied, then slammed the door and stomped into the front office.

"Going to the homecoming with me Saturday?" Larry asked Katie.

Katie froze for a moment, then answered without raising her head to address him.

"I told you before that I'm already going with somebody else."

"Oh, yeah? Who is it?"

"Like I said before, nobody you'd know."

"That was yesterday, and I didn't. Today I do."

"You mind your own business," she said coldly, shooting a chilly look in his direction.

"I always do." He laughed as he walked away, slamming the heavy metal door behind him.

After a few minutes, Dutch pushed back from his desk and stood up slowly, a little concerned by the stiffness in his neck. He placed his hands on his hips, arched his back slightly, then rocked his head from side to side until he heard the crack of vertebrae and felt the unwelcome pressure subside. Closing fists on his two large thumbs, he popped the joints, then laced his fingers together, turned his elbows outward, and knuckled off a few more cracks. Joints that he missed with the mass approach, he twisted and pried individually, down to the tips of each finger, until all had been serviced and snapped.

He leaned on his desk for a few minutes while the blood found its way to his feet. He attempted to curl his toes inside his shoes, but the steel caps of the safety boots frustrated adequate flexing. It seemed that if he sat for too long nowadays, at least one leg would numb up and both feet would feel like clubs until he had walked a-ways. A sharp tingling raced from his hips to his ankles, signaling that it was okay to take the first step. He headed down the hallway, gaining strength in his legs with each stride.

He opened the shop door to the ratcheting rhythm of an air hammer, accompanied in the distance by the deep tympani of paired sledgehammers breaking loose a rubber tire from its rim. He stood by the back stairs for a few moments, bit off the end of a cigar, blinked at the flare of the match, and luxuriated in the squinting smoke before climbing the steps to the engineering office overhead.

Inside, three men huddled over a variety of maps spread across the wide drafting table. Don was reviewing the property lines and permit area with the mine's field engineer and the company land agent. The rod man sat respectfully in the corner, rewriting his field numbers into the office notebook while his elder colleague represented their efforts of the last week to the new man.

"Here are the stations that we shoot everything off of," said Lee Wagner, the surveyor, pointing to dots on a topographic map with coordinates laid down beside them. He then pulled a larger scale aerial photo over the first map and pointed to a series of white crosses clearly visible on the blue tinted sheet. "And as you can see," he hesitated, throwing back both of these maps to reveal an even larger scale map taped to the top of the table, "we use these stations to figure the pit advance and everything that's taken out of the pit. Those numbers are compared with the haul truck cycles, the coal in the stockpiles, the loads in the unit train, and the tipple figures to determine the amount of coal produced for the month and the royalties to be paid. In other words, they've got to remain undisturbed ... in the same place."

"I understand," Don said apologetically, "but one of those stations is outside the area the company wants to permit, and the other is within one hundred feet of a riparian zone, so it has to be moved."

"What's the problem?" Dutch asked as he shut the office door, muting the cacophony of the shop in the process.

"We're going to have to relocate some of our survey stations," Don said.

"Why's that?" Dutch asked, looking at the concerned faces of the surveyor and his rod man.

"They're not within the area the company wants to permit for one thing, and this one's actually near an environmentally sensitive area," Don said, pointing to the map. "The inspectors will pick up on that right away."

"Is a station going to cause that much environmental damage?" the surveyor said sarcastically.

"I don't think so," Don said, "but the inspectors will think so, and that's what counts."

"He's right, Lee," Clarence Gilmer, the land agent said. "They'll figure that there'll be traffic in and out of the station. I've seen them threaten to shut down a mine over lesser things."

"What about the one outside the permit area?" Dutch asked.

"Well, we could permit a little strip over to it, but the company would have to pay bond on the ground and then reclaim it later. It's in old spoil, so that'd be a dead cost," Don said.

"What do you think, Bud?" the superintendent asked Clarence. "Aren't we eventually going to mine in that direction?"

"That's true," Clarence replied, "but not within the next five years, and the company only wants to permit what the mine will disturb in the next five years. Saves them a lot of bond money."

"So, what's the problem?" the Dutchman asked, tipping the ash from his cigar into the wastebasket. No reply was offered. "Look, men," Dutch said, "this boy's not here to give us a hard time. As I see it, he's here to point out our shortcomings in order to save our butts occasionally. What's the problem with moving the stations, Lee?"

"Not a thing, Dutch," replied the surveyor. "We'll get 'er done before we leave today." He joined the rod man who was already halfway out the door, and the two men disappeared into the reverberations of the garage. Dutch watched them leave, then turned toward the engineer.

"You let me know when you're about to change the way we do things around here, you understand?"

Don was taken off guard, but managed to nod and stammer, "Yes sir."

"Now, down to the business of redrawing the permit lines. Bud here been giving you the maps you need?" Dutch asked.

"Yes sir. I'd like to draw the rough lines on the aerial first, then, with your approval, transfer them on to a base topographic map. All I need is to locate the present position of the pit on the topo and project the area of disturbance over the next five years."

"What does 'disturbance' mean?" Clarence asked.

"Any part of the operation," Don responded. "Cable routes, sediment ponds, access to monitoring stations, things like that."

"Well," Dutch said, flipping over and slowly smoothing out the aerial photo. "With our present rate of progress, the pit ought to be right around here in five years," he said while pressing his thumb to the map. "We've got a color-coded map from corporate which shows that. It's down in my office."

"Okay, we'll work from that, then," Don said. "The trick will be to allow enough room within the permit area to accommodate all of our activities."

"I'll get you a copy of our property maps," Clarence said. "I guess we'll need to own everything we permit, right?"

"Not necessarily. Is there any property within the mine plan that the company doesn't own?" Don asked.

The superintendent and the land agent exchanged knowing looks.

"Only a little ten-acre parcel south of the office," Dutch said. "Over by where you're living. It's Conner Owens' place, and he's not likely to sell."

Don stared at the map thoughtfully, trying to locate Conner's house on the blurred blue photo.

"Claims he don't need the money," the land agent said.

"No, I think he's just got an attitude about the company," Dutch replied. "Son, are you going to have the draft permit line to me by tomorrow evening?"

"I've got to run the perimeter. How long will that take?" Don asked Clarence.

"Rest of today, probably most of tomorrow morning," was the reply.

"I'll have to check it with the property maps, do some field scouting for potential problem areas, "Don said.

"Okay," Dutch said. "Under the circumstances, I'll give you an extra day, but I expect you to be in here early Saturday morning and have ten copies of the map on my desk by five o'clock Saturday night before I leave for home."

"Yes sir," Don replied, relieved that Dutch had extended the deadline.

"Let's go," Clarence said. "Time's a-wastin'."

By dusk the two men had driven in and around a five hundred acre area, stopping occasionally to unroll Don's map on the Bronco's hood, penciling in the projected area of disturbance. Along the way Clarence pointed out features he thought might be of importance to the engineer and some that were of obvious importance to him.

"See that patch of woods?" Clarence asked.

"Uh-huh," Don said.

"Best mushrooming in the county. Yellow and brown morels, big damn peckerheads."

"Peckerheads?" Don said.

"Don't you know what peckerheads are? Christ Almighty, where you from, boy? They're a type of mushroom. Ever went ginsenging?"

"Went what?"

"Hunting for ginseng. It's a root that looks like a man; sells for beaucoup a pound. See them hills back into the woods? You dig it at the foot of the hill."

The day passed quickly. Much to the young man's surprise, they arrived back at the parking lot, entering from an unfamiliar road behind the hopper. It was dark and under the mercury vapor lights, Don thought the mine office looked almost benevolent, if not just familiar.

"Don't worry," Clarence said, laughing, "after a week out here you'll know your way around."

"Thanks for the help," Don said, shaking the older man's hand.

"Reckon you'll be needing me tomorrow?"

"No, I think I'll spend the morning out in the field doing a little scouting," Don replied.

"Okay. I'll drop the property maps off before noon. Be careful out there," he said. "It's deer season."

"Isn't it a little early for deer?" Don asked.

"Not in Sullivan County. Open season all year long in the Bottoms. Good night."

Don retrieved the rolled-up maps from the back seat and started for the engineering office. He walked through the open shop door and into the hiss of escaping air and the rhythmic clang of a hammer tolling on some resisting metal part far back in the darkened garage. He nodded his respects to the two mechanics who leaned against the supply counter and then walked up the stairs, passing the foreman's office where a few men relaxed with the day's last cup of coffee before heading home. Entering the room, he shut out most of the shop noise when he closed the door, but the vibrations were still noticeable underfoot.

He unrolled the map on the drafting table and attempted to familiarize himself with the mining area one more time before leaving. Straining to recall the route the land agent had driven earlier in the afternoon, he reviewed his shakily-written notes on the map indicating areas which he would have to investigate the following day – an ancient homestead at the edge of a field with an abandoned graveyard hidden in the woods behind it; an open air shaft from an old deep mine, half-collapsed and filled with rotting timbers, trash, and water; the broad border of swamp white oak, maples, and river birch, framing a stream which began as a bubble under the roots of clustering birches, then retreated slowly westward into the Bottoms and away from the mine.

Finally, he noted the dashed lines which set Conner's property apart from the company's land, a narrow strip of woods nine hundred feet long and half as wide. From the photo, the old man's house was not visible through the overstory of leaves, but he knew that the cabin was near the front of the blue rectangle.

Don was curious as to why Conner still hung onto such a small piece of land. He shuffled through the maps until he found the one with the color-coded mine plan, then he compared it to the aerial photo. *Well*, he thought, *the old boy's pretty sharp. His property is situated almost dead center in the middle of where the pit will be five years from now. He's got the company by the short hairs and is just biding his time.* The thought brought a smile to Don's face, and he resolved to bring up the subject to Conner that night over supper. He looked at the clock on the wall. *Uh-oh*, he thought, *I was supposed to call the old man about supper. Better do it right now.* Picking up the phone on the drafting table, he dialed Conner's house. *I'll just take him out for supper. Too tired to cook anything, and it's my turn anyway.*

As the phone on the other end of the line started to ring, Don heard a noise from the garage as someone entered the office. He turned to see Larry Miller's face, looking around the room through the slightly opened door. Satisfied that Don was alone, the big man opened the door and walked over to the side of the drafting table.

"Be with you in a minute," Don said, cupping the phone with his right hand. Conner answered on the other end.

"Yep?"

"Conner? This is Don."

"Hey, boy. Working late?"

"Yeah. What do you want to do for dinner?"

"What you got in mind?"

"My turn to cook. How's about we go out tonight?"

"Any place in particular?"

"You know the area better than me. You make the choice and I'll buy."

"Hell of a deal. Let me get scrubbed. How long you going to be?"

"Not more than fifteen minutes," Don said.

"Good. I'll see you in a bit."

"Okay, I'll pick you up."

Don hung up the phone and turned to face Larry. "What can I do for you?"

"Them the new permit maps?"

"No, not yet. Just some rough lines where the permit line will be."

"We gonna have them tomorrow?"

"No. I'll have them to Dutch by Saturday afternoon."

Larry took a pack of Marlboros from his jacket pocket and shook out the one cigarette that was left. Leaning his left elbow on the drafting table, he offered Don a smoke.

"No thanks, trying to quit," Don said, even though he had never smoked in his life. Larry lipped the last cigarette out, crushed the pack in his hand, and placed it on the table. He took a silver lighter from his pocket, clicked open the top with a flick of his wrist, at the same time sparking the flint with his thumb. He raised one eyebrow and stared at Don through the broad orange flame before lighting his cigarette. He drew half an inch of ash then flipped the lighter shut, placing it on the table beside the empty pack.

"You play basketball?"

"I played in high school, but I don't play much anymore," Don replied warily.

"Why not?"

"Bad knee."

"No kidding. Me, too."

"Did you hurt it playing ball?"

"Naw," Larry said, looking down at his knee in disgust. "Got kicked in a fight by some little bastard. He was aiming a little higher."

Don almost laughed until he realized that Larry meant his words to be taken seriously.

"You know, there's a big ball game in town Saturday night. You want to go with me and the boys?"

Don looked at Larry's face. It was almost without expression, but there was a steely gray coldness in his eyes which matched the tone of his voice. The engineer turned away from the miner's stare and began to roll up his maps.

"Thanks, anyway," Don said. "I've already got plans."

He pulled one map out from under a metal weight, one of four which he used to hold the maps down. The cylinder thumped on the table then rolled slowly toward the edge where Larry leaned. Don reached out with his left hand to grab it before it fell to the floor. As his hand closed over the cylinder, Larry's right hand arched across the engineer's wrist, pinning his arm to the desk. Larry smiled slowly as he leaned into Don's face, his cigarette swaggering with his words.

"I think maybe you should change your plans."

Don looked down at his arm, then back up at Larry. For the first time, he noticed the resemblance between Larry and the Dutchman. But there was something about the man in front of him that seemed less controlled, and more dangerous. Then he remembered Dutch's handshake and felt a coldness developing behind his eyes. It spread to his temples and down his neck, and he felt the muscles in the back of his jaw bulge outward as he gritted his teeth. In one motion he levered his arm and wrist out from beneath Larry's grip, replacing the map weight upright on the table with a deliberate thump.

"I'm not going to get into a pissing contest with you."

"That's good. That's real good, because I piss like a racehorse, and around here I'm stud."

"You misunderstand me," Don said, taking the roll of maps in one hand and heading for the door.

"Oh, yeah?" Larry said, rising from his slouch and grinding his cigarette on the floor.

"Yeah. Go peddle your stuff to somebody else. I go where I want. Turn the lights out when you leave."

Don slammed the door behind him and walked down the hallway, fully expecting the big man to be right behind him. *If there was to be a fight*, he thought, *I want it out in the open*. He hurried past the foreman's office. The room was quiet, but he knew that there were men inside who had overheard his words with Larry.

He turned to go down the stairs. Still, no sound came from behind him. Breathing quickly, he walked through the garage and out the side door into the parking lot. He slowed his pace slightly upon seeing his truck, imagining a sense of security. Unlocking the door, he tossed in the maps and climbed behind the wheel. He pulled on the handle to swing the door shut, but halfway through its arc, the door stopped. A huge, dismembered hand seemed to attach itself to the window frame. Illuminated by the interior light of the truck, the hand forced the door back open, and slowly a denim shirted figure positioned itself in the flickering light. The man's face was hidden by the shadows.

"Maybe I didn't make myself real clear," said the voice in the dark. "You ain't going to the game or the dance with her!"

Don looked toward the office where a group of men stood by the open garage door. *Surely, he's not dumb enough to start something out here in front of these men*, he thought. *He's just trying to intimidate me*. Don turned the key in the ignition and started the truck.

Putting the gearshift into reverse, he eased off the brake until the open door pressed against Larry's side, threatening to pull the big man along with it. With the door angled acutely, Larry had no choice but to move his feet to remain upright. With his left hand on the window frame and his right hand clamped on the top of the cab, he faced forward and leaned his weight against the truck's motion. Don responded by letting off the brake a little more, and Larry's feet began to slip on the gravel as the truck began to roll. Larry glared with a mixture of embarrassment and panic at the engineer.

"Stop this truck you son of a bitch," Larry said, trying to keep his balance.

"You can come along if you want, or you can stay," Don said, quickly shifting into first gear and starting forward, a move that nearly pitched Larry on his nose and forced him to release his grip on the truck. "But I go where I want," he said, punctuating his statement by slamming the door shut.

Driving past the garage, Don waved to the men standing by the open door. To his surprise, a couple of them waved back.

Larry stood in the darkness, watching the taillights of the engineer's truck turn onto the access road and disappear. Then he stared at the men in the open door who scattered into the garage at his approach. Halfway to the shop, he stopped and looked back over his shoulder, toward the distant sound of Don's truck on the gravel road.

"It ain't over, you bastard," he muttered. "It ain't over."

Chapter Thirteen

The Ash Grove
Traditional Welsh Folk Song

The ash grove, the ash grove, how plainly 'tis speaking,
The harp through it playing, has memories for me,
When over its branches the sunlight is playing,
A host of kind faces are gazing on me.

The friends of my childhood again are before me,
As I lift my eyes up to yon leafy dome,
And others are there looking downward to greet me,
The ash grove, the ash grove, alone is my home.

Don picked up Conner, and the two men drove into Linton to a little restaurant that the older man favored. It was on the main street in town across from the fire station. They sat in a booth by the window and ordered the special with iced tea. Don stared out the window at the trickle of cars and trucks that alternately stopped and started with the automatic signal on the corner.

"You're not very talkative tonight," Conner said. "Ain't heard two words out of you since we got here. Cat got your tongue?"

Don took a deep breath and let out an audible sigh. "Nope," he said, "just had a little trouble at the mine today. It's nothing."

The waitress brought over the two iced teas and a coffee cup stuffed with packaged sugar. Conner lined up three packs in his left hand and tore the top off all of them simultaneously, dumping the contents in his tea. He stirred the ice with the long spoon, took a test sip, then added three more.

"That there waitress," he said, taking a drink of his tea before continuing his thought, "is a handsome woman. Her name's Suzy. Used to work up in Jasonville at the bank. Guess she makes more money waiting tables." He stirred his tea a little more and looked across the table at Don who still stared out the window. "Yes sir, the older I get, the better they look. They claim the eyes is the second thing to go, you know."

Don smiled and turned his attention to the old man. "And what's the first?"

"Well, you'll have to wait and find out for yourself."

Don glanced at the waitress who leaned on the end of the counter, talking to the cook. She looked to be in her mid-thirties.

"I never look for any trouble, but since coming up here, it just seems to find me."

"Dutch jump you?"

"Yep, but that's not it. He was right. I need to clear things with him before I go off on my own."

"Somebody else then?"

"Yeah, his spawn."

"You must mean old Larry," and Conner chuckled. "He's a pretty good-sized fellow, ain't he?"

"I think he's got something going with Katie, or had, anyway."

"Why's that?"

"He more or less told me to stay away from her."

"You going to?"

"It's none of his business what I do. Besides, she's the one that asked me to the dance Saturday night. You don't think?"

"What? That she's been using you to pimp old Larry?"

"Yeah."

"Now that's just plain stupid, boy. She wouldn't do anything like that."

"You're right, I know you're right. It was a stupid thought."

"Listen. You've been spending a lot of time with her lately, going up to Terre Haute and all. Does she seem like the type to do that sort of thing?"

"No."

"Damn straight, and you know it, too. Larry just feels like she's his personal property, that's all."

"You know her pretty well, don't you?"

Don couldn't be sure, but it seemed that Conner's face appeared to slightly flush. He looked down at a plate the waitress had just set in front of him, scratched himself behind his left ear then reached for the salt and pepper. His eyes followed the waitress back to the counter, then he turned his attention back to Don.

"Known her since she was born."

"I've never met anybody like her."

"Special, ain't she?"

"I don't know what it is. I've hardly known her a few days, but man - " Don shook his head and turned his thoughts inward. His mind began to touch the fringes of emotions he had felt on their drive to see Tommie in the hospital and the sleepless night that followed.

"Listen. She ain't never had nothing to do with Larry. And he's run off practically everyone who ever had a conversation with her. Don't let him get to you, but don't turn your back on him, neither. Guys like him don't mind cold cocking you when you ain't looking. And if it comes to a fight, get in the first blow. I reckon a smashed nose takes the swagger outa guys like Larry, real fast."

"You sound like a corner man," Don chuckled.

"You're going to learn that around here, you've got to stick up for yourself. Nobody else is going to."

"I'm not much into fighting."

"I'm not saying to go looking for it, just be ready when it comes. And believe me, it's going to come."

Don stirred his tea slowly and looked out the window, focusing on a blood memory, reliving the tactile sensation of what it felt like to pummel another human being. Involuntarily he made a tight fist with his right hand. He looked down at his whitening knuckles and deliberately relaxed his grip, fanning his fingers a few times then drumming them on the table. He hoped Conner hadn't noticed, but he knew better.

"I appreciate the advice, really, but you don't have to worry about me," Don said softly. "I used to have a pretty bad temper, and I've fought bigger guys than old Larry. I'd just like to avoid it, that's all."

"But if it comes looking for you?"

"Then we'll see."

Don looked away, out the window, and thought about the accident that took his brother's life. Conner slipped into the booth beside the young man and draped his arm protectively over Don's shoulders, and the young man buried his face in his hands, shivering deep breaths.

"It's all right, Suzy," Conner said to the waitress who had hurried over. "Could you bring us some coffee?" and after a few moments, "You want to get out of here, boy? We can go if you like."

"No, I'm okay," Don replied, sighing heavily. "I was just thinking about my brother and my parents."

The old man moved back into the booth across from Don.

"How are your parents doing?"

"Oh, they've both been dead for a few years; killed in an auto accident. I thought of them the other day when I met Ernie's folks," Don said.

"Got any other family?"

"Nope. But what I was meaning to tell you, before I got all stupid, was that when they took my parents to the hospital after the accident and all, I followed the ambulance and beat the hell out of the drunk that killed them. I guess the guy was pretty much uninjured up until that point; that always seems to be the case with drunks."

"Seems a reasonable thing to do."

"Well, they weren't short of blood for his sobriety test. But my point is that I lost more than my parents on the side of that road and whipping up on some drunk didn't bring the balance back to zero."

"So, you came up here to get away from it?"

"I buried my parents on a cold day late fall. It was hard. Since then I've felt like a cold, hard man. But I'm not running from anything anymore. I've still got the house in Newburgh. I'll go back some day."

Conner took a deep breath and sat back. *Everyone has their demons to deal with,* he thought. *This boy appears to have more than his share. Can he overcome them? For Katie's sake, I hope so.* Suzy brought the coffees, slipped an unnoticed sympathetic look at Don, smiled at Conner, and went back to the counter.

"But you know, boy, there are some things worth fighting for, where standing up for yourself does make a difference."

"I know, but I'm not sure Larry's one of them."

"Maybe not him, but maybe Katie. And besides, I happen to know that she really likes you."

"Really? She told you?"

"Yep," and Conner chuckled, starting to eat his supper.

"She talks to you a lot?"

Conner hesitated for a moment, sipping his tea. "Sometimes about the damndest things, too."

"You sound like you're pretty close. You two related or something?"

"I knew her daddy. He's been dead for awhile now. If you look hard enough, you'll find most people around here connected by something. But you generally don't ask. It ain't polite."

"So, it seems like you're her adopted father; is that it?"

"In a manner of speaking. Me and her mother were close. Eat your supper, boy; it's gettin' cold."

The two men finished their supper in a practical silence. Don looked up from his plate occasionally thinking to ask Conner a question, but the old man ducked his glance. So Don concentrated on his supper and later, the apple pie with a slice of cheese on top.

On the drive back to the house, Don ventured a question.

"I was looking at the property maps today, you know, getting ready to submit the permit."

"I always liked maps. Looked forward to the *National Geographic* magazines that had the big foldout ones."

"Well, I noticed that they have your property outlined."

"Really?"

"Yeah. How much land have you got; about ten acres?"

"Right around that."

"Why haven't you sold out like everybody else?"

"A lot of people ask me that, and they think they already know the answer before they ask. But they're wrong."

"What do you mean?"

"Well, they think I've got something against the coal company, or they think I'm just holdin' out for more money. But that ain't it at all."

"No?"

"Nope, not that those wouldn't be fair reasons in themselves." Conner remembered how the bottomland around his home had looked before the company opened the Daggett Mine, how he and his neighbors had talked about holding out as long as possible to get the best settlement on their property. Some took the cash and moved into town, and others held out a little longer for more money as well as residual income from the coal. He had let them know from the beginning that he would never sell out. Most of those neighbors were dead now, with their land chewed up and soulless.

"How's that?" Don asked.

"Huh? Sorry, I must have dozed off, there."

"You were saying why you're keeping the land."

"Oh, yeah," Conner said, finding his bookmark. "I'll tell you something. The companies get pretty much what they want around here; everybody has their price and eventually the companies pay it. But the land is everything. If you don't have ground, you ain't got nothin'."

"How about you?"

"What do you mean?"

"Do you have a price?"

"I ain't any different. I've got my price, but they can't afford it."

"But you're not talking about money, are you?"

"That's right."

"What is it then?"

"Control, boy, and a few other things. For most of my life I've been told what to do, and so have you. Anybody who owns the land controls the people who live on it. At my age, who needs the money?"

Don recognized the truth in the old man's statement. A descendent of Irish immigrants on his mother's side, Don had been told the story of how his family had lost their country to the British, their farms to the aristocracy and their lives to the potato blight. *Everyone, in one way or another*, he thought, *is connected to the soil on which they live.*

They passed Milo Decker's house on the red shale road. A pale light squeezed through the edges of the shades.

"Take old Milo there," Conner said. "Sold off a while back. Now he don't own the ground he sets on."

"Yeah, but I understand his boys got jobs at the mine."

"Probably would've anyway. They were dumber than a box of rocks. You seen the high school yet?"

"Yeah."

"Nice football field, ain't it?"

"Yeah, real nice; lights, bleachers. Looks like a new track."

"Wait till you see the new gym on Saturday night. Seats over three thousand."

"What's your point?"

"Well, the companies always toss money in on sports facilities, but they won't pay a dime for a new library, or computers, or anything like that."

"Is that true?"

"I'm here to tell you," Conner said with conviction.

"Why do you suppose that is?"

"'Cause they don't want to educate their future labor force beyond their needs. Got to keep workers at the face."

"Come on!"

"It's true. Take old Ernie, rest his soul. Smart kid, but they grabbed him before he got a sense of the world around him; so he stayed."

"But surely that was his choice."

"The money was good, and he was young enough not to know the difference."

"The difference in what?" Don asked.

"The difference between money and opportunity. All my life, I never had any doubts about where I'd be workin', and I never had any other opportunity. Kids nowadays ought to have more of a choice; see what's out there and then come back if they want."

"What does that have to do with you not selling?"

"Pull up to the house, and I'll show you the other reasons."

Don parked in front of Conner's cabin and followed the old man around the side to the back porch. Conner took down the gas lantern from its hook on the back porch, set it on the railing, stroked the pump a few times, lit a kitchen match, and rotated the valve a quarter turn open. The gas cracked and bubbled through the stem and briefly flamed orange around the mantles. A few more strokes on the pump and the bubbling turned into an even hiss and the mantles threw a bright yellowed light out from beneath the smoking green hood of the lantern. He screwed the pump down against the tank, lifted the light by its wire handle and stepped off the porch. Walking around the newly turned earth of his small garden, he opened the door to a small shed at the edge of the woods and rattled out a leaf rake.

"Used to be an outhouse," he said, while latching the door. "Still is in an emergency. Come on; you follow me. Watch your step."

Don followed Conner into the woods, hanging back a respectful distance after being smacked in the face by a few invisible branches that parted in front of the old man, then whipped backward as he passed. He watched the ground at Conner's feet. Once his eyes adjusted to a midrange of dark and lantern light, he noticed that they were on a small, depressed path almost hidden by the leaf fall. Once through the smaller maples and sumac at the wood's edge, the understory cleared out, and they walked through a grove of tall, straight trees. The path disappeared beneath a carpet of leaves, but Conner looked straight ahead as he crunched along. Don jogged a little to catch up with the glaring lantern which had disappeared over the edge of a ravine and now glowed and swung along the gully bottom.

Don missed the trail down to the stream and side-hilled as best he could along the ravine, catching up with Conner as he crossed a log foot bridge and started up the other side. The bank was steeply eroded, and the two men passed one another on short switchbacks until the old man gained the top through a tangle of exposed tree roots. Conner held the light over the edge of the ravine until Don scrambled up the trail to join him on the plateau. While Don brushed the leaves and dirt from his pants, Conner extinguished the lantern and took a few steps into a dark hollow that seemed to grow in the fading light.

"Where are you going?" Don called out; his eyes not yet adjusted to the darkness. The crunching of leaves underfoot stopped, and he heard the long scrape of the rake across the ground and the rustle of leaves.

"You stay right where you are for a minute," the old man called back, drawing the leaves into a pile around his legs, occasionally stomping them down into the shallow, rock-filled pit where he stood. After clearing the ground for a good six feet around the pit, he stepped out. Finding a dry branch close by, he started breaking it up and throwing foot-long pieces into the pit.

A diffuse, pale light filtered into the glade, as the veil of clouds overhead, pushed by a high wind, yielded to the waning moon. Don looked up through the framework of empty branches at the circle around the moon and the clustering stars that shimmered like faceted diamonds. *Ice crystals*, he thought. Then slowly and without warning, he felt the compass of his heart turn on the wind, and Katie's memory walked the night sky. He brought his hands to his face, pressing his thumbs into the hollow of his cheeks and rubbing his fingertips against his forehead as he felt the pulse of his heart quicken and heard the surge pass through his ears. He pulled his hands away from his face and was surprised by the slight trembling he saw in his fingers. He rotated his wrists so that his palms faced outward, revealing their involuntary movement in the yellow light that was growing from the center of the glade. Conner had started a fire in the pit, and the flames were rising above the ground level.

"Come on over here," Conner said, rising from his crouch, his face and front illuminated by the flames while the rest of him merged with the blue shadows behind. He raised his head slowly to watch the sparks spiral upward, looked toward Don, and offered a broad, contented smile.

"Look around you, boy. What do you see?"

Don stopped a short distance from the fire and looked at Conner's face through the wavering heat. The old man had raised his arms up slightly above his shoulders and was slowly turning in a circle. Don traced Conner's line of sight to the cathedral of rough-barked white oaks which enclosed the glade. They seemed to dance in the growing light at their feet while their upper branches were caught in a web of celestial fire. The gnarled tiers of lower branches were broad and rigorred with age and somewhere between the earth and sky, they watched; and they knew. The young man felt the drumming in his ears reach its peak and then slowly subside.

"I see the reason you can't sell this place."

Conner lowered his arms and smiled. He sat down on a log near the fire and motioned for Don to join him.

"Seven of them," the old man said, shaking his head. "You know about these things. How old are they?"

"Haven't you ever asked them?"

"Good answer," and Conner chuckled. "Nope, never thought that was very polite."

"I'd imagine they were here before the white man."

"That's what I figured. The place has a special feel, don't it?"

"Oh, yeah. Kind of sets on you when you first step in."

"Like a nine-pound hammer?"

"What do you mean?"

"Oh, it's an old minin' song, about things being too much for the body sometimes. Occasionally, when I think I'm gettin' old, I come out here and sit with my friends. On these trees' scale, I'm just a sprout." They both laughed.

"See that field out there?" Conner said, pointing out from the darkness beneath the oaks to an open cornfield lit up by the moonlight.

"Yeah."

"Well, that's as far as the company owns. I figure at the present rate of minin', they'll be there in about five years. Am I right?"

"Just about," Don said, shaking his head in amazement. "What then?"

"I guess they'll just have to go around, won't they?" Conner laughed.

"I guess so," Don said, smiling at the thought.

The men sat in silence for a while. Don poked the fire with a thin green stick of sassafras and savored the aroma of the smoke. Conner watched the young man's actions intently as if the weak light from the fire pit might illuminate some scarred aspect of Don's character that had not yet been revealed. *No shadows following this boy around that can't be dispelled by a little companionship,* he thought. *Been through some hard times, but he'll be stronger for it.*

"Sassafras," Don said, setting the stick beside the pit. "I should dig up some roots and dry them this winter."

"Makes a dandy tea," Conner said. "Supposed to have magical, restorative powers." He hesitated for a few moments. "So, what do you think about Katie?"

"I find myself thinking a lot about her lately," Don said, maintaining his gaze into the fire. "Even here tonight, right before you lit the fire."

"That's not surprising. This is one of her favorite places."

"Really."

"Yeah, used to bring her here when she was a little girl. Roast weenies and marshmallows over the pit."

"Well, I like her a lot. More than I'd like to say right now. I just don't know if I'm going to stay in this area for very long, and I'd hate to start something up and leave."

"You act like a man that don't know where he's going."

"Sometimes I wonder. When I came up here from Newburgh, I felt pretty much like I was casting myself adrift from everything I knew and was comfortable with, you know, my family, my home."

"That's in the past. How do you feel now?"

Don thought about how his lost feeling had intensified with the initial reception he got at the mine with Dutch, the nature of the work he would have to do, and the resistance he would encounter. Then there was the specter of Larry, the possibility of deadly sabotage, and finally, the accident itself. But now, all that was harsh potential seemed to be balanced by the kindness of the old man sitting here beside him and quiet respect at the mining community he could not have imagined. *Yet all this, it seems, came as a result of Ernie's misfortune. Can I live with that?*

"I'm not sure that I've earned the right to feel this way yet, but I think I belong here just as much as anybody else. You're a big part of that, you know. You, Ray - and especially Katie. I just want to make sure that what I feel for Katie is real and not some emotional overreaction to recent events."

"Hell, a guy your age don't need to know exactly where his future lies, just got to have some idea. I don't think anybody around here's about to run you off. You're quite the hero, you know but don't let that go to yer head." *I know at least one old man and a beautiful girl that hope you'll stay,* he thought. "If you do decide to leave, I reckon wherever you go you'll do just fine. But take my word for it: you need somebody to go along with you. Believe you me."

"But if I decide to leave here, you think she'd come along? She's lived here all her life, hasn't she?"

"Yeah, but I think she'd go with you."

"Has she told you that?"

"No, but I know. Sometimes folks have to leave other folks in order for one of them - sometimes both of them, to grow."

Don picked up the stick again and poked it in the dying fire, stirring a few sparks into the air. "You know, it's a thought I've had before," he said softly. "But I've tried not to think about it too much."

"You mean with what happened to your parents? Son, I didn't have the pleasure of knowing them, but if they were here, they'd probably agree with me that their passing opened up a door for them and a door for you."

Don stirred the coals a little more. He remembered the maps he'd prepared for Dutch and considered the inevitable progression of the giant dragline. He heard the wind in the tops of the trees; when it blew from the right direction, he could just make out the electric whine of the extending cables and the low thunder of cast rock. He tilted his head slightly and looked back through the darkened forest to the west. "What are you going to do when the mine gets to this ground?"

"I imagine I'll be long gone by then."

"What do you mean?"

"Giving up the ghost, boy. Why, dead, of course. Drivin' the brass-handled sedan. The groundhogs'll be bringing my mail!"

"Hell, you'll outlive me, old man. Besides, who'll look after these trees?"

"Oh, I got that all planned out."

"You got family?"

"A daughter, the prettiest girl you ever laid eyes on."

"Does she live around here?"

"I guess so. You're taking her to the dance Saturday night."

Don hesitated for a moment. *No,* he thought, *I'm not hearing this right. Then again, they're pretty close, but he said her father was dead, didn't he?* He looked at Conner. The old man had a smile that his mother would have described as "the cat that ate the canary." From that smile and the twinkle of the old man's eyes in the firelight he saw the resemblance to Katie. If Don hadn't been sitting down already, he would have collapsed into a heap. *Oh my God,* he thought, panning through a slide show of time spent with Conner over the last few days; *have I said anything about his daughter that might have offended this man?*

As if he had read his thoughts, Conner laughed and slapped his thigh. "Aw, don't worry, you ain't done nothing yet to be ashamed of, have ye?"

"I'm confused. I don't understand. You mind explaining this to me?"

"Well, it's like this. Old Bill Johnson, the man Katie thinks is her daddy, was a mean bastard. Drank a lot, beat his wife, hard on the boys, too. Katie has two brothers, and Bill took each of them to the mine the day they finished high school and put them to work."

"They still around?"

"Nope. Bill and the oldest boy, Bill junior, were killed in a mine explosion when Katie was around three years old. The younger boy, Danny's his name, good-looking kid, he up and joined the service. He comes around once in awhile. Him and Ernie were pals."

Conner looked into the pit and stirred the coals with the stick. The fire had nearly died, so he broke the stick in half and threw it on the ashes. After a few seconds, a small blaze erupted, illuminating, and emphasizing the creases in his face.

"Old Bill was a womanizer, too," he continued. "Funny about these miners sometimes. They're always off foolin' around with some other man's wife; they don't ever think that with the limited number of women around here, their wife might be doing the same thing. Anyway, I knew Rose long before she married Bill Johnson. I wanted to move out of here and take her with me, but she wouldn't go. Married Bill instead. Said I had too many dreams to suit her. After Danny was born, the old man treated Rose more like a housekeeper than a wife. One time after he came home real drunk and beat her up bad, she came to see me. Asked me if anything happened to her to look after her boys."

"How old were they."

"Eight and ten, I think. Anyway, one thing led to another, and we started seein' each other, regular like, when Bill would take the boys off hunting or something."

"Kind of dangerous, wasn't it?"

"I suppose, but there's other things in life a lot worse. You know, they say in the mines that if a man's light goes out while he's working, his wife's with someone else."

"Really. Did the old man's light ever go out?"

"Yep, the night Katie was born. I was workin' the same shift with him and the boys. He went nuts."

"Do you think he knew?"

"That the girl wasn't his? I think so, but he was never sure who the father was, even on the day he died."

"Does Katie know?"

"Nope, and I ain't gonna tell her neither."

"Don't you think she'd like to know?"

"No. That knowledge has made her mother a bitter person. She lives in a world where old man Johnson never did no wrong. The strange thing is, on the night he died, I might as well have died, too. She's shunned me ever since."

"But you have Katie."

"I have Katie, and for every hundred mistakes a man makes in his life, sometimes there's somethin' good comes out of one."

Conner stood up from the log and raked some dirt into the pit. "It's late," he said. "Get the lantern. You've got to be to work in the mornin'. We'd better get goin'."

Don fired up the lantern and handed it to Conner.

"Sir, I love your daughter."

"I know you do," Conner said, placing his big hand on Don's shoulder. "And that's a good thing."

The old man led the way back down the ravine. At the edge of the circle of trees, Don stopped and looked back into the glade. The ancient trees seemed to bend inward toward the soft glow of the dying embers.

Chapter Fourteen

The Witness Tree

To the children it was a game, one of many that they played unaware of its importance to the survival of the tribe in the coming months, but their mothers understood. Carrying baskets woven of rush and reed with frames and handles made of hickory and willow withes, the matriarchs led the small ones up from the fertile bottoms, past the fields of yellowing maize and into the forests which overshadowed the village, deep green in the summertime, now slowly changing to a somber brown. The signs had foretold a bountiful crop in this season, and last night they had heard the God of the Air crashing about the trees on the terrace, shaking down the acorns for the People. The women sang a prayer of hope as they walked, for who has seen the wind?

The sun had not yet risen above the forest rim when they reached the hall of the monarchs. The group dispersed beneath the wide spreading branches of the ancient oaks and began to fill their baskets. The women bent low to the ground, picking up every acorn that they could see and turning the leaf litter aside to search for more. They twisted the scaly caps from the fruit before tossing it in their basket, singing a quiet song of thanksgiving as they gathered. The older children marauded in small groups to the outer edge of the glade, returning with handfuls of hickory and butternut. The infants were set on piles of rustling leaves, within arms' reach of their mothers.

By the time the sun had climbed into the treetops, the people had squirreled enough nuts to fill their needs. The women slung the deep, narrow baskets across their backs and lifted the short, square bushels to one shoulder. Then, straddling their babies on one hip, they led the clan out from the forest and back to the village. The children paired themselves on each side of the wide, shallow baskets and followed, swinging them as they walked.

Emerging from the forest's shadow, the group passed along the edge of a field overgrown and orange with broom sedge. Saplings of maple, shingle oak, and elm struggled to push their leaves above the waving grass, to succeed where others of their species had failed to compete and survive on the burned-over field.

Struggling to carry her full basket of acorns, a young female of the group tripped on the vines of dense fox grape that reached out from the forest's edge. One by one she retrieved the spilled acorns and placed them back into her basket; except for one, which had rolled away and remained hidden beneath a leaf by the trail. Other members of the group passed her as she knelt, and one of them stepped on the leaf, pressing the acorn into the soft, warm earth. Readjusting the basket on her shoulder, the girl rejoined the group as they descended the terrace toward the village. The fields of maize whisked golden in the midday sun, and the old women were tending the cooking fires. There would be much work in the coming days, but there would be food for winter.

In the spring, the lost seed germinated, its taproot burrowing into the moist soil while the shoot climbed into the weak sun. By the time the first frost dusted the field that fall, the single stem of the young oak was protected by a thick mulch of leaves, and its roots reached deep enough into the earth to survive the winter freeze.

With the passage of time, the tree grew tall and straight at the edge of the field. In the spring the villagers combed the forest's border for wild berries and stalked its dank interior for mushrooms. In the summer, they dug the root of young sassafras, *drying it in the sun. When autumn painted the poplar a cadmium orange, the people of the earth passed by with empty baskets on their way to the grove of oaks. Some years they returned with full baskets, other years with half-empty hearts.*

Over the years the forest crept onto the grassy field, then retreated again as the people cut down the young saplings for lodge poles. Sometimes the field was set ablaze and maize planted in the ashes. And when the last crop of maize withered and the village moved farther down the river, the oak reached maturity and began bearing seed of its own. Sometimes the people would return and gather the acorns from about its feet. More often, its fruit sustained the inhabitants of the deep woods - the deer, the squirrel, and the turkey.

In time the people of the earth were diminished, only to be followed by men with primitive compasses and two-pole chains. They measured off sections of land and described what they saw in terms of how the ground could be used. In their entries they wrote, "forest thin, broken by gullies," and "good white oaks, land suitable for growing wheat." They were paid two dollars a mile, the land was worth ten cents an acre in "hard" money, and missing a few acres was not that important.

What these men had in common was the practice of using conspicuous trees at section corners for reference points. Compass bearings and distances from the corner to two trees were often recorded in the surveyor's field notes. Sometimes the surveyor described the trees in his notes. He also took an ax and hacked a large blaze on the trunk of the tree. And in this manner the tall oak at the edge of the field became a "witness tree."

The mutilation of its bark notwithstanding, the chief advantage of being a witness tree is that you didn't have to worry about being cut for building someone's house, split up for firewood, or converted in later years to charcoal and railroad ties. By the time the oak had gained a full and magnificent form, its broad-skirted trunk defied the largest cross-cut saw of the day and it was safe for all time.

Don got up shortly after daybreak. He hadn't slept well and had been awakened several times by a ghosting wind that shuffled the loose shingles on the roof and howled through the treetops of the woods behind the house. The more he thought about it, the more concerned he was that by some misreading of a map Conner's grove of trees might be endangered. On his trip around the property with Clarence, he had heard the scream of bulldozers crashing through the woods behind Conner's land. Clarence said they were clearing a line for a new electrical substation.

After a cup of coffee, he went out to the Bronco and retrieved a roll of bright orange surveyor's tape and his maps. It had been his intention to use the tape on Monday to mark the permit line once the Dutchman approved it. But in the meantime, he'd flag Conner's property line so that at least someone would call the foreman or the mine office before they got onto an area where they didn't belong.

He stepped off the back porch and headed for the pole bridge to Conner's house. On the other side of the ravine, he picked up the fence line which separated the two properties. It was an old woven wire affair with two strands of barbed wire on top of the fence posts, and he followed it back into the woods, attaching a bow-tie of orange ribbon on each post and letting a three foot section of tape flutter in the early morning breeze.

When he reached the first corner of the property, he found that he was standing in the field that Conner had pointed out to him by moonlight. A large creosote railroad tie marked the property corner. It was braced by a deadman wire, buried in the ground to hold it upright against the strain of the tight wire fence pulling to the south and to the west. Unrolling the maps, he noted that the post was near the corner of a section. *Well,* he thought, *that ought to be easy enough for the surveyors to locate. I'll just put a few ribbons around this post and mark the fence back to the west with tape, and everything should be safe.*

He rolled up the maps and looked across the field in the direction of the distant sound of bulldozers. Shading his eyes to the rising sun, he noticed the vague form of a large tree which set back into the woods and seemed to swallow up all the light around it. My God, he thought, that's a huge tree, probably the granddaddy of Conner's grove. Deciding to investigate, he walked toward it through the tall, dewy grass.

It was the biggest oak tree he'd ever seen; almost eighty feet tall, he estimated, and the area inside the drip line of the branches had to be at least as wide. The forest floor beneath it was devoid of any other vegetation, except for dead leaves which were ankle deep and acorns that fell so often from the high rattling limbs that they sounded like rain. Its base spread out like a cone from beneath massive lower branches, and tentacles of roots rippled across the ground surface.

Don circled the base and noticed the cat-face scar running up the trunk from the ground, the result of a fire which swept the hillside, probably before Conner was born. A large part of the trunk appeared to be hollow. The ground on the far side of the trunk was disturbed, and a straight line of dirt about ten feet wide and two feet high had been pushed almost to the base of the tree.

Don followed the track of the dozer back into the woods. A road had been blazed through the smaller timber until it stopped at the base of the big oak. Ash, maple, and poplar trees, two feet in diameter and straight as arrows, were uprooted and pushed to the side of the path. Many of the trees leaned against others, their branches entangled high above. He considered following the path back to its source, but the high wind and swaying, tangled trees caused him to reconsider.

Walking back toward the big oak, he noticed the horizontal scar at its base. Before, he had thought that the operator had enough sense to stop when he got to the tree, but now it was painfully obvious that whoever was in the dozer meant to destroy the tree. A deep groove had been slashed in the trunk about two feet from the ground. Someone had backed up and repeatedly assaulted the tree after failing to uproot it in the conventional manner.

But why? The mine might never come this far. He'd have to check and locate its position on the mine plan to determine if the pit extended this far south, but he didn't think so. He sat down on a root and looked at the scar. The tree was so broad and rounded at the base that the cut was deep but not very wide. It wasn't close to girdling the tree. The oak would probably survive.

He took the surveyor's tape out of his pocket, tucked the end under a piece of bark and walked around the tree, unrolling the tape as he went. After reaching his starting point, he tied it off, hesitated for a moment, and then wrapped one more band around the trunk. *There*, he thought, *that should at least make somebody think before they do anything. I'll see Dutch about this today.*

He stood for a moment on one of the buttressing roots and looked up into the tree. Placing his hand on the trunk, he spread his fingers over the rough, gray bark. For a moment he imagined that he could feel the pulse of the tree, the rush of the life that was moving down from the branches and into the root system with the onset of winter. He imagined an ancient intelligence that could accept an end to life that he could not. And he felt the vibrations beneath the bark, but was it from the swaying branches overhead or from the distant grumbling of bulldozers?

He walked back across the open field and used the rest of his tape to mark Conner's northern property line before heading back through the woods to the house.

John and Roger followed Larry's truck along the new road being dozed through the woods, west of the mine.

"Will you look at all that ash!" John exclaimed. "Straight as a die and just the right size for splittin', too."

"Cut in here all winter long," Roger said.

"Damn straight. I told you old Larry would take care of us, didn't I?"

Roger leaned out the window to spit out his chew. Up ahead, Larry pulled over to the side of the track, got out of the cab, and lit a cigarette. John pulled in behind him.

"So, what do you boys think about this area?"

"Some fine-lookin' timber, Larry," John said.

"Yeah. The land department generally gets their hands on it and sells it off. Pockets the money themselves, I figure. Come on up ahead. I got something to show you."

"Reckon it's safe to run back through here?" John said, glancing up at the crowns of the uprooted trees, swaying in the wind.

"You're so chicken. C'mon!"

The three men followed the road down through a small stream and climbed up the opposite side. When they reached the top of the bank, Larry stopped, put his hands on his hips, and glared straight ahead. John and Roger kept their eyes on the branches overhead.

"What the hell is this?" Larry asked.

"A white oak," John said, "and I mean a big damn white oak."

"Yeah, but what's with the flagging?" Larry asked as he stalked up to the tree.

"Maybe it ain't supposed to be cut," John said. "It does look historical, don't it, Roger?"

"I 'magine," Roger said.

Larry reached the tree ahead of the other two men when his attention was drawn to the open field a few yards ahead. Without taking his eyes from the field he cupped his right hand over his mouth and in a low voice called back over his shoulder.

"Hey, Roger, did you bring your shotgun?"

"It's in the truck," Roger said.

"Go get it for me, will ya?"

The two men caught up with Larry who was standing underneath the tree looking out into the open field. They thought maybe he had seen a deer. Instead, they saw Don tying the last of the surveyor's tape on Conner's fence about a hundred yards away.

"Get your gun, Roger."

"What for?"

"I think I can drop him from here. Whadya think, John?"

"Sure, you could, Larry, but why would you want to?"

"Because I don't like him, that's why. Go get your gun, Roger."

A tense silence followed as they watched Don walk back down the fence line and turn into the woods in the direction of Conner's house. The three men followed his progress, each with different thoughts, until he disappeared into the shadows. Roger didn't move.

"You candyass," Larry said, glaring at Roger. "I was just gonna put the fear of God in him that's all."

"Not with my gun," Roger said calmly.

"Why don't you just drop a tree on him?" John said, trying to lift the tension. "This one here ought to do the trick, but I don't think she'll come down."

Larry ripped the orange tape away from the oak tree. "Oh, I reckon she'll come down all right, just needs a little persuasion. Took the dozer the other day and banged her a few times, and man did the acorns fall. I'm afraid one of these lower branches might crack and come down through the cab though. That's why I want you boys to climb up there today and see them off."

"Sure, Larry," John said, "we can do that. But maybe that orange ribbon means that the tree's protected or somethin'. Maybe we ought to check with your old man first."

"To hell with my old man. You want firewood, there it is; cut it down and haul it off. I'll be back this evenin' with the dozer and it better be done."

He threw the orange tape down and stomped back to his truck. Turning around in the road, he bumped back out of the woods. When the noise of his truck had faded, Roger and John looked up at the oak's massive branches, then down at the scar made by the bulldozer's blade. Roger knelt on the ground, and ran his hand along the white, splintered wood.

"Why do you figure he wants to take down this old tree, anyway?" John asked. "There's plenty of easier ones back along the road."

"Because it got in his way."

After flagging Conner's property, Don began a survey of the permit area adjacent to the pit, stopping occasionally along the backroads to unroll the aerial photo on the Bronco's hood. A broad, black line on the map marked the mine area and circled numbers indicated points of special interest that would require some additional investigation before the company could move through the area.

One problem was an old airshaft. It was an opening in the earth about four feet square, filled almost to the top with water. Looking much like a natural sinkhole, the earth around it had slumped, and the timbers that braced the sides were nearly obscured by the talus and weeds that covered them. *If someone fell into it*, he thought, *they would have one hell of a time climbing up the vertical walls.* He wondered how deep it was and threw a chunk of cinder block into the black square. It made a deep sound as it hit the surface of the water, drawing air down with it before fluttering to the bottom of the shaft. Some distant memory from his boyhood told him that a deeper sound meant deeper water, and the thought attracted him to the edge of the pit. There was a long tree branch lying on the ground next to the shaft with its smaller limbs. *Someone else has been here already,* he thought and *wanted to test the depth of the water as well.*

He shuffled his feet down the slope of loose dirt, getting as close to the edge as he dared. Holding the limb by the smaller end, he plunged the butt down into the inky water. It went down about eight feet and touched nothing; the only resistance was the weight of the water pressing upward. He leaned forward and pushed against the corking action. The branch bowed slightly as the butt caught in the side of the shaft, then abruptly gave way. Caught off balance, Don nearly fell headlong into the pit. He windmilled his arms and dropped back on his heels, scuttling up the bank like a crab. Sitting down in the grass at the top, he heard the loose dirt fall over the side into the water. The limb rose slowly out of the water and bobbed up and down, as if someone in the thick water below were using it to try to snag him.

Back at the truck, Don marked the spot on the map in red as a definite safety concern and wondered if anyone had ever fallen into the shaft. He had heard of archaeologists finding animal skeletons and human artifacts in the cold bottom of sinkholes in Central America, and the thought gave him the shivers.

Nearby lay the remains of an abandoned house that had been dismantled for its siding and usable lumber by the miners. Behind the house was a rotting log barn. Scattered at the field's edge and all around the stone foundation there were rusting metal skeletons of ancient farm implements: a wheat drill with its weathered wooden seed boxes lay worm-eaten, bleaching in the sun; a two-bottom plow with a broken moldboard and a coulter missing; there were paint cans, soup cans, pie pans, some pocked by bullet holes and all oxidized to a burnt brown. By the shards of pop bottles and Mason jars that colored the ground, the place seemed to be a favorite spot for target practice.

Next he drove to the church south of the mine. Don walked back into the woods behind the church, estimating the distance indicated on the property map as the location of the graveyard. He looked around in the mottled shade but could find no gravestones. Then off to his right, he noticed a green line of cedars growing close together, so he headed in that direction. When he reached the area, he realized the cedars squared off a small weedy lot distinct from the undergrowth beneath the yellowing poplar. *This had to be the cemetery*, he thought, although there seemed to be no stones to indicate the extent of the burials. The ground was a tangle of honeysuckle. Rooting his boot beneath the vines, he pulled away a section by dragging his foot across the ground like a hoe.

The steel toe of his boot bumped into a low stone. Pulling back the vines, he exposed a piece of marble about twelve inches wide and six inches deep. Removing the tendrils of the honeysuckle from the weathered white stone, he discovered that the top had been carved in the shape of what appeared to be a lamb. With his pocketknife, Don scratched at the black mold on the front of the stone, and the initials I.B. appeared under his blade. Infant boy, he thought, and the baby didn't survive long enough to be given a name. Don put one knee to the ground and took a deep breath.

From his crouch, Don raised his head and glanced quickly around the plot, feeling like the unholy invader of a private sanctum, then got up and carefully replaced the vines over the child's grave. At one corner of the graveyard, there was a large cedar whose broken-out top splintered gray within the low, green branches.

Walking carefully up to the tree, he noticed thin, bone-white slabs of marble stacked against its trunk like cards. They seemed to be uneven slashes of stone. But a few of the headstones appeared intact, and their tops were still arched gracefully. The engraved testaments on their grainy surfaces were almost eroded away by a black deteriorating fungus that ate away at their immortality. Don began to lever them back against his legs, indexing through generations of the vertical memorials until he could no longer support their weight against his knees. This would be a job for the experts, he thought. Most of these graves would be unmarked.

Paper rubbings would be taken of the tombstones, and any names that might be revealed would have to be researched in the court records and living relatives notified. Most likely, no descendants would be found. The top six inches of soil would be scraped away with a small dozer, revealing the dark rectangles of each grave. He imagined that within the slumped soil there would be nothing left of the antique tenants, so the archeologists would excavate down about six feet into each grave and take enough representative dirt to fill a small metal box. All the boxes from the graveyard would then be placed in a containerized coffin designed expressly for this purpose. Finally, the pioneers of this small reliquary would be found a new resting place for the next hundred years, in another cemetery close by. What remained of the old haunt would be picked up and moved by the dragline.

By late Friday afternoon, Don managed to confirm the locations of all questionable areas at the mine that would require additional investigation. That evening, he began the transfer of information from his field map to a finished series of large linen drafting sheets for Dutch's inspection and approval. He called Katie to let her know that he needed to work late in order to finish on time.

"The five o' clock deadline is a good thing to work against, but I want to make doubly sure that I get done on time. So, I've got to work late tonight."

"Can I come in to help out?"

"Thanks, but it's just a matter of drawing up a bunch of maps. Tedious detail work, but I need to do it myself."

"Alright, but I can't wait 'til tomorrow night. I want to show you off."

"Wild horses," he laughed. "I'll see you tomorrow about six o'clock."

Chapter Fifteen

One of These Days
Words and Music by Earl Montgomery

One of these days it'll soon be all over, cut and dried,
And I won't have this urge to go all bottled up inside,
One of these days, I'll look back and I'll say I left in time,
'Cause somewhere for me I know there's peace of mind,
There's gonna be peace of mind for me, one of these days.

"Rosie, get out of that bathrobe and start gettin' ready ta go," Dolores Cooper scolded, as she pulled the kitchen chair away from the table. She cupped her left hand under Rose's elbow and gently helped the frail woman to her feet. Then she placed her right arm around Rose's thin waist and guided her out of the kitchen and toward the bedroom.

"Now you get in there and put a nice dress on," she said while opening the door. "I'll send Katie in directly to help you with your hair." Rose shuffled across the bedroom floor and sat down in front of her vanity. Dolores closed the door quietly and walked back to the kitchen where Katie was taking the pies out of the oven.

"You know, there ain't nothin' wrong with that mother of yours, don't you?" Dolores said.

Katie put one pie on the counter to cool, shook her head in resignation, and returned to the oven for another.

"You ought to make her shift for herself, then she'd come around, I'd bet. Did she make those pies, or did you?"

"She trimmed the crust."

"That's just what I mean. I can remember a time when she'd whip up a batch of pies without even thinkin' about it."

"I'm tired of fighting her on it." Katie sighed. "Sometimes it's just a lot easier to do it myself."

"You got to make her start doin' things for herself, or she ain't gonna get any better."

"We both know she's never going to get any better; she likes the way she is."

Dolores took a wet rag from the sink and began to wipe off the kitchen table, a habit she had acquired through years of running her own restaurant. She gathered up the glass salt and pepper shakers in one hand and rubbed small circles over the faded Formica. Then she sat down heavily in Rose's vacant chair, neatly folding the rag on the tabletop.

"I know you're trying to help, Mrs. Cooper," Katie said after a few minutes, "but she's not going to change."

"I know, child, just as sure as you do. I just don't like to see you spendin' all your time takin' care of that old woman when she can take care of herself."

"I don't mind."

"Yes, you do, and you know it. Why, when's the last time you went somewheres?"

"I go to Terre Haute about once a week. Lately, a little more, since the accident."

"That ain't nowhere. I mean a real trip!"

Katie looked out the kitchen window; it was almost dark. She walked to the back door and turned on the porch light, then sat down at the table beside the older woman.

"See, you can't even remember, can you?" Dolores said, and before Katie could answer, she continued her lecture.

"There ain't nothin' worse than havin' somebody dependin' on you for everything, Katie; not having a life of their own, I mean, or you either." She slapped the edge of the table with her fingers. "I guess I'm one to talk; my boy's still around the house, and with that wife and baby, too."

"He does a good job helping out, doesn't he?"

"I don't give him no choice in the matter. If it weren't for the grocery and restaurant, he'd be out on the street. But he's my only child, and that's a little different."

"Kind of the opposite of me and Momma, huh?"

"He ain't never been real smart like some. I don't know how he ever graduated. But he sure could play some basketball, though, couldn't he?"

"Yes, he could. He was really something."

Katie remembered Bobby Cooper from high school. *He was a block of wood, really*, she thought. All her girlfriends had crushes on him at one time or another, but it was that little sophomore cheerleader Patty that intentionally got pregnant by him – thought he was her meal ticket out of Dugger. *Well, he was her meal ticket, but not in the way either of them imagined,* she mused.

"I always thought he'd go on to school," Dolores said, shaking her head. "At least to Vincennes for junior college. They got a good basketball program. I used to think they didn't want him because they recruit all them jumping-jack black kids from the ghetto, but I know now it's because he couldn't make the grades. I blame myself for that."

"How can you think like that?" Katie asked.

"I was just so busy tryin' to get the restaurant up and goin' after his daddy died that I let the school do what they wanted with him. I never checked because he seemed to be doin' fine. His grades were good."

"It would have been hard for you to know, Mrs. Cooper. Sometimes the teachers go easy on the athletes."

"I know that now; I just wish I'd a known it then. Anyway, I'm thinkin' about sendin' him to night school over in Linton to catch back up. You figure that's a good idea?"

"I think that would be wonderful. What does Bobby say?"

"He ain't real crazy about the idea, but he don't have a choice. I ain't gonna have him hangin' around the store talkin' basketball all his life. How about you?"

"What do you mean?"

"When are you going to get out of here and do somethin' on your own?"

Katie sighed. "Well, I used to think I couldn't leave my momma, but maybe my reasons to go weren't better than my reasons to stay."

"Havin' somebody dependent on you is a stiflin' thing," Dolores said, shaking her head. "Even more so if it's somebody like your mother. I mean, somebody that don't really need no help."

"You think she'd be okay if I decided to go?"

"Why, child, she'd be just fine. She'd have to adjust, that's for sure, but she has friends. We'd look after her 'till she got on her feet, don't you worry about that."

Katie got up and went to the counter to check on the pies, lightly touching the sugar-crusted tops with the tips of her fingers. Then she filled up the tea kettle and set it on the stove to boil. Retrieving the coffee and sugar from the cabinet, she brought it back to the table and set them in front of Dolores, then went back to the cabinet and brought out four cups.

"You expecting somebody?" Dolores said.

Katie looked at the fourth cup and smiled. "Yes," she said. "He's supposed to be by in a little bit. He's taking me to the dance."

"Anybody I know?"

"You may have seen him. He just started to work at the mine this week. Company man; he's living over by Conner in the old Goodman place."

"I know who you mean," Dolores said, her eyes sparkling. "He's a good lookin' fella. Conner was in the other day, says he's real nice."

"He is, Mrs. Cooper. He went up to the hospital with me a couple of times this week to see Tommie and Ray. We had dinner once."

"And you didn't stop by my place?" Dolores laughed. "I'm hurt."

"Well, no," Katie said, blushing. "We went to a real nice place to eat up in Terre Haute." When she saw Dolores' eyes crinkle, she hastily added: "Not that your place ain't nice. I mean, it was late; you would've been closed by the time we got back."

"This boy got a name?"

"His name's Don, Donald Rodgers."

"Don Rogers," Dolores repeated softly, looking toward Rose's bedroom. "Am I gonna get to meet him?" Dolores knew full well that she already had met the young man at her restaurant, but she wanted to encourage Katie's excitement. "He's comin' by here, ain't he?"

Katie looked up at the clock. "I hope so," she said. "He might be running a little late. Dutch gave him a bunch of work to do today. But he said he'd come by as soon as he got off work and went home to change clothes. He's supposed to be here by six o'clock."

"Well, it's six now. You'd better go help your mother with her hair. I'll start loadin' up the baskets. Then we can all sit here and wait to meet Mr. Rodgers."

"I don't know if he's expecting to walk in on three women when he picks me up," Katie laughed. "You might run him off!"

"I won't let him," Dolores chuckled. "Have you told your mother about him?"

"Hell, no. She thinks I should be going with Larry Miller. I wouldn't want to shock her."

"You was always too good for Larry, and your mother ought to know that by now," Dolores giggled. "I'm glad you found somebody else, sweetie. Now, go help her with her hair."

There was no answer when Katie knocked on the door, so she opened it slowly and peeked into the bedroom. Rose was seated on the embroidered stool in front of her vanity. She had on the new yellow dress Katie pressed for her earlier that afternoon. Katie took a brush from the vanity and began to remove the rollers and brush out her mother's hair. Both women stared ahead into the mirror.

"That's a real pretty dress, Momma," Katie said softly. "Goes real well with the purse Danny sent you for Christmas."

Rose looked at her image in the mirror; the soft eyes with the dark circles underneath, the thin expressionless lips. She raised her chin slightly, trying to find her daughter's reflection in the glass, but the crystal light from the lamp on the nightstand illuminated only a pair of hands; they gently pulled and patted her thinning white hair.

"I used to be young and pretty once too, you know," Rose said softly. "I had my share of beaus - Daddy used to say he had to beat them off with a stick."

"I'm sure that's right, Momma."

"Your daddy - I met him at the homecoming dance when I was eighteen. He was tall, handsome, had that Irish red hair."

Katie removed the last roller and brushed her mother's hair up from the bottom to give it more fullness. She stepped around to the side to evaluate her efforts. Rose glanced up at her.

"I heard you're goin' to the dance with somebody besides Larry," Rose said.

"That's right, Momma." *Who did she hear that from?* Katie thought. *Oh well, she was going to find out sooner or later.*

"What's wrong with Larry Miller? Don't you like him?"

"No, I don't like Larry Miller, Momma."

"Well, he's not gonna be very happy about you showing up with somebody else, is he?"

"It's none of his business."

"He'll make it his business, you know that. You're just gonna cause a lot of trouble, and what for? Because some stranger tells you stories about things."

"What are you talking about? What things?"

"You know exactly what I mean. Getting you all excited about places you ain't never gonna go, things you ain't never gonna see."

"What are you talking about, Momma? You don't even know Don."

"You think I don't? Well, you're wrong. I know exactly what these young bucks say to try and have their way with a young girl."

"Don's not like that, Momma. And besides, I'm old enough to think and do for myself."

"You ain't near old enough or half as smart as you think. Larry's the one you ought to be goin' with, not puttin' him off like you been doin'."

"I've never been interested in Larry!"

"Well, you ought to be. There comes a time when a girl has to make a choice and settle down. It might not be the best choice, but you learn to live with it. Your daddy and I didn't always see eye to eye in the beginning, but we managed and we got along," Rose said.

"There," Katie said, patting the underside of her mother's short hair. She was shocked at her mother's denunciation but mystified as to its origins. What was she talking about? She wanted to ask, but she was in a hurry. She'd wait until this weekend when things weren't so rushed, she thought. "Finish your makeup," Katie said. "It's time to leave."

"Mark my words, girl. Don't be listening to no foolishness from some stranger."

Katie left the room without responding to her mother. The older woman looked into the mirror and whispered to the eyes in front of her: "One of these days," she said softly, "he'll say he'll take you away, but he won't mean it, not one word of it."

"Poured you a cup of coffee," Dolores said as Katie rushed through the kitchen. "Is your mother ready yet? It's almost six-thirty."

Katie looked out the kitchen window. It was dark, and the streetlight had switched on down at the corner. "You'd better take Momma and get going," Katie suggested. "I'll stay until Don gets here."

"What? And miss meetin' Mr. Right?"

"Mrs. Cooper, please take Momma with you. I don't want her giving Don the once over when he gets here. Besides, he's already late. You run along. I'll introduce you to him at the dance."

"Okay, sweetie," Dolores replied. "And don't worry about your mother; I'll take care of her. You just promise me I'll get to meet this fella."

"I promise, really."

"Okay. Rosie? Rosie!" Dolores called, stomping toward the bedroom. "Time to go! Get a move on."

Katie was in the bathroom brushing her hair when she heard her mother and Dolores leave. After touching up her lipstick, she went back into the kitchen to finish cleaning up the sink. She refilled the tea kettle with cold water, put it back on the burner, and sat down at the table, readjusting the coffee cups. She looked up at the clock. *Six thirty-five,* she thought. *Maybe he tried to call but the phone might be out.* She hurried into the dark living room and pulled the chain on the floor lamp next to the couch. Finding the phone on the end table, she picked up the heavy black receiver and held it to her ear. She heard a click and then the dial tone. Hanging up the phone, she walked back into the kitchen.

She sat at the table for a few more minutes, watching the clock, before she went back into the living room. She sat down at the end of the couch and hesitated for a moment before calling the mine. The front office was closed, but a clerk from the supply room answered the night phone.

The new engineer? Saw him leave about an hour ago, right around dark. The lights are out upstairs, but I can check for you, the man said. No, that's all right; she thanked the voice on the other end as she hung up the phone. She waited another minute and called Conner's house.

"No, he hasn't pulled in yet. Left the mine when? Maybe he's had a flat or broke down on the road. Don't worry, you go on and help your mother. I'll run up the road and see if he's off in a ditch somewhere."

She turned off the gas under the boiling tea kettle and stepped out onto the back porch. At six forty-five she went back into her bedroom, changed her blouse, and put on a jacket. Walking into the living room, she checked one more time to make sure the sure the phone was working. Then, turning off most of the lights in the house, she grabbed her purse, locked the back door, and drove to the high school.

Chapter Sixteen

Red Dog Road

Earlier in the day, Don had made his last field inspection - a small stream which flowed westward from the pit. Parking his truck in a side ditch off the county road, he followed the meander as it alternately pooled and cut through the banks of river birch and soft maple. At one point it forked, and he took the drier branch to the south and soon came across a bridge on the red shale road, just west of his house. Staying in the wet-leafed bottom of the creek, he climbed through the dank coolness of the road culvert before continuing upstream along the steepening banks. Crossing Conner's property line Don passed the glade of oaks that rose on the plateau behind the cut bank of the creek. From that point, the stream turned back toward the north. A few yards from this bend, it was crosscut by a newly bulldozed road that Don recognized as the one leading to the old oak. He decided to check on the tree.

Climbing up the bank, it seemed that the morning chatter of birds had become suddenly quiet, and the usual scatter of squirrels across the dry leaves didn't precede his approach. Up ahead he noticed a light area in the trees that should have been the dark form of the oak. As yellowed beams spidered through the overhanging branches, webbing the forest floor in a linen-filtered light, Don recognized the oak and fell to his knees in bewilderment.

At the feet of the oak, the ground was littered with its massive branches, hacked off its body, nearly to the top of the crown. The stumps exposed by the amputations were white and wet with sap; wood chips lay in piles at precise intervals along the ground, indicating where the chainsaws had carved away firewood-sized pieces. The air smelled of wood dust and death. Don walked over to the tree and sat on one of the great arms. He saw a flash of orange under a pile of chips and reached down to retrieve the flagging he had so hopefully wrapped around the tree the day before.

Don considered waiting for the killers to come back; he thought about barging into Dutch's office and complaining about it; maybe he should go to Conner's house and bring him back to see the slaughter. But in the end, his mind couldn't think at all.

Considering the futility of any action he might take, Don stood up and placed both of his hands on the tree and for a few moments, pressed his fingers against the cold, gray bark. Clambering back into the creek bed, he stumbled along the winding track back to the truck. And it seemed that along the way, he passed through many generations of life and death, of thought and emptiness, and he felt the terror in the land around him.

It was now late afternoon as Don glanced out the window of his office. His room overlooked the garage, and through the open bay doors he could see the approaching dark outside. He looked up at the clock - ten till five. *Finished it with time to spare*, he thought. It had been a long week, but the maps were done; all he had to do was roll them up and take them down to Dutch's office. He walked over to the drafting table and looked them over one last time.

Even now, hours later, as he rolled up the maps, Don sensed the dull pain of his morning discovery. He resolved to make some sense out of his ignorance and to determine if he could continue to work in a situation that seemed to be larger than his capacity to understand it.

Stretching a rubber band around the roll of maps, Don put on his hardhat and turned out the light before heading down the dark stairs to the Dutchman's office.

Through the open door, Don could see the superintendent talking to someone seated against the wall, so he waited a respectful distance outside in the hallway until Dutch motioned for him to enter.

"Anything else?" Dutch said to the man in the folding chair.

"Not right now. We can talk later," Larry said. "How long you gonna be?"

"Not more than fifteen minutes. Got to stop by the house before I go to the game, though."

"All right," Larry said, lighting a cigarette and smiling at Don through the blue smoke. "I'll try to catch you later this evenin'." He left the office and walked down the hallway toward the garage.

"These the maps?" Dutch asked Don.

"Yes, sir. If you have a few minutes, there's a couple of things I'd like to point out."

"Start pointing!"

Don proceeded to trace the boundary of the permit line, explaining potential locations for topsoil stockpiles and sediment ponds. He also pointed out the safety hazard of the air shaft and the need to call the corporate office about the old graveyard. The two men discussed the need to reroute the south branch of the creek Don had followed into the woods.

"According to Clarence's maps, we own this area outside the permit line," Don said, pointing to the area where the oak had been savaged. "Am I right?"

"Yep," Dutch said. "That's the old Bedwell place. Seems to me the company bought that back when I was a kid. What's your point?"

"Well, we're not going to mine it anytime near soon, so I think we should stay off of it."

"The electricians are locating a new substation back there."

"I know; I saw their road. That's not the problem."

"What's the problem?"

Don took a deep breath. "I don't think we need to be taking out a bunch of trees in areas that we're not going to mine."

"Why's that?"

"Well, for one thing, it's a waste of resources and secondly, there's plenty of good wood out in front of the pit."

"That's true," Dutch said. "Any other reasons?"

"Well, the more intact we keep the perimeter, the quicker the mined area will regenerate as soon as we're through. Acts like a seed area mostly; for birds and animals, as well as trees."

"This something that corporate is supporting, or just your idea?"

"I've got support for it."

"Okay. You get me a map of the area where the men can cut wood and I'll have Katie type up a memo to make sure they stay within our boundaries. Will that suit you?" Dutch said.

"Yes, sir." Don said.

"Anything else?"

"No, sir."

"Good. I'm outa here," Dutch said, leading Don out the side door. "You going to the game?"

"Yes, sir."

"Good. Enjoy yourself. Maybe I'll see you at the dance afterwards."

Don watched as Dutch started up his truck and backed out of the parking space. Before the truck had stopped rolling backward, he turned on his headlights and shifted into first gear and high-tailed it out of the lot. Don hurried to his Bronco, satisfied that he had met the superintendent's deadline on the maps, and happy to have made his point about disturbance outside the mining area. He looked down at his watch. It was five forty-five. Time to get a move on. He had to change clothes and pick up Katie by six.

Don jumped in the Bronco and headed out of the mine and down the red shale road, eventually turning onto the roller coaster of gravel that undulated westward to his house. Rolling down into the last hollow before his drive, he passed an old pickup overloaded with firewood. He eased his truck over toward the side of the road and waved. The men in the truck returned his salute as they passed. Don recognized the driver as one of the two men he had seen in the restaurant earlier in the week. He wondered if they might be the ones who cut up the oak. *I'll make a point to talk to them at Cooper's*, he thought. *There was no need to cut up that tree - much easier pickin's laying right nearby. And those two guys sure don't seem like the types that would go out of their way to cause themselves more work. Something else is going on.*

As the taillights of their truck disappeared in the dust of his rearview mirror, his headlights illuminated low, dark shapes up ahead, strung across the road in an irregular dashed line. He slowed the truck down and stopped far enough back so that he could see them clearly. *Logs - must have fallen off that truck I passed,* he thought. *I'm late already, but I'd better clear them off the road before someone comes along and hits them.* Leaving the truck running with its lights on, Don jogged toward the logs, watching his shadow grow longer with each stride.

Don bent over to examine one of the logs and found that it was white oak. Standing the piece up on its end, the cross-section was nearly elliptical rather than round. He understood immediately; these sections were part of the branches of the old oak. He felt as if he'd walked across someone's grave.

He tried to kick and roll the heavy logs off the road into the ditch, but the cam-like shape fought against him, so he was forced to lift each piece and carry it to the side. Partly because his mind was off in the woods with the mangled oak and partly because he was blinded by the bright lights and engine noise of his truck, he didn't notice the truck that pulled up behind the Bronco. He struggled to remove the last log from the road.

Bent over, with his back to the headlights, Don felt a shadow approaching from behind. As he stood up and began to turn around, something hit him hard on the side of his head, sending his hardhat bouncing into the weeds and knocking him sprawling on the gravel. He raised himself to his hands and knees and tried to squint his swelling eye into the headlights at the dark silhouette above him. But before he could focus, a big boot stomped on his left hand, and he was lifted off the ground by a violent kick to his ribs. Dizzy and gasping for breath, he curled into a fetal position. The shadow bent down, picked up the oak log and raised it slowly, directly above Don's head. Unable to move, he blinked up at the menacing figure, then closed his eyes in resignation. *This is it,* Don thought; *he's going to kill me.* He flinched in expectation when he heard the man grunt and the thump of the wood as it was thrown into the roadside ditch. He felt what seemed like hot embers on his skin as an invisible boot kicked loose gravel at his face. Then the stalker-shadow turned around, and he heard it run back up the road. It disappeared beyond the headlights.

Don felt something warm and thick rise in his throat and flow out of his mouth. He tried to raise his head, but the headlights from the truck began a binary swirl. Struggling to his feet, the swirl shrilled into a thin white line that turned black and silent as he fell in the middle of the road.

His lantern swinging by his side, Conner walked toward the soft glow rising out of the hollow where the road crossed Barren Fork. Shadows played on the underside of the arching branches, and he understood that something was moving between himself and the light. When he reached the top of the rise and looked down the grade into the ravine, he saw the rough outline of a man silhouetted against the glare of headlights. The man bent down, then raised a large object over his head. The auroral light from behind him magnified his movements, and Conner at once understood the threat.

In the roadbed, a dark shape moved and tried to separate itself from the shadows.

"Hey, there," Conner shouted. "What the hell do you think you're doin'!"

He heard the standing man utter an obscenity, then saw him throw the object into the ditch. By the thump, Conner figured it must have been a log. The man picked up something from the road, then ran back through the headlights. Conner heard the slam of a door and the slip of tires on the loose gravel as he slammed a vehicle into reverse. The driver careened back up the road without switching on the headlights. Then, turning the wheel sharply, he backed into the side ditch and jammed the truck into first gear, jacking a turn and jumping back out onto the road, spitting gravel as he headed away from the hollow. Only when the driver had sped down the road for some distance did Conner see the truck's head and taillights come on.

The figure of a man rose from the road shadows and immediately dropped back down. Deliberately, the old man shuffled down to the bottom of the hollow and set his lantern down by the collapsed man, who lay on his side, one arm stretched out toward the sound of the idling truck. His face was in shadow, but Conner knew that it was Don before he pushed on the upraised shoulder and gently rolled him over onto his back.

Conner went down on one knee and shook out a red handkerchief from his back pocket. Lifting the back of the young man's head with his left hand, he began to carefully wipe away the blood from the corner of Don's mouth and dab at the small, sharp pieces of gravel embedded in the young man's face.

"Hey, boy," he said softly. "Wake up, son. It's me, Conner. Wake up."

Don's left eye was already swollen shut, the result of a savage blow to the side of his head that had also cut his ear. His right eyelid trembled slightly and after a moment or two, Don squinted into the harsh light.

"Damn, boy," Conner said, "you had me scared for a minute there. I thought you was a goner."

Don gurgled and then rolled onto his side, coughed, and spit blood into the dry dust by his face. With the old man's help, he rose into a sitting position, lightly touching the bloody fingers of his left hand to the crease of his swelling eye. Struggling to his feet, he doubled over, grabbing his lower rib cage with his right hand. He coughed tightly, swayed a bit then slowly eased himself up straight. Conner steadied him.

"Rough day at the office," Don said, shivering and coughing.

Conner chuckled. "Well, I see they didn't knock the sense of humor out of you!"

"They? Was there more than one? Came at me from behind, I only saw one."

"That's all I saw. Big guy, too."

Conner left the lantern in the road. Lifting Don's right arm, he tried to place it over his own shoulder. But the engineer winced at the pulling on his ribs, so Conner lowered the young man's arm around his waist. Then the two men limped over to the truck.

"Have any idea who it was?" Conner said.

"Oh, I have a rough idea."

"Yeah, me, too. Let's get you back to the house. Can you drive?"

"Yeah, no problem," Don said, easing up behind the wheel.

"Good. I'll get my lantern and follow you down."

"You don't want to ride?"

"It ain't that far, boy. You was almost there."

Don pulled up in front of his porch, shut off the truck, and switched off the lights. He rested for a moment until Conner's bobbing light turned onto the driveway and approached the side of the truck. Then he opened the door and slid down out of the cab. His knees buckled slightly, and he leaned against the door to shut it.

"You gonna be all right?" Conner asked.

"Yeah, I think I'll just go in and lie down for a bit," Don said.

"Need any help?"

"No, thanks anyway. I've got to get cleaned up. I've got to pick up Katie."

"You ain't goin' nowhere, son," Conner said.

"She's going to wonder what happened to me. Probably thinks I stood her up," Don said.

"Don't you worry about that. I'll drive into the gym; I've got some things to tend to: you go on inside."

"You wanna take my truck?"

"Naw, I'll take my old clunker," Conner said, and chuckled. "Looks like it might be safer. Besides, I was gonna go to the dance, too. May be gettin' home late, you never know."

"Okay, but let Katie know I'll be along in a little bit."

"I'll let her know you're home. You stay put."

Don climbed the steps to the front porch and rattled open the front door. The only light in the house came from the bulb under the suspended metal shade in the kitchen that threw its triangular beam hard against the kitchen table. Once inside, Don felt the pain welling up in his gut. Placing his shoulder to the door, he pushed it shut, then slid down onto the floor with his back against it.

Chapter Seventeen

Save the Last Dance for Me
Doc Pomus and Mort Shuman

*You can dance, go and carry on 'til the night is gone
And it's time to go,
If he asks, are you all alone can he take you home?
You must tell him no,
And don't forget who's takin' you home
And in whose arms you're gonna be,
Oh, darlin', save the last dance for me.*

Halftime at the basketball game, and Dugger was leading Linton thirty-eight to twenty-two. The smokers filed out of the new gym and teenagers gathered in knots along the sideline as the announcer began to read the roll call of glory. The crowd rose to its feet as the band began to moan the alma mater. The homecoming queen and her court were introduced and escorted to the middle of the floor by tall, slightly embarrassed boys gangling in oversized suits. The announcer read their names over the public address system. The girls' parents joined them on the court, the mothers holding a single yellow rose presented to them just for the occasion.

Over in the old gym, the women set out the food and punch bowls for the homecoming dance that would follow the game. A few refugees from the game clustered at the doorway and peered into the gold and black draped hall. The disc jockey set up his equipment on the stage and tested the sound system.

Dolores pulled Katie off to the side of the gym, behind a big piece of plywood with a bulldog painted on it.

"Where's that boy of yours?" she asked.

"I don't know. He should have been here by now."

"Well, it's halftime and I got to run across to the gym," Dolores said, with obvious delight. "They're gonna introduce Bobby and he gets to escort me on to the court!"

"That's wonderful. I wish I could see it, but I'd better stay here and help with the refreshments."

"All right, but as soon as he gets here, you bring him over and introduce him to me. You promised."

"I promise. Now, run on, it sounds like the band's starting to play."

"I won't be long. I'll see you in a bit."

Entering the damp heat of the new gym, Dolores looked around the entrance to the concession area. Bobby was leaned up against the wall, running down the game's progress with his former teammates. Their conversation was framed in the context of a game played six years ago. There was no comparison between this night's scrimmage and the game they had played, they all agreed. These boys couldn't hold a candle to their team. *But these boys are a bunch of scrappers*, someone offered, and everybody agreed to that, too.

Bobby's wife stood with a group of other young women her age, talking about babies and mothers-in-law, while her six-year-old son ran under the bleachers with a rowdy band of grade school boys, looking down on the floor for money, toward the bleacher seats, and up girls' dresses.

With an accent on tremoling clarinets and bass drums, the band began to blare the school fight song. Somewhere overhead, two trumpets fought to raise the melody above the overpowering accompaniment. The school principal hurried to the side of the gym and motioned frantically with his program to the young men waiting in the concession area. They swaggered out from behind the bleachers, showing the poor man the same, slow disdain they had developed for him while in school. This was their night, and they knew it.

One by one, as the announcer blared their names over the loudspeaker, each boy took his mother by the arm and escorted her to the middle of the court. There they faced the frenzied faithful who were half-singing, half-screaming the school song. Finally, with one team member left on the sideline, the crowd began to chant: "Bob-ee! Bob-ee! Bob-ee!"

Bobby Cooper waited until the announcer screamed his points and pedigree into the microphone. Bending over to hand Dolores a yellow rose, Bobby took her by the arm and walked slowly out to the jump circle at midcourt, waving to the crowd with his free hand. On this Saturday night, Bobby Cooper didn't have to strip and wax the floors in the restaurant. Instead, he reveled in the brief reflection of his youth. And his mother was radiant.

Katie watched Rose thread her way through the crowd at the entrance and past a leering Larry Miller. A few yards away from the door, she saw him whisper something in John Hick's ear, something that made both men laugh. Roger was there, too, but when she shot him a questioning glance, he looked down at the floor, turned, and disappeared into the parking lot. Larry stepped over the thick rope between the doors and eased across the corner of the gym to the table where Katie was setting out the pies and cookies her mother had retrieved from the car. Leaning down to the table, he snorted at one of the pies.

"These sure look good," he said. "Did you make 'em?"

"Some of them," Katie replied, turning her back on him to take some more pies out of the basket. *He seems to be awful sure of himself,* she thought; *even more than usual, if that's possible. I wonder what he said to John, and why did Roger look away?* She turned to place another pie on the table, but Larry grabbed it out of her hands.

"How about givin' me a little piece," he said, "of pie that is."

"You buy a ticket like everybody else," she said. "Now, go on."

"Oh, I think I'll hang around here. Might pick up a dance or two with some eligible female types,"

"I don't know of any cripples or blind ladies here tonight, but I suppose there's always that chance."

Larry hesitated for a moment, then sneered at her. "Where's your date?"

"He'll be here," Katie replied, turning back to the basket.

"I wouldn't be too sure about that."

Katie felt the blood drain from her face as she turned around to confront Larry. In a voice tinged with barely restrained hatred, she asked: "Just what do you mean?"

"Oh, I don't know. Maybe he had an accident or somethin'. He ain't real familiar with the roads around here yet. You know how things happen."

"What did you do to him?"

"Me? Why, we just had a little talk, that's all. He gave me the impression he wasn't coming. I told him I thought that was a good idea."

"You son of a bitch!" Katie screamed, picking up a pie and hitting Larry squarely in the chest with it. She ran down the length of the gym to where her mother and a few other women were setting up the punch bowls. Larry glared at the group of strangers who laughed at him from behind the door ropes, then he stalked off after Katie.

"Momma! I've got to leave!"

"You can't leave now, child," Rose replied. "Where's Dolores?"

"She's across the way," Katie said frantically. "She'll be back directly."

Larry came up from behind and grabbed the young woman by the arm. Evenin' Mrs. Johnson," he said tightly through clinched teeth. "I need to speak with your daughter here."

"Mother ... " Katie said.

"Why, hello, Larry," Rose said. "What's happened to the front of your shirt? Come on over here and let me clean you up."

She took Larry's arm away from her daughter and pulled him toward the water fountain. Katie broke free and ran for the door, scavenging her purse from under one of the tables. She ran across the parking lot and opened the door to her Jeep, feeling the shadow of someone who approached her from behind, silhouetted against the light from the open gym door. Reaching into the Jeep, she found the handle of the bat and jerked it out from behind the driver's seat, brandishing it in front of her, both hands on the handle.

The figure stopped. "You ain't going to use that on me, now?"

"I will if you had anything to do with Larry this evening, Roger," she said.

"Nope ... just came to see the game," Roger replied, looking back toward the gym so that his face was eclipsed in the light.

"But you do know what happened ... right?"

"I 'magine."

"Couldn't you do anything to stop him?"

"You know how he is."

"Where's Don now?"

"Out at his house, I reckon," Roger said.

"I'm real surprised at you, Roger," she said coldly, turning her back on him. Suddenly, she wheeled around clutching the bat in her hands, causing Roger to jump back out of her reach.

"Did you ride in with Larry?"

"John did. I drove myself."

"Is Larry driving the company truck?"

"Nope, his Ford, but - "

"Where is it? Come on, I don't have much time."

Roger pointed to a new Ford truck a few yards away, glistening peacefully within a cone of mercury vapor light near the baseball field backstop. "Katie don't even think about it - " Roger said, but it was too late. As she ran through the grass toward the truck, Roger frowned, put his hands in his pockets, looked down at the ground, and spat. Then he turned away and walked back toward the sound of the game.

Conner pulled into the parking lot at the high school. Easing his truck through the loose crowd, he drove up to the old gym. Creaking open the door, he got out and circled the knot of people at the entrance and hurried toward the broad light coming from a side door. Just inside the door, he paused, letting his eyes adjust to the brightness and found himself on the perimeter of a group of women preparing tables for the dance. Rose stood a few feet away, swiping at a large purple stain on Larry Miller's shirt.

Larry glanced at Conner in surprise and backed up, trying to put the water fountain between him and the older man bearing down on him. But Rose, bent over attending to the stain, held on to his shirt as if it were his ear, pulling the tails of his shirt out of his pants.

"Now you hold still," Rose said without looking up from her work. "This'll only take a minute. You better soak it when you get home."

Larry pressed himself against the wall, his arms at his sides and his palms flat against the painted brick. He looked into Conner's narrowed stare then turned his head from side to side. There was nowhere to go. The old woman tugged and worked at the stain without knowing that she separated and protected the two men from each other. Larry realized his advantage and eased away from the wall a little bit.

"I don't know what's come over that girl," Rose said. "Her temper ... I think she gets that from her father."

"You're damn sure right she does," Conner said. "Where is she now?"

Rose turned around, dropping her cleaning rag, and gaping up at Conner, who had not taken his eyes off Larry.

"Why, Mr. Owen," she said. "What brings you into town?"

Conner moved to Rose's side, hemming Larry against the fountain and the wall. Then, for just a moment, he broke eye contact with Larry, and taking Rose's fingers gently between his huge hands, he bent toward her and smiled into her soft eyes.

"Why, I figured to come in and catch me a dance with some pretty little girl," he said.

Rose blushed and looked down at the floor.

"Where's Katie? I thought she'd be here helping you."

"Well, she was, but she ran off," Rose said. She bent her knees and squatted to retrieve the rag from the floor. Conner leaned over and gently helped her back to her feet. "Her and Larry had a spat."

"They did? Wonder what for?" Conner grinned, re-affixing his eyes on the young man pressed against the water fountain.

"I don't know, but she hit him with a pie, right square in the belly," Rose said.

"And it looks like it was one of your famous raspberry ones at that; what a shame," he said gently to Rose. His eyes shifted to Larry. "At least you saw it comin'."

"What are you sayin', old man."

"You know exactly what I mean, you young punk."

"I don't know what you're talking about. I'm getting out of here!" Larry said, threatening to move away from the wall.

"You just stay put!" Larry hedged back against the wall.

"What's goin' on here?" Rose asked.

"Nothing for you to worry about, Rosie. Now, where's Katie?" Conner asked.

"I saw her pull out of the parkin' lot and head toward the mine," someone volunteered from the small crowd that had gathered behind Conner. Conner glanced behind him; but the group stood firm and questioning. Then he turned back to Rose.

"Now, don't you worry about the girl," he said softly. "I got an idea where she's goin', she'll be just fine. You go on back to work. This here young man and me's gonna have a little talk."

Rose turned her sad, wide eyes toward Larry then back to Conner. She smiled at the older man, then shuffled away toward the crowd at the tables, which broke up into smaller discussion groups and went back to work mixing the punch and setting out the cups and bowls.

"Thought you was pretty smart, didn't you?" Conner chuckled grimly.

"What do you mean?" Larry said.

"Don't take no kind of a man to beat another over the head from behind with a club."

"You don't know what you're talkin' about."

"The hell I don't. Who do you think came over the hill with the lantern?"

"How you know it was me?" Larry asked contemptuously. "You can't see for nothin', old man."

"Maybe not at night on a dark road, but I saw how you acted when I came in, and how you're actin' now."

Larry realized how he must be appearing to the people who stared and laughed at his predicament. *Wait a minute*, he thought. *I don't have to take anything off this old man. I could whip him in a heartbeat.* Larry straightened up and leaned toward Conner, attempting to physically intimidate the older man.

"I'm getting' out of here. You ain't got nothin' on me!" Larry said.

"You stay put," Conner said, gripping Larry's arm and leaning as hard as he could against the younger man.

Larry shook off the old man's grasp, raised his hands to his sides, tightened his fingers into fists, and leered at Conner.

"How you gonna stop me, old man?" Larry said.

"Look over there," Conner said, nodding his head toward the front door of the gym. "Sheriff Hoaglund's off duty, taking tickets at the door for the PTA. I figure he's supposed to be in charge of crowd control, too. Maybe we ought to go ask him, to make sure, I mean."

"You ain't got nothin' on me, old man."

"You want to go see? Well, son of a bitch. Look who he's talkin' to now ... your daddy. Let's go take a walk."

"Wait a minute," Larry said quickly, dropping his arms and looking at the floor. "What you want me to do?"

"You'll leave here tonight when I do, and I plan to stay for quite awhile."

"It's a big gym, a lot of people will be milling around. How you gonna know if I leave?"

"You better make sure you stay where I can see you, or I'll have you in the pokie slicker than deer guts on a doorknob. And that boy'll press charges, too. He's got an eyewitness, don't forget."

"I need to go home and change my shirt," Larry said glumly.

"You look just fine. Why, the girls'll be throwin' gravels at the other guys tryin' to get to you!" Conner chuckled. "Now get. And you better be turnin' out the lights when I go to leave!"

Larry slid down into a sitting position by the cooler, with his shoulders against the wall, deflated. Frustrated, he jerked his head backward, cracking his head against the rough brick. He winced at the sudden pain as Conner turned and walked toward the women behind the folding table.

"My, my, my!" he said. "Looks like it's gonna be a humdinger of a party, yes, sirree. Rosie, that's the prettiest yellow dress I ever did see. Why, they're playin' our song! May I have this dance?"

Before she could answer, Conner gently took Rose's hand and led her out into the middle of the gym floor. And as the band played *Tennessee Rose*, Conner sang what words he could remember softly in her ear:

Well, it's a sweet dream that keeps me close to you, dear,
And it's a sad thing, when we're apart I'm blue,
And there are times now and then I thank the heavens up above
When I'm with the one that I love.

Now there are diamonds that some may long to see,
And they may shine, but not bright enough for me,
I wouldn't take the whole world if it was dipped in gold,
For a night with my Tennessee Rose

Take this love I am giving,
For it's truly the lasting kind,
The gift I hold is believing,
That you will always be mine.

Tennessee Rose
By Karen Brooks and Hank DeVito

Chapter Eighteen

Easy from Now On
Carlene Carter and Suzanna Clark

Quarter moon in a ten-cent town,
Time for me to lay my heartache down,
Saturday nigh, I'm gonna make myself a name,
Take a month of Sundays
To try and explain,
It's gonna be easy to fill,
The heart of a thirsty woman, harder to kill,
The ghost of a no-good man,
But I'll be ridin' high,
In a fan-dangled sky,
It's gonna be easy,
It's gonna be easy from now on.

The rearview mirror stayed black and lightless, so Katie turned her attention and the Jeep onto the red shale road. She had anticipated the appearance of headlights behind her, but it was apparent that Larry hadn't followed her out of town - at least not in his own truck. Smiling, almost laughing off her anxiety, she wondered if her mother realized, by fussing over Larry's pie-damaged shirt, how she had aided her daughter's escape. The corrugations in the road hammered and fish-tailed the jeep violently until she let off the gas and downshifted to gain traction. Relaxing her grip on the wheel, her troubles at the dance bottomed out, and new apprehensions began to rise inside her, as she considered what she might find at the end of her run.

In the dark hollow, just before the Goodman place, she saw a white object reflect her headlights. She hit the brakes and skidded to a stop, then got out. By the edge of the road, she found a hardhat lying in the weeds. Not a scratch, she thought, rotating it in front of the headlights. Why'd he go off and leave it? Climbing back into the Jeep, she placed it crown-up on the seat, then skittered out of the hollow and pulled into the drive, parking next to the Bronco.

She reached over, grabbed the hardhat, and climbed out the canvas door. A light breeze rustled the carpet of leaves on the ground, and except for a returning whisper from the branches overhead, silence surrounded her. She looked up through the swaying limbs, black-etched on a dark, velvet sky; breathed the cool air in through her nostrils, held it for a moment; then exhaled the warmed vapor from her lips. A dim light glowed from somewhere inside Don's cabin.

Stepping onto the porch, she put the hard hat under one arm. Cupping her hands around her eyes and standing on her toes, she peered through the small square of glass in the wooden door. She rapped on the wooden door with her fist, much more loudly than she had intended, and the glass rattled loosely in the frame. In the night's stillness, the knocking seemed harsh and intrusive.

She waited a few seconds for a response, then tapped on the glass with the tips of her fingers.

"Don? Don? Are you in there?" she asked, forcing down her rising anxiety. There was no answer, so she knocked again, this time a little louder. But before she could speak, she heard a muffled cough and felt a slight movement against the bottom of the door. Looking downward through the glass into the dimly lit room, she saw two legs sticking out away from the door. She knelt on the porch and moved her face close to the bottom of the door, so that her cheek touched where she thought Don's head would be.

"Don, it's me!" she said softly. "Can you hear me?"

A body shifted on the other side of the panel, and the glass chattered lightly.

"Katie?" a voice rasped through the wood.

"Yes, it's me."

"Oh, geez," Don said, "I'm sorry I didn't pick you up. I, uh, had some trouble with my truck."

"Are you all right?"

On the other side of the door, the young man struggled to keep his words from slurring. Touching a hand to his face, Don was able to detect the swelling that was affecting his ability to speak. More importantly, his thoughts were not clear and the voice from the other side of the door seemed to alternately fade beyond hearing and grow louder and rasping.

"I'm just a little tired," he said, "that's all."

"Why are you sitting on the floor?" Katie asked worriedly. From the tenor of his speech, it was obvious that Larry had injured him in some way. She needed to get inside. *I'll go around to the back door,* she thought. *Maybe it's open.* She stood up to go.

"Are you mad at me?" he said, his voice rising and quavering at the question.

"For what?"

"Standing you up, on our first date."

"No ... no, I'm not mad. You sound hurt. What's wrong?"

"I didn't mean to be late. Give me a few minutes. I'll get ready. Damn, my head hurts."

Katie hurried around the house to the back porch and tried the door. She twisted the old doorknob with all her strength and shook the door, but it was securely locked. She ran back to the front porch in a panic and peered in through a large window in the log wall nearest the door. The window was draped with a sheer curtain, but by pressing her cheek to the cold glass she could see through a small, shadowed slit between the curtain and the wall. Don lay crumpled against the front door, half-sitting with his back to the door, his head cocked to one side.

"Don, open the door for me," she said, rapping on the windowpane. *I'll break this if I have to,* she thought.

"Oh, I don't know," he replied in a reedy voice. "I don't think I'm such a pretty sight."

"I don't care. Don, please open the door."

"You sure?"

He's starting to sound really disoriented, Kathy thought. She knelt by the front door and forced herself to sound calm. "Please, Don, open the door for me," she said. "Or I'll break the window."

Don grasped the doorknob and pulled himself upright. Going back to the window, she saw his shadow on the curtain, heard the latch bolt slide free, and felt the stumble of his footsteps across the wooden floor toward the back of the house. When they stopped, she walked to the door and slowly pushed it open.

Don felt hot, and when he got up from the floor, he headed toward the bathroom to put some cold water on his face. Halfway across the room the kitchen light began to sway inside his head. He steadied himself against the back of a kitchen chair that wavered at the edge of the lamp light. Pulling it back away from the table, he collapsed into the seat, bent over toward the floor as far as the pain in his ribs would allow, and cradled his head in his hands.

Katie walked quietly over toward the cone of light and knelt beside his bent shadow and placed her hand on his knee. She cradled his battered hand on her fingers and feathered her right hand toward his face, still half in shadow. She pressed her cheek lightly against his bloodied knuckles and started to cry.

Her tears stung the raw flesh of his fingers, and he turned toward her, straining to clear the fog from his head. She reached toward the blindness on the left side of his face and he felt her fingers slide behind his neck and her thumb trace the outline of his ear.

"I'm so sorry," she said.

"For what?" Don asked.

"I know who did this to you. It's my fault."

"I think I know who it was, too, and it's not your fault."

"I should have warned you about him."

"You did. The first day I met you at the mine."

"I did?"

"Yeah, everybody else told me about him, too. Hell, Larry even told me. It's nobody's fault. I should've been looking," Don said, reaching up toward the back of his head.

"Maybe we better go see Doc Bennett. The game's over, he's probably at the dance."

"Don't know if there's much he could do. Besides, I don't feel like going into town just now. I haven't looked in the mirror lately, but ..." He pressed his palm against his forehead and tried to laugh, but the effort constricted into a tight coughing. "My head's clearing up. I may have cracked some ribs."

"Can you move your hand?"

He lifted his arm up to the light and flexed his fingers slowly. "It's numb across the top, but I don't think anything's broken."

"I'm going next door to get Conner," she said.

"He's not there," he said.

"How do you know?"

"He's the one that found me on the road ... brought me back here. He took off for town. I don't know how long ago; said he'd tell you what happened."

"I didn't see him. I must have passed him on the road."

"Then how'd you know to come?"

Katie hesitated for a moment. "Larry showed up at the gym; said you and him had a little talk, and that you weren't coming. I figured it out."

"Some discussion," Don winced, touching the swollen area around his left eye. "He came at me from behind with some kind of club. The bastard blind-sided me."

"Just like him, too. Big as he is, he's still a sneak."

"What time is it? Look at my watch."

"It's about eight thirty."

"You say the ballgame's over by now?"

"Probably; why?"

"You still want to go to the dance?"

Katie got up and walked over to the refrigerator. "No, silly. Let's get you cleaned up. You're not going anywhere tonight. Do you have any frozen peas or stuff like that?"

"What for?"

"For your eye. It takes the swelling down." She opened the door of the freezer and found it was empty, except for one ice cube tray.

"There's hardly any food in the house," he said. "I guess I need to go to the grocery store this week."

"I'll run next door to Conner's. He has a big freezer on the back porch. Don't move till I get back," she said, and hurried out the backdoor.

She returned in a few minutes with two plastic bags. The peas were frozen together, hard as a brick, so she took a metal pot from the stove and started pounding them on the counter with the bottom of the pot until they broke apart and rolled around inside the bag.

She looked past the kitchen table and saw the couch in the living room, in front of the fireplace.

"Let's go over to the sofa," she said, helping Don to his feet and guiding him by his elbow across the room.

She took off his jacket and laid him down so that his head was supported by the sofa arm, then she knelt on the floor beside him. She gently molded the bag of peas over his forehead, around his eye and down the side of his face. He winced, and his body stiffened at the coldness.

"Sorry ... sorry," Katie apologized as she placed his jacket over his chest and tucked it in around his shoulders. She looked at Don's face and felt the bruising across her heart. *I love this man*, she thought, and asked herself how feelings could be so intense after such a short period of time. But there was no denying that the emotions were there, conflicted as they were just now with guilt for Don's condition and her deep anger at Larry's actions. "You lie still," she said. "I'll get a fire going in the stove. It's colder than hell in here!"

From the back porch, Katie brought in an armload of sticks and split firewood and in a short time had kindled a fire inside the big Florence stove. Don lifted the peas from his forehead and watched. After the crackling flames had turned the pipe above the stove cherry red, she cut back the air vent, toggled the damper, and heat began to surge out into the room. In the kitchen, she turned out the overhead lamp and came back into the room by the glow of orange flame behind the isinglass, sitting down on the floor beside the couch.

"You did that like you've done it a few times before," Don said.

"Guess so," Katie laughed, looking toward the stove. "We've got one just about like it at home."

Don watched the young woman's face as the warm light flickered around her, gilding her hair and reflecting in her dark eyes. He reached over and touched her cheek with his fingertips, and she turned toward him, smiled softly, and placed the palm of his hand against her cheek. Sliding his hand behind her slender neck, he drew her closer to his face. Katie leaned toward him, and feathering her hair back with her hand, pressed her lips to his mouth, then laid her head on his chest.

After awhile, she raised her head and carefully repositioned the compress on his head. "It's warmer now," she said. "How's about I get a fire going in the fireplace? Wouldn't that be nice?"

From the back porch, she brought in more wood and sticks, and within a few minutes the stringy hickory popped and hissed, and the room expanded with a warm, flickering light. A plastic dishpan on the kitchen counter she filled with warm water and brought it over to the couch. She removed his jacket and hung it on the back of the kitchen chair.

"Do you have a first aid kit out in your truck?" she asked.

"Yeah, we have to carry them," he said. "It's in the back by the spare tire."

Katie hurried to the Bronco, retrieving the box. She had Don sit up, then unbuttoned and slowly slipped the shirt off his back and gentled it over his damaged hand. The young woman tried to suppress her emotions as she touched his bare skin. But the sensuality of undressing him made the heat rise in her forehead, and she felt a light stinging on the skin between her breasts. She laid his head back on the sofa arm and sat down on the floor by the dishpan.

"This may sting a little bit," she said, lowering his hand into the warm water and struggling to get her emotions in check, "but I've got to clean you up."

Don's body stiffened as Katie gently worked the cloth around his fingers. She sponged his arm with warm water all the way to his shoulder, then rinsing out the cloth, folded and placed it over the left side of his chest. Even through his pain, Don was beginning to feel aroused, and he cursed himself mentally, willing his body to relax.

"Is this where it hurts?" she asked, pressing her fingers lightly against the warm cloth.

"Yeah, but not if I stay still," he said. "Is it bruised?"

"Not at all," she responded, lifting the cloth to look more closely, then replacing it.

"Maybe it's not so bad, then."

She lifted his hand from the water and dabbed a dry towel on his knuckles. "I need to put some antiseptic on this hand. Let me know if it stings and I'll stop," she said, while applying the white cream to his wounds. When she finished, she took the dishpan back to the kitchen, changed the water, and returned to the couch.

"Sit up, and let's look at this face," she said, removing the compress from his head and the cloth from his chest. Warming the rag in the water, she wrung it out and gently stroked the side of his head, cleaning the wound on his ear.

"Here, let me do something," he said, taking the rag from her hand. He covered his face and breathed in the steam before briskly rubbing it over his cheeks and forehead. She saw him run his tongue around between his teeth and lips, then he blinked at her and smiled. "Still got all my teeth," he said. She smiled and kissed him above his puffy eyelid.

"Would you like me to fix you something to eat?" she asked.

"How about some aspirin, over easy," he replied. "Are you hungry?"

"No, but I could go for some coffee. How about you?"

"Sounds good. You need some help?"

"No, I'll get the coffee, just this once!" she laughed, remembering their first meeting at the mine office. She walked into the kitchen, set some water to boil on the stove, then brought back a glass of water. Don took the bottle of aspirin from the first aid kit as she sat down on the floor.

Don moved to the edge of the couch, choked down four aspirins, and handed the glass back to Katie. He looked longingly into the fire, then into her soft, brown eyes. He reached out and cradled her cheek in his hand.

"I love you," he said softly.

She smiled, squeezing his hand gently. "And I, you," she whispered, rising to her knees and leaning her body upward toward his. He moved his feet apart and encircled her waist with his arms, drawing her against him. And they kissed; softly at first, then more passionately and heated until he felt her smile on his lips. She put her chin on his shoulder and cradled the back of his head in her hands, lacing her fingers through his thick hair.

"When did you know?" he asked.

"The very first time I saw you in the office."

They held onto each other in the firelight, neither one of them speaking for a long time; Don tried to recall every detail of their brief time together, while Katie relived her first impressions of the man who held her and luxuriated in the newborn sensations. Finally, she answered his unasked question.

"It wasn't anything in particular; I just knew."

Chapter Nineteen

Late Last Night
Anonymous

*Oh, me, oh, my,
What's gonna become of me?
I's downtown just foolin' around,
No one to stand by me.*

Following the Monday morning shuffle of men going to and from the mine, a quiet, sentimental veneer from the weekend's homecoming settled like dust on the patrons of Cooper's Gas, Grocery and Cafe.

Bobby, feeling vindicated, replayed the Bulldogs' win over Linton two nights before, but only in his mind. Mopping the floor, he waited for John to mention the game so he could wade into the older man's skepticism. John knew the trick and read his newspaper silently, snapping the pages open for emphasis when he thought Bobby didn't get the message that he was being ignored. Patiently, Bobby worked and waited for an opening. Roger stared out the window.

The only sounds were the occasional clatter of the compressor fan from the freezer in the grocery and the slow, rhythmic swish of Bobby's mop. Behind the counter, Dolores broke open a carton of cigarettes and refilled a half-empty rack. She smiled at the game being played around the table by the window but allowed her son to gloat and throw knowing glances at John without distraction. She, too, was enjoying the afterglow of Saturday night's celebration, but it was a slow Monday morning; by tomorrow, the feeling would be swept away and things would get back to normal.

"Hey, easy money," Bobby cried out as Larry rattled the front door shut and stomped across the floor toward Roger and John. "How 'bout that game Saturday night?"

"Yeah, some game," Larry said. "Get me some coffee, will ya, kid?"

"Well, good morning to you, too," John laughed.

"Sure, sure," Bobby sighed. "I'll make a new pot ... be a couple of minutes." Dropping the mop into its bucket, Bobby dried his hands on his apron and disappeared through the swinging doors into the kitchen.

"I hear tell you sent that new truck back to the body shop for some customizing," Roger said dryly.

"You just wait till I catch the bastard that trashed my truck," Larry said. "Broke out every window, head light, and taillight. Beat the hell out of the front fenders," Larry fumed. "You were out there, Roger. Guess you didn't see anything, huh? Nobody seems to have seen anything."

"You'd think with all the friends you got," Roger said.

"It could've been anybody, Larry," John said. "Probably some people from Linton pissed off about the game."

"Hey ... maybe it's that new guy at the mine, Mr. Miller," Bobby said as he poured the coffee. "The one who you said almost ran you over with his truck."

"Naw, it couldn't have been him; at least I don't think so," Larry said thoughtfully. "And I think she spent the weekend with the son of a bitch," he said loudly, slamming his fist on the table.

"Keep your voice down," John said.

"What the hell for!" Larry exclaimed. "There ain't nobody here gives a damn anyway."

"Deputy was in here this morning," Roger said without altering his stare out the window. "Asked if anybody'd been out on Red Dog Road Saturday night."

Larry first glared at Roger then looked back to John.

"We didn't say nothin'," John said quietly. "Hell, nobody did. Nobody knows nothin' about it."

Larry shook a cigarette out of his pack, and looked menacingly toward Roger, squinting in the smoke as he lit up.

"Nobody knows about what?" Larry asked.

"You messin' up that company man, that's what," Roger said.

"So, what if I did. Who around here gives a damn? And besides, how they gonna prove it was me?"

"Deputy claims he's got a witness that came in yesterday to report it; claims he thinks there might have been more than one person involved."

"Oh, yeah? I don't need no help with kickin' somebody's ass. Where'd they come up with that idea?" Larry asked.

"Seems like they think maybe somebody blocked the road with logs so's they could ambush the guy when he got out of his truck to move them," John said nervously.

"Well, I'll be damned!" Larry chuckled. "You boys were back there cutting wood, weren't you? That'd make you accessories, wouldn't it? That's good ... that's real good."

"We don't know anything about logs on the road, and we didn't know anything about your beating up the guy," John said.

"Well, you better keep on knowin' nothin', or it'll be your ass, same as mine," Larry said. "You boys understand me?"

"That we do," John said.

"Roger? How about you, dammit?"

"I 'magine."

"Damn," Larry said, standing up and pretending to glance at his wristwatch. "I got to get out to the bench. Got to look over the shot before noon. I hear tell you boys are startin' work tomorrow," he said glancing toward Roger.

"That's right," John replied. "Safety training this afternoon at the office, then we meet the blasting foreman tomorrow mornin' for the first shift."

"So, you'll be in on the big blast tomorrow, huh?" Larry asked. "It goes off at the end of the first shift."

"What do you mean?" John asked.

"Aw, the engineers have been messin' around with some new angle drillin' technique… timed detonations and all that," Larry said. "Tryin' to save more time and money by shootin' the rock across the pit rather than movin' it with the drag. The first test is tomorrow."

"Sounds a little complicated for the likes of us," John said, apprehensively. "Sounds pretty technical."

"Hey, you wanted the work," Larry snickered, then narrowed his gaze toward Roger. "Besides, you two don't need to know much. It's all been taken care of by people a lot smarter than you. Just do what you're told."

"Kiss my ass," Roger said.

"You just remember what I said about talkin' to the deputy," Larry said darkly.

"Don't you want some coffee?" Bobby asked.

"Naw, just set her on the table there for the boys," he said, walking toward the door. "And put it on my bill."

"Some homecomin', huh," Bobby said after him.

"Yeah, kid," Larry replied. "Some night." *And I've got one stop to make on the way to the pit*, he thought.

Chapter Twenty

Billy in the Low Ground
Traditional Bluegrass Instrumental

Monday morning. Yellow, a light, dusty yellow is how he felt. Warm, up to the neck; toes on one foot cold. The old man used to buy dill pickles in gallon jugs ... sliced smooth, not serrated. Glass gallon jugs ... from Kohler's, he thought. Why was that? A melody wound its way up into his consciousness, between the light and the warmth.

He turned his head toward the fading music, which slowly dissolved into the buzz and tap of a fly, caught between the drawn shade and the glass of the bedroom window. He squinted into the triangle of light escaping from the bottom edge of the shade and followed the movements of the shadow-dancing fly along the cold, wooden floor. Working the blanket over his legs with his exposed left foot, he curled its edge around his toes, pulled the upper part over his head, and drew his knees to his chest to gain warmth. Monday morning, he thought, better get a move on; lots to do today. Just a few more minutes and I'm up ... here we go. Just another couple of minutes ....

"I don't know how long I'll be down there; maybe just a few days, maybe as long as a week," Don had said last night.

"I think you need a few days off, and when they get a look at you tomorrow, they're going to demand that you take them," Katie replied.

"Do I really look that bad?"

"You look marvelous."

"No, really."

"Sweetheart, your left eye's practically swelled shut; your hand looks like it went through a meat grinder, and you can't move without your ribs hurting. Other than that, I'd say you're fine."

"Maybe I need somebody to look after me, that is, until I get back in fighting form," he said.

"Is that an invitation?"

"I'd like to think of it as something a little more formal than that."

She laughed lightly and nervously. "Just what do you mean by that?"

"Well, I know we haven't known each other very long ...."

"A week."

"A week, I suppose. But I feel like I've known you a lot longer than that; I feel like I want to be with you ... a lot longer than that."

"What are you saying?" Katie asked.

"Come away with me," Don said.

"Where?"

"Down south. I've got a house in Newburgh. I'll report into the company first thing and tell them I'm taking a few days off ... you said they'd probably make me anyway."

"Then what?" she said.

Don pictured quiet walks along the levee above the Ohio River, sitting on the bank with her, watching the barges and paddle wheelers working their way upstream to the lock and dam.

"We'll spend all our time together ... for a few days, away from here."

"And afterwards?"

"We'll come back here and get your things."

Can I be hearing him right? Katie thought. *Oh, Jesus ... let me hear him say what I hope he's going to say.*

"My things?" she asked, her heartbeat accelerating.

"Well, I suppose we should ask your mother."

"Ask my mother what?"

"Oh geez!" he said, closing his eyes tight with embarrassment. He looked up and she was smiling.

"Maybe you should ask me first."

He quickly averted his eyes downward and looked for the words.

"What I meant was ... I didn't mean to presume ...."

"Don," she said, and smiled, "look me in the eyes."

She lightly raised his chin with her fingers. "I love you," she said. "Now what do you want to say?"

"I love you. Can we get married?"

"Yes."

Immersed in the memory, Don rolled over onto his back and stretched his arms and legs out from under the covers. *Yes,* she had said. He looked at the alarm clock on the nightstand. *Seven thirty,* he thought. *Better get moving; she'll be here at eight.* Climbing out of bed, he reached under the shade and raised the window slightly, brushing the fly out into the cold morning air. Then he skittered across the frigid floor on the balls of his feet, jogging in place on the bathmat until the shower water was hot.

Stepping out of the shower, Don heard loud voices coming from across the ravine, in the direction of Conner's house. He slid the bathroom window upwards slightly and chocked it with the piece of two-by-four left on the sill for just such a purpose. Sensing some urgency, he hurriedly toweled himself off while trying to catch as much of the verbal sparring as he could.

"I ain't afraid of you, old man," Larry said.

"Maybe not, but you damn well ought to be!" Conner replied evenly.

"You got no one around to take your side now, so tell me where she is!"

"You mean she's not at the mine?"

"You know damn well she ain't. Is she over there with him?"

"Don't rightly know; and if she is, it ain't none of your business," Conner said.

Both men looked across the ravine when the screen to Don's door slammed as the engineer came out on the back porch.

"Conner," Don called through the trees. "Are you okay?"

"Just fine, boy," Conner said. "Got me a visitor; you go on back inside."

"I'm coming over," came the reply, and the sound of Don's boots echoed from the porch.

"You stay here, old man," Larry said. "I'll be back to deal with you directly," and he ran toward the footbridge across the ravine.

"I wouldn't be too sure about that," Conner chuckled, then followed at a walk.

Before Don got to the edge of the ravine, he saw Larry standing on the other side with one foot up on the bridge, but instead of hesitating, he lengthened his stride and nearly stumbled as he stepped onto the deck.

"Come on, you son of a bitch!" Larry said as he walked across toward Don. "Ain't had enough?"

The two men came together at the center of the bridge. Larry, with his left foot forward, drew back his right arm to strike, but it never flew forward. At the apex of Larry's draw, Don threw his entire weight into a straight right-hand punch that caught Larry squarely on the nose, dropping him to his knees.

"You broke my damned nose," Larry screamed through the blood, grasping his face with both hands.

Don clasped both of his hands together and with all his strength swung at the side of Larry's head, knocking him off the bridge and into the bottom of the ravine. Then he met Conner at his end of the bridge.

"Too bad it's only five feet to the bottom," Conner laughed as he clapped Don across the back. "But it looks like a knockout."

"Damn! I think I broke my hand!" Don exclaimed.

"Small price, small price," Conner said, and chuckled. "Let's see. Hmm, yep, I'd say it don't look so good. Let's lock up and go see Doc Bennett. I'll drive."

"What about him? Think he'll cause any trouble if we leave?" Don asked.

"I don't imagine so. I have a feelin' we won't be seeing him around much anymore," Conner said. "Come on, let's get some ice on that hand before we go. You're just a regular mess, you are."

Halfway to the pit, wiping the blood from his face with a handkerchief and still feeling somewhat groggy, Larry got the call.

"Daggett Mine to Car Eleven, Daggett Mine to Car Eleven."

"This is Car Eleven," he responded. "Go ahead."

"Dutch needs to see you in his office," said the man's voice on the other end.

Damn! Was there a meeting this morning? He couldn't remember. *No*, he thought, *that was last Monday*. He looked at his face in the rearview mirror. His nose was slightly crooked to one side and the area under his left eye was starting to turn purple and swell. *Damn!* he thought; *I can't let anybody see me like this.*

"This is Car Eleven," he said into the mike. "I'm headed to the bench. Can this wait until after dinner?"

"Get in here now, pronto." It was the Dutchman's voice on the other end.

Larry swerved the truck to the right, downshifted, and making a wide loop in the middle of the haul road, sped back toward the mine office.

Jerking the truck into its assigned parking place, he waited for the road dust to settle, then climbed out and stalked toward the side entrance to the superintendent's office.

Inside, Dutch was at his desk. On his right sat a man a little over dressed for a day at the mine, Larry thought. He was a small man, and his dark suit seemed close-hangered to his thin shoulders and chest.

"What's up?" Larry asked, as he strode to the Dutchman's desk.

"What happened to your face?" his father asked. "You been in an accident?"

"Not a damn thing. Who's this guy?" Larry asked.

"This here's Bob Glennon, Vice President of Human Resources," Dutch said, indicating the man with a slight nod, while keeping his eyes on Larry.

Larry glanced over at the man, who sat motionless and without expression. A feeling of contempt rose up inside him as he appraised the small, bloodless face under the white hardhat, punctuated by the thin lips and wire-rimmed glasses. *Either an accountant or a damned lawyer*, he thought, turning back toward the superintendent, a barely concealed smirk on his face.

"What's he want?" he asked Dutch.

"He came up from corporate this morning ... been here since seven," Dutch said, looking past Larry to the wall clock. He pushed his chair away from the desk and stood up slowly.

"He wants to talk to you."

Stealing a few seconds to gain his balance before heading for the door, Dutch took a cigar from his pocket, bit off the end, lit up, and raised one eyebrow through the smoke.

"I told him you'd give him your full cooperation," he said, and walked out of the room, closing the door behind him.

Larry heard the footsteps disappear down the hall and had the sensation that he was beginning to shrink inside his clothes. A small feeling of panic fluttered up in his chest, but he swallowed hard and forced it down along with the bitter taste of blood in his mouth. When he turned back toward the visitor, the man had already moved to where the Dutchman had stood, positioning the desk between himself and the big miner.

"Have a seat, Mr. Miller," the man said.

"I'll stand," Larry said defensively. "What's this all about?"

"Suit yourself; this shouldn't take too long."

"Good, I'm a busy man."

The visitor sat down in Dutch's chair, and placed his leather briefcase on the desk, flipped each latch individually, raised the lid, and took out a manila folder. He leaned back in Dutch's chair with an easiness that offended the man standing on the other side of the desk, and opened the folder carefully, as if a light were inside that might momentarily blind him.

"Where were you on Saturday night?" the visitor asked without looking up.

"In town, at the game," Larry answered sharply. "Is this an inquisition?"

"I mean before the game."

"I was here, I worked late. Hey, I don't have to answer these questions," Larry said.

"No, you don't. That your hardhat?" the man asked, pointing to Larry's head.

"Yeah, what of it?" Larry asked.

"You lose that Saturday night, maybe on the shale road south of here?"

"Obviously not. It's on my head, ain't it?"

"That it is."

Larry struggled for a moment to understand the point of the questioning, fighting back the urge to take off his hardhat and examine it. It came off when he was kicking the engineer around, but he retrieved it from the road before he left. Now his fingers worked the sides of his pant legs and he wondered.

"Look son," the visitor said, "we know it was you. We got a call on Sunday from someone who saw you there. Out of respect for your old man, I flew up here this morning to take care of this before the sheriff's office gets in on it."

"Oh, yeah? Well maybe the sheriff don't know nothin'. Besides, he's my mother's cousin."

"We're well aware of the difficulties in trying to bring charges in this county."

"So there! You can't prove nothin'! I got my rights!"

"As I was saying, we're aware of the difficulties, but we'll bring charges; at the very least, you'll lose your job."

Now Larry's face darkened, and the fingers on both his hands clenched into fists. The visitor, unmoved by the posturing, closed the folder and replaced it in the briefcase. Then he stood up, and placing his hands on the desk, leaned into the miner's anger.

"Sit down, Larry," he said sternly. "There are a few other alternatives if you want to stay with the company. Sit down."

Stay with the company? Larry thought. *From the tone of this guy's voice, that could mean anything; even work underground. Oh damn! They wouldn't put me in an underground operation, would they?* Larry had a deep and abiding fear of working in narrow tunnels and dark rooms with tons of rock overhead. He felt a bead of cold sweat slide from his left armpit toward his elbow as he took a seat in the offered chair.

When Larry left the office, he went out the same door by which his father had left. Passing the reception area, he noticed his father inspecting the pictures on the walls. As Larry walked into the room, the Dutchman reached up to adjust the frame of one photo above the bronzed torch trophy. The older man stepped back, and placing his hands on his hips, regarded the picture through the smoke of his cigar.

"Got my first safety award the year you were born," he said without turning around. "Shift boss at the old Number Three. No lost time accidents for that year."

"They can't do this to me," Larry said.

"Four years later, well ... that's another story. I was in West Virginia at the time; got to be willing to go if the company says so."

"But they want to send me to Wyoming. Some damn mine in the middle of nowhere!"

"Didn't see your momma much, or you either, when you was little," Dutch sighed, moving over to look out the window. "Still, got to look at it as an opportunity. Work hard, the rewards'll come later."

"But I don't want to move out west! Can't we fight them on this?" Larry cried. "This is my home, Daddy."

Dutch turned around to face his son and ground his cigar out in the ashtray on the receptionist's desk.

"There ain't no other way. If you go, you still have a job, and a life; if you stay, they'll prosecute. No telling what the outcome might be," Dutch said.

"But my life is here," Larry said.

"And so is mine. We can get a lawyer, but do you want to hold your family up to the kind of contempt that would come if this went to court?"

"That weasley little bastard in your office ain't got the guts to take this to court. He's bluffin.'"

Dutch eyed his son coldly for a moment, then continued.

"That *'weasley little bastard'* as you called him used to be one of the finest foremen in the company until he decided to get an education and worked his way up into labor negotiations. He's taken on tougher men than you over the last thirty years. He means business."

"So, what am I supposed to do?"

"Take his offer; go to Wyoming. Everything's moving out West now anyways," Dutch said, turning toward the window. "I've been 'asked' to retire myself."

Larry was caught off guard by his father's last words. The full import of his actions over the last week began to roll over him and Larry fought against his confusion.

"Where's Katie today?" he blurted out. "Her desk seems awful neat."

"Gone," Dutch said. "Took a few days off, heading south, she said. You better get going too. Give Ray your keys. They want you off this mine by noon tomorrow and out at Pronghorn Mine by the end of the week. Ray's already made the arrangements."

Larry stomped down the hallway and kicked open the swinging door to the shop. He stopped at the water cooler to get a drink. Bumping his hardhat on the stainless-steel splash wall, he took it off. The white plastic was slightly scratched, and the Deane Coal Company sticker on the side still looked new. He turned it over. On the inside, neatly printed on the bill was the name *"D. Rodgers."* He flung it the length of the garage.

Chapter Twenty-One

Dark Hollow
Wilmer "Bill" Browning

I'd rather be in some dark hollow,
Where the sun don't ever shine,
Than to be here alone, knowin' that you're gone,
Would cause me to lose my mind.

So, blow your whistle, freight train
Carry me far on down the track,
I'm goin' away, I'm leavin' today,
I'm goin', and I ain't comin' back.

Larry slouched on his barstool, running his index finger around the wet edge of a whiskey glass until it started to vibrate and whine. The barkeep brought over the bottle and started to pour another shot.

"Hell, jus' leave the whole damn bottle," Larry said, grabbing the bourbon from the man's hand and pouring a large volume of amber liquid into his glass. "And some more ice, too, if ya don't mind."

Mitch brought Larry a small dish of ice then walked to the other end of the counter where he turned up the volume of the television above the bar. Monday Night Football was on, but there were few patrons in the lounge. *Too early for dinner just yet,* he thought, *and way too early for Larry to have as many drinks as he's already had.* Mitch took a rag and rubbed the polished top of the dark-wooded bar and watched Larry sulk. *Soon the regulars will be showing up,* he thought; *maybe Larry would leave before he got out of hand.*

"Hey, you," Suzy Hutchins said as she came through the front door. "Who's playin' tonight, Mitch?"

"I think it's the Packers and the Cowboys," the bartender replied, smiling at the attractive woman as she walked across the wooden floor to the bar, the sound of her high-heeled cowboy boots punctuating a blue jean skirt that was perhaps a little short for a woman in her thirties. As Suzy climbed onto the barstool, Mitch noticed there were white stars on the back of her skirt where pockets might have been. She wore a matching denim jacket over an open-collared white blouse and a red kerchief was knotted around her slender neck. He remembered seeing the outfit advertised on sale at K-Mart last summer, around the Fourth of July. *Damn, she looks good tonight,* he thought. *I should ask her out sometime, instead of always watching her leave with some miner or trucker she doesn't even know, but for one night. She's attractive and obviously looking for company.*

"Oughta be a good game," he said, noticing that Suzy had one eyebrow cocked and was looking at him, as if reading his mind. "When did you ever take an interest in football?"

"My ex never missed it on Monday night," Suzy said. "I never liked it back then, bein's how it was my only night off. Couldn't get him outta the chair to do nothin,' though. Since he run off, I kinda miss it."

Mitch pulled a pilsner glass off the mirrored stack behind the bar and filled it from the tap.

"I know what you mean," he said, placing the beer on a paper coaster in front of the woman. "When I first moved down here to Sullivan from Chicago, I missed the sounds of the city. Couldn't get to sleep without hearing a train, car horns or police sirens ... and the occasional gun shot, too. Now I'm okay, though. Enough noise in this joint to take home with me after work." Mitch briefly fantasized about taking Suzy home after work. "By the way, how's the new job in Linton?"

"Just fine," she said, sipping her beer and wiping the foam from her upper lip with the back of her hand. "The pay's actually a little better than up in Jasonville, but I don't have to tell ya, miners are notoriously small tippers." She smiled and looked down the bar toward Larry. "That who I think it is?"

"Himself. Been in here since around noon ... drinkin' his lunch I guess," Mitch said, turning to look at the wall clock. "Guess he's started on supper, now."

Suzy leaned over the bar to check her hair and makeup in the mirror behind where Mitch stood. With her right hand she reached inside her blouse, cupped her left breast, and adjusted her bra. Repeating the process with her left hand and right breast, she pursed her lacquered lips at the mirror then ran her index finger down the thin-lipsticked edge of her open mouth. She winked at Mitch then slid off the barstool, adjusted her skirt, picked up her drink and sauntered down the bar toward Larry. *So, he's had supper already,* she thought. *I wonder if he's ready for some dessert.*

It was after midnight when Suzy pulled her rusting Chevy Camaro into the trailer park where she lived south of Sullivan. She leaned forward over the steering wheel, squinting through her alcohol haze and slowly crunched to a stop on the gravel drive next to her double wide. Turning off the car's engine, she kept the headlights on and fumbled through her purse until she found the single key to her front door. Larry slumped in the passenger seat. He had been awake when they left the bar; now his head was thrown back and he snored loudly.

The door hinge squealed when she emerged from the hot, humid interior of the car into the cold night air. A dog chained beneath a nearby trailer barked in protest. Larry stirred as she opened the passenger door. *Well,* she thought, *the dead do come back to life. The evening might not be a total waste after all.*

"Come on, stud," she said, leaning into the car. She slid her hands under the big man's armpits and pulled him toward her. "Let's get you into bed."

Larry opened his eyes and grinned in her face.

"Sounds like a good idea to me," he said. "Get outa my way; I gotta piss."

Suzy stepped back away from the car and climbed the wooden steps to her front porch, fumbling to unlock the thin aluminum door. Larry leaned against the corner of her trailer and unzipped his trousers, producing a steamy arc that crackled long and loudly on the cold gravel. *Jesus,* Suzy thought, *how much did he have to drink?* And for a moment, she felt a sobering anxiety about bringing the big man back to her place. She hesitated for a few seconds, then opened the front door.

"Don't take too long … or I'll think yer playin' with yourself. I'll be waitin' inside."

After a few minutes, Larry zippered his fly and lumbered up the steps. The trailer shook slightly as he stumbled across the threshold and into the living area, knocking over an end table and a lamp, its bulb briefly flaring before popping. A light was on at the far end of the trailer, dimly illuminating the narrow hallway leading to the bedroom and the kitchen. Larry opened the refrigerator door and fished out a can of beer. Popping the top, he took a long pull, emptying the contents. He crushed the can in the frame of the refrigerator door, and the light inside flickered off, then stayed on, the door held partially open by the wedged beer.

Larry waited in the half-light of the kitchen. A belch rolled up from his stomach, and with some satisfaction, he let it escape, loud and unrestrained. Most of his senses were dulled by the alcohol but his hearing remained acute. Somewhere within the darkened trailer the squeak of faucets reduced hissing shower water to silence. A toilet flushed in the bathroom, and Larry heard a door open, then close. He moved around the kitchen counter to follow the sound of bare feet padding down the hallway.

Before he reached the bedroom, the light inside was extinguished. Larry stepped through the doorway, his eyes adjusting to the darkness after a few moments. The woman from the bar was sitting on the side of the bed with a towel wrapped around her, but she let it fall away when she saw Larry take his coat off.

The big man staggered to the side of the bed and stood in front of her, weaving slightly. He reached out to steady himself, grasping the ponytail of hair she had twisted into a bun behind her head. Suzy looked up at him and smiled knowingly. His rough right hand stroked her wet cheek.

After a few moments, much to his surprise and humiliation, Larry felt nothing. No arousal, no heated anticipation. Suzy started to laugh but stopped when Larry pulled her head back roughly, his left-hand squeezing and bunching her hair. She looked up at him, her shadowy, smiling eyes quickly widening as

Larry drew back his right arm. She took a deep breath and was about to scream when his open right hand crashed into the side of her head, knocking her sprawling across the bed.

In less than a heartbeat he was on top of her, straddling the stunned woman's chest, pinning her arms to her sides with his legs. Shouting obscenities, he beat the woman savagely about the face and shoulders. Suzy tried to cry out, but her chest was compressed by Larry's bulk and mercifully, after an eternity of excruciating minutes, she passed out. When her body finally went limp and offered no resistance, Larry climbed off the bed, flipped on the light switch by the door, and regarded his handwork.

"Slut," he said. The woman's purse was on the nightstand, and he picked it up, and stumbled back into the kitchen. He took another beer from the refrigerator and left the door open. Dumping the contents of the woman's purse onto the kitchen counter, he found her car keys, seven dollars in her wallet, and half a pack of generic cigarettes. Larry turned on a burner to the gas stove, hearing the hiss of propane and the rhythmic crack of the sparking ignition. After a few moments the gas fired up. Shaking out a cigarette, he stuck the cigarette in his mouth and the pack into his shirt pocket. Steadying himself with both hands on the oven handle, he leaned over the stove, tentatively aiming the tip of his smoke toward the edge of the circular ring of blue flame.

The end of the cigarette flared but so did his eyebrows; Larry smelled his burning hair long before he felt the stinging heat on his forehead. He flew into a rage, knocking dishes off the counter and crashing into pots that hung low beneath the wall cabinets. Careening out of the discordant kitchen, he bumped into the arm of Suzy's worn-out couch, and fell face forward onto the cushions. He pushed himself up and rolled over onto his back, his cigarette bent but still burning. The gas of the stove continued to hiss blue.

Lighting a second smoke with the butt of his first, Larry settled into a pattern that would last for the next hour. *He would stay in the trailer for a little while,* he thought, *then drive the woman's car back to the bar in Sullivan and get his company truck.* There'd be time to stop by his dad's house for a few of his things while it was still dark; *I'll go back for the rest later when it's time to clear out,* he reassured himself. *There's some unfinished business to take care of first.* The crimson glow of the cigarette tip illuminated and accentuated his angry features. Through his inebriant fog he heard a cough, then a low, continuous moan coming from the bedroom.

"Tease!" he shouted down the hallway. "Somebody should've done this long 'fore now." The coughing began to fade but the moaning grew audibly, irritatingly louder. *Maybe I will,* he thought. *Maybe I will a few times before the sun comes up.*

"Shut up!" Larry cried, cracking the top off his beer, and flicking the ash from his cigarette on the floor. He took a sip from the can, then alternately a drag from his cigarette. "I'll be in directly, you whore. We'll see if that new boyfriend still wants you when I'm done with ya."

Larry left the trailer a few hours before dawn, parking Suzy's car on a side street and walking the final few blocks to the bar where his company truck still waited. He drove to his father's farm, turned off his headlights and engine, and coasted past the big house in silence. He came to a stop near the barn, where he lived in the remodeled tack room. Dawn was beginning to gray the eastern horizon when he finished loading the truck.

Across the drive, a light came on in the farmhouse kitchen. Instinctively Larry ducked behind the side of his truck and waited. After less than a minute, the kitchen light was extinguished. A few moments later, another light shone through the curtains of the upstairs bathroom window. *Just like the old man,* he thought. *Always up early.* Confident in the knowledge of his father's clockwork habits, Larry waited until he was certain that Dutch was in the shower. Then he started his truck and nudged it slowly down the driveway, disappearing from beneath the cone of mercury vapor light.

From an unlit upstairs bedroom window Dutch watched his son slink away from his home and wondered.

Larry skirted the Daggett Mine property and turned into an old field less than a mile south of the pit. He turned off the headlights, then drove slowly and cautiously through the tall, invasive grass that scraped against the undercarriage and softly brushed the sides of the truck. Occasionally a sapling snapped unseen against the side mirrors. A few deer bounded near the perimeter of his surging vision; the truck's tires slipped and spun on a flattened, frosted mat of vegetation. *No poachers out here yet*, he thought. *Probably will be a real good season this year, too. I'll get my share of shooting in early*, he thought.

After a few minutes he came to a line of wire fence and turned left, following it to the corner of the field where tall, dense bushes of multiflora roses covered an area the size of a two-car garage. There were open areas beneath the thorny arches, carved out over time by grazing cattle and deer. Larry had used the area before as a hunting blind. Now he spun the truck around, threw it in reverse and backed quickly into the dark, brushy hollow, stopping when he felt an elastic resistance where the clinging branches would let him go no further. *That's the fence,* he thought, and shut down the engine.

Except for the steaming of the engine, a shadowy silence gloomed beneath the bushes. Forcing open his door into the resisting, unseen branches, Larry grabbed his lunchbox and squeezed out of the truck cab, working his way toward the open field, now visible in the growing light. He waited until he had walked halfway across the field then turned around to look toward his hideout. The trampled grass was already starting to spring back up from where the tires had pushed it toward the ground and the truck appeared totally hidden in the brush. He smiled at the success of its concealment.

Larry emerged on the road and walked in the growing light toward the abandoned church near the old cemetery. He could see the church's narrow steeple angled above the cluster of cedars nearby. He would have some breakfast from his lunch bucket and wait.

"Sonofabitch," he said out loud, patting his jacket pockets: *no more cigarettes. Maybe there's some stashed with my stuff,* he thought. *If not, I'll just have to hold out for a smoke until later... the sun will be up soon.* Larry lengthened his stride toward the church and hustling up the overgrown drive, he entered the structure from the back.

Inside the church, something skittered across the floor when he came through the choir door at the back entrance. In the half-light he walked carefully across the raised platform to the baptismal, a window-like opening in the back wall behind the pulpit. He pulled the supernal, pleated curtain to one side and from the front retrieved a large green duffel and his high-powered rifle. The bag was packed solid and heavy. With some difficulty, he stepped down from the platform into the congregational area and took a moment to balance the disproportional load.

Ranks of wooden pews were aligned in parallel as if awaiting the arrival of a ghostly congregation. The simple arched windows in the walls were dirty, but intact. Most miners, and the community in general, were either extraordinarily reverent or superstitious about churches. The company had scheduled the demolition of this one shortly after acquiring the property from a local Pentecostal group, but nearly two years later the men at Daggett had yet to tear it down.

Larry sat down in one of the front pews, dug into his bag and found a carton of cigarettes and some matches. Removing the cellophane from a pack, he crushed the crackling plastic in his hand and dropped it on the floor. Lighting his cigarette, he slouched against a wooden bench, extending his arms across the rolled top. He crossed his ankles in counterfeit contempt of the crucifixion scene painted on the wall above the baptismal font.

Grinding out his cigarette butt on the dusty floor with the heel of his boot, Larry reached for his lunch box. He took out the stainless-steel thermos and unscrewed the top. raising the container to his lips, he choked on the bitter black liquid as it rushed into his mouth. The coffee was cold, and in a fit of rage he threw the thermos through one of the brightening windows in the side wall, shattering the glass and part of the wooden framing. Then he stood up, took a deep breath, and slung the duffel over one shoulder and his rifle over the other.

He stalked down the aisle toward the front of the church and mounted the enclosed stairway that led to the steeple loft. The bell that had once called the faithful to worship was no longer there, but the sound of the big man's passing rang hollow in the House of God.

Chapter Twenty-Two

Drill ye Tarriers
American Folk Song

Every mornin' 'round seven o'clock,
There are four and twenty men workin' on the rock,
And the boss comes 'round and he says keep still,
And bear down heavy on that ol' steam drill,

So, drill ye tarriers, drill (drill ye tarriers),
Drill, drill and blast,
Ye work all day for the sugar in your tay,
And ye stand by your drill,
And ye blast away,
Oh, drill ye tarriers drill

Roger waited in the truck with the engine running while John tapped on the screen door at Cooper's Café. It was a few minutes before six in the morning, but there was a light in the kitchen, so he pounded a little harder on the wooden frame with his fist. Still no answer; I'll just go around back, he thought... somebody must be up. He stumbled around the side of the building in the dark and upon reaching the back door, peered through the glass into the kitchen. Dolores was at the sink doing dishes and John noticed the percolating coffee on the counter next to the sink. He tapped tentatively on the window.

Dolores looked over her shoulder then sauntered toward the back door, drying her hands with the dish towel. Opening the door, she walked across the kitchen and back to the sink.

"Ya might as well come in," she said. "I've been half expectin' you."

John entered the warm kitchen holding a thermos at his side.

"I reckon ya got no time for breakfast anymore," Dolores said. "I heard you boys got called back to the mine."

"That's right, ma'am," John said. "I wonder if I might trouble you for a little coffee; for me 'n Roger."

He held out a quart thermos bottle that Dolores took to the sink and rinsed out with hot water before filling it full of coffee. She handed it back to John with a smile.

"You boys oughta get yourselves a coffee maker, and that don't mean marryin' one," she said.

"Thank you, ma'am," John said, opening the back door. "Maybe we'll do just that. I mean, we'll still be comin' in for breakfast regular-like ... we just need to be out at the blastin' shed early this morning. Got some company bigwigs comin' up from Evansville to see the shot, so we're loadin' the holes early."

Dolores followed John out the door, the shadows masking the concern on her face. She called to him as he disappeared around the corner of the building:

"Y'all be careful out there," she said. "You still owe me a cord 'a wood."

"Yes, ma'am," John called back. Dolores heard the truck door's metallic slam. The worn clutch caused a sharp grinding of the gears as John gunned the engine and accelerated toward the mine.

Ammonium nitrate, a common component of agricultural fertilizer, was used for blasting the rock that lay above the coal. It was brought in by rail spur to a storage area southeast of the mine that the miners called the "fertilizer plant." The company owned all the land within a mile of the off-loading area, a buffer against any accidental explosions. Several abandoned farmhouses decayed within this company-imposed blast zone, but it was likely that they would be blown to splinters if one of the railroad tank cars was accidentally touched off. Roads leading to the blasting shed were blocked off with enormous boulders brought up from the pit by a rubber-tired loader. The sharp-edged rocks were also reminders of the power generated from a detonated mixture of pelletized ammonium nitrate and fuel oil, known by miners as "anfo" for short.

This powerful elixir was loaded into special plastic sacks as thick as a loaf of bread and three times as long. Bulldozers and earthmovers removed the topsoil from above the underlying rock, then holes were drilled on the bench in a pattern designed by the blasting engineer. A prescribed number of anfo bags, with a detonator attached, were lowered into each hole. When the blast was electrically touched off, rock strata above the coal seam was lifted upward a few feet and fractured for removal by the dragline's giant bucket. The spread and efficiency of the blast depended on the depth of the bore, the amount of anfo in the hole and a few milliseconds of difference in the ignition sequence.

The blast that was to be touched off today was different from an ordinary configuration. The holes had been drilled at a slight angle and the powder charges were to be substantially larger, with correspondingly shorter ignition delays. This carefully designed procedure would result in the overburden being hurled across the pit toward the spoil side, reducing the amount of dragline hours needed to move the overburden. But everything had to go just right, and every blast was a controlled experiment.

By the time John and Roger arrived at the fertilizer plant, the lot was already crowded with company vehicles that could be distinguished by the unique paint scheme and company logo on each door panel. Half a dozen men clustered at the far end of the gravel lot, conspicuous in their pressed pants, dress shoes and matching windbreakers. They formed a semi-circle around the mine superintendent, who was providing a safety briefing for the day's demonstration. A few of them, Dutch explained, would observe the blast from the end of the pit. He would take the remainder up to the dragline for a closer look. Seismometers were in place at increasing distances away from the pit, extending east into the town of Linton and as far away as Sullivan to the west. Cameras were also in strategic positions on top of the dragline as well as on the spoil side of the pit. Time sequence photos would record the throw characteristics of the cast blast and help the engineers not only estimate the amount of rock that was moved, but the resulting cost-savings as well. Such documentation was necessary to prove that cast-blasting could be done safely and efficiently, with little impact on the surrounding area.

"Christ," John said as they parked their truck. "Larry said this was gonna be a big deal today, but I sure didn't expect to see this many white hats up from corporate, did you?"

"I 'magine," said Roger.

The two men got out of the truck and walked over to where the warehouse foreman was counting bundles of plastic sacks that would be filled with the white anfo pellets. John went inside to clock in for Roger and himself. The foreman looked toward the cluster of men to ensure that they weren't within earshot, then confided to Roger:

"These are special bags, just for today's shot," he said, pointing to the pallet of sacks. "See how they're marked with the yellow squares?"

Roger leaned down and inspected the bags.

"Well ... we're missin' a bundle," the foreman continued. "Goddamnit, I told everybody to use the old bags if they needed fertilizer. Now we're short."

It was a common practice at the Daggett for the miners to "borrow" a few pounds of ammonium nitrate to fertilize their lawns or gardens ... and a little bit went a long way. There was no official sanction for the practice, but it was considered part of doing business. Dipping into the anfo wasn't stealing; the miners considered the waste material down by the tracks as fair game for the taking. Besides, they figured, it didn't do any good to hide. You could always tell who had been to the "powder room" at Daggett because their lawns were always a brilliant emerald green.

"Listen," the foreman said conspiratorially to Roger. "You and John get ta sackin' up that damn anfo right away. I'll bring over a dozen of the old bags, and you fill and put 'em on the damn truck when them suits ain't lookin.' Bury 'em in among the new sacks."

Roger looked over his shoulder toward the gaggle of men at the end of the lot. He spit on the ground and frowned at the foreman.

"Look," the foreman hissed. "Those damn bags are the same, just a different marking. It ain't gonna affect the shot, and I'll take care of the damn inventory sheet ... don't you worry."

Something's off, Roger thought, but he couldn't figure what it was. He stood still for a few moments, his mind working the question like the chaw of tobacco in his cheek. *Maybe it's just the jitters*, he rationalized. *Why would a man take those bags unless he was filling them with anfo to fertilize his ground, and this time of year, nobody fertilizes their ground ... do they?*

The foreman waited impatiently for Roger to make up his mind. There was nothing the man could do if the miner refused to go along. He vowed to himself to make it hard on both new men if Roger blew the whistle over such a small issue, and the shot was postponed as a result. The foreman was responsible for all the blasting materials, and Dutch would have his ass.

"Well?" he asked.

"All right," Roger said. "But you check the inventory of blastin' caps while we're loadin.' I wanna know the count before we take this powder to the pit." *If a man's loaded those bags with anfo intent on blowing something up, he'd need the blasting caps. That'd be a dead giveaway.*

The foreman's face turned as white as the anfo he handled. Like all the other miners at Daggett, Ernie's recent death had raised everyone's awareness of the saboteur.

"I'll be damned," he said slowly. "You bet yer ass I will."

"Okay, then," Roger said, picking up a few bundles of powder bags and heading toward the loading hopper. "Bring over the old bags pronto before this hits the fan. This is between you and me."

"Done," said the foreman hurrying back into the storage barn.

Roger and John filled the appropriate number of bags with anfo and loaded them onto the truck. John didn't notice the unmarked replacement bags and Roger didn't volunteer any information. It was going to be a slow, cautious drive to the bench this morning and John climbed into the passenger side, anxious to get going.

"Shotgun," John said. "You drive this pig out and I'll bring her in."

"I'll be right back," Roger said, heading for the warehouse. The foreman emerged from his office, meeting Roger halfway across the lot with a box of blasting caps for the day's job.

"Well?" Roger asked.

"I checked the inventory sheet twice and went into the locker where we keep 'em," the foreman said. He glanced quickly toward where the company men were sitting in their vehicles with the heaters running. "Ain't nothin' missin;' I reckon it's just somebody gettin' some fertilizer for home, dammit."

Roger hawked his chew out on the ground.

"You tell John?" the foreman asked.

"No dammit, I said this was between me and you."

"Okay, then," the foreman said. "We good ta go?"

Roger hesitated for a few moments, glancing to where Dutch's truck was pulling to the head of the convoy of company vehicles.

"Hell, yeah," Roger said. "We're good ta go."

"Damn, skippy," the foreman said. "Now get outa here."

The string of company cars tagged along behind Dutch's truck as he drove toward the pit. Roger and John followed in the heavily loaded truck while the blasting superintendent brought up the rear. The convoy proceeded slowly, barely stirring the dust of the poorly graveled road. Every vehicle had turned on its emergency flashers; the red lights strobed into Roger's consciousness, and he couldn't escape the impression that the whole thing reminded him of a funeral procession … and he was driving the hearse.

It took most of the morning to load the holes. John attached the blasting caps to the bags before Roger gently lowered them into the bores. The blasting superintendent checked the procedure against a chart on his clipboard to ensure that the proper number of bags were loaded in the correct sequence. After the anfo had been placed, the holes were backfilled to the surface with driller's mud. Flaming orange-colored detonator cords stuck vertically out of each hole like colorful candlewicks. With metal clips and short segments of blasting cord, the men connected these deadly sprouts to a central spur. A red surveyor's flag was pushed into the loose drill cuttings beside each hole to designate its dangerous status.

It was a few minutes before noon when all the holes were finally loaded. Roger and the blasting superintendent walked away from the pattern and down the bench, unrolling the primary cord. They moved toward a shed at the end of the bench that would shelter them from the blast. The small building was only large enough to hold two men and the electrical detonating device, but it was constructed of welded metal and was so heavy that a bulldozer was needed to move it along. While Roger and the superintendent connected the wires to the detonator, John drove the blasting truck off the bench and along the cable route. Where the road crossed at the end of the pit, his progress was blocked by the company cars he had seen earlier in the morning. Their occupants were standing along the road eagerly awaiting the show. John pulled the truck off to the side, turned into the spoil berm to chock the wheels then hopped out and walked toward the group.

"'Mornin' gentlemen," he said as he joined them. "A fine day for a picnic, wouldn't you say?"

A few of them looked in his direction, one even smiled and was about to respond when the warning whistle shrilled from the bench. A second later, Roger touched off the cataclysm.

From his perch in the church steeple, Larry saw the explosion through the scope of his rifle. A second later, the undulating ground wave snapped the tops off some nearby trees, and he heard the quick, whisking sound of the branches raking against each other. The steeple shook from the engineered earthquake; shards of glass and shattered window frames tinseled the tender grass along the church walls. A deep rumble rolled from the direction of the billowing blast cloud that now obscured the dragline, and Larry knew his plan had worked: he had dropped a few extra bags of anfo down some holes the night before.

"I bet that got those company pukes' attention," he said to himself. That Roger had been added to the blasting crew was a bonus he hadn't counted on during his weeks of planning leading up to the blasting demonstration. *I hope it scared the hell out of him,* Larry thought. *He'll probably lose his job, too ... the arrogant bastard.*

On the bench, the upheaval flipped the heavy blasting shed over on top of the two miners. Roger was unhurt, but the blasting superintendent had a foot pinned under one of the sidewalls. Rocks thunderstormed on top of the metal plate and a choking gray dust talcumed the two men's sweating faces. After a few moments, the heavy air grew deathly quiet. A muffled siren wailed from the direction of the dragline.

"You alright?" Roger asked.

"I'm okay," the superintendent replied. "Just my boot caught under the edge, there."

Roger traced the man's leg, digging in the loose ground with his hands and freeing the trapped foot.

"Thank God for steel toes," the man said, inspecting the large gash in the leather of his boot that exposed the protective metal cap beneath. "I'm not gonna complain about safety boots again … that's for damn sure."

"I 'magine," Roger said. *I think we just learned where them extra bags went*, he thought.

In the bowels of the dragline, men were huddled around Emory Jones who lay on the greasy metal floor. The operator had been struck by a basketball-sized blast fragment as he sat in his control seat. For three years during World War II, Captain Jones piloted B-24 bombers on extraordinarily dangerous missions in the South Pacific. Now a chunk of compacted mud accomplished what Japanese Zeros and antiaircraft batteries had failed to do, and the old man lay dead. There had been no time to react, and the men standing behind him, including Dutch, were cut and bruised by the flak-like explosion of glass and rock.

In the panicked moments immediately following the blast, Dutch had sensed a small, almost imperceptible movement of the massive machine. As the company men tended their wounds, the mine superintendent climbed up to the operator's chair on the front of the dragline. The fractured cab extended precariously over the edge of the pit. Taking off his jacket, Dutch spread it over the blood-soaked seat, sat down and placed his hands on the control levers.

His experienced eyes quickly scanned the gauges. There it is again, he thought. A slight vibration danced through the machine and Dutch felt the strain in the metal. Through the haze of dust and smoke, he walked his eyes up the rocking boom, its cables still swaying from the concussive wind. His gaze ended at the American flag, its torn stripes lashing the end of the point shive. I need a horizon he thought, fighting through the gray vertigo: God, just give me a horizon.

A moment later, as if in answer, a freshening breeze from the west cleared the dust from the bench area. Dutch glanced quickly at the vertical angle of the boom. Like the minute hand of some giant clock, the flagpole at the boom end was moving slowly away from the vertical. From his windy perch, Dutch felt a slight change in the angle of his seat and knew the machine was pitching toward the pit. He knew the bench beneath him had been fractured by the blast and he saw a ravel of rocks begin to break away from the bulging vertical high wall beneath the tub. He watched as chunks of shale fell into the pit one hundred feet below. There was only one thing to do, Dutch thought, if the drag and all the men inside weren't to follow those rocks down to the coal: he shivered slightly and committed himself to the drastic, but unavoidable action.

Positioning his boots on the foot pedals, Dutch pulled back on the hoist controls with his right hand and raised the bucket from where it had rested on the bench. He waited a few heartbeats, then stomped on the left pedal, and the boom began to swing toward the pit, picking up speed as the electric motors inside began to whine.

Ninety degrees into the swing; the boom extended completely over the pit. Dutch glanced down quickly and saw the high wall beginning to rupture from the weight and torque of the dragline.

One hundred-eighty degrees; in the windblown cab, Dutch shoved the lever in his left hand forward, and the centrifugal force and weight of the bucket played out the screaming cables.

Two hundred degrees ... two hundred fifty degrees and Dutch stomped the right foot pedal. The metal beast screamed and bucked as he paid out the ropes like a monstrous fly cast. The huge bucket crashed through the oak woods on the west side of the bench, its attached cables wrapping around the base of shattered tree trunks, the teeth of the bucket biting into the ground.

Before the rotation of the machine had completely stopped, Dutch began hauling in the loose ropes, attempting to anchor the bucket and stop the slipping dragline. The electric motors screeched in protest as the cables spooled inward then smoked to a stop. Dutch waited helplessly as the cables grew taut and the machine continued its slow slide toward the pit. *Would they hold?* he wondered. The thick cables groaned, the boom stretched and cracked; the metal sheeting on the front of the machine buckled, but after a few minutes the dragline's movement toward the precipice stopped.

For a few moments, Dutch imagined that he was still drifting backwards and reflexively grabbed the armrests in anticipation of his final, fatal tumble. Realizing the illusion, he released his grip and reached overhead for the microphone to the company radio.

"Daggett Mine," he said calmly, wondering if the radio still worked. "Daggett Mine."

"This is Daggett Mine," came the reply. "That you Dutch?"

"Yep," he answered, thinking that his voice sounded strained and different. "We need some help here on the bench. Get all the dozers we got movin' to the number two incline ... I'll meet 'em there. Call the hospital and get some ambulances out to the county road; we've got injured and we'll need to take 'em out that way. "

"Got the ambulances already," the voice answered. "Dozers comin' directly."

"One other thing," Dutch remembered. "Any word from the company crew that was on the ground?"

"Yeah," the voice answered. "The blast didn't go their way. They called back here to the office; that's how we knew."

"Okay," Dutch said. "Drag out."

Replacing the microphone in its clip, Dutch winced at the sudden pain in his left shoulder. He clutched at the spasm with his right hand and waited for the burning to subside... but this time it only got worse. An iron band tightened around his chest and ferrous-tasting fluid surged into his mouth. He tried to pull his leaden legs out from under the control panel to stand but was knocked back into the operator's seat by a heavy pain that slammed into his chest. He heard his heart start to jack-hammer and passed out. They found him barely breathing, his eyes rolled back into his head and his hands clutching the dragline's control levers.

Chapter Twenty-Three

Fox on the Run
Tony Hazzard

We'll have a glass of wine, boy to fortify our souls,
We'll talk about the world and the friends we used to know,
I've seen a string of girls that have put me on the floor,
The game is nearly over, and the hounds are at the door.

She walks through the corn leadin' down to the river,
Her hair shone like gold in the hot mornin' sun,
She took all the love that a poor boy could giver her,
And left me to die like a fox on the run.

At first Conner didn't recognize the man who showed up after dark outside his cabin door the evening following the blasting accident. Once he realized it was Roger, he invited the miner inside. Katie and Roger had grown up together, and Katie's brother, Danny, considered him one his best friends. Roger took Katie to the prom when they were in high school and since then, Conner knew that in his own way, the young man had always looked out for his daughter. The two miners talked for a few hours, Roger taking up residence on the couch, briefing Conner on the recent happenings at the mine and his suspicions concerning Larry's involvement in the troubles.

"Larry's on the run," Roger said in his abbreviated clip. "Been trying to track him down since this afternoon. Whole thing's got out of hand and my guess is that he'll go after Katie next. Noticed her Jeep's next door and that engineer's Bronco's gone, too. Stopped by her mom's earlier, but Mrs. Johnson wasn't home."

"Rose is out with Dolores Copper, I 'spect," said Conner. "Halloween's tomorrow and most of the widder-women spend the day out at the nursin' home decoratin'; or so they say. I think they're just prospectin'."

"You're bad," Roger said. "Where's Katie?"

"She went south with Don," Conner said. "I think you'll like him when you get to know him; he's a good man."

"Maybe so. When they comin' back?"

"Tomorrow. I called down to Don's house in Newburgh and told him about the accident today; spoke to Katie about old Dutch bein' in bad shape. They're gonna stop by here tomorrow in the afternoon to pick me up before goin' up to the hospital in Terre Haute to see the Dutchman. He's been very good to her, ya know."

"His boy's not been very good, huh?" Roger asked.

"Larry? What did you expect?" Conner asked.

"Didn't expect him to kill one of my best friends."

Conner remembered that Roger, Danny, and Ernie had hung out together from the time each was able to walk. *I guess I forgot about that over the years*, he thought. *Roger must be as grieved as anyone outside of Ernie's immediate family.*

"I don't think he meant to kill Ernie, son," Conner said.

"Maybe, but between what he meant to do and what actually happened don't make much difference, now does it?" Roger replied. "He pre-charged them blasting holes last night knowin' full well that people could get killed, and he also knew that John and me would be workin' on the crew."

"You're probably right there."

"Probably would've killed that engineer if you hadn't happened along."

"Yep, that's fer damn sure," Conner said. "Do you have any idea where he's gone to ground?"

"Talked to the sheriff earlier this evening, and he claims to have no clue where Larry might be," Roger said. "'Course, they're related ya know."

But you know where he might be, don't you? Conner thought.

"Sheriff did say Larry was at some tavern in Sullivan last night," Roger said. "Left with a waitress from Linton named Suzy Hutchins. Found her beat up in her trailer south of town. Can't see, can't talk … but between her and the bartender, it's a pretty good guess that it was Larry that bashed her face in."

This was the first Conner had heard about the incident, and he was shocked. His face flushed dark in anger. "She gonna be alright?" he asked.

"That's what they claim, anyway," Roger said.

But how can any woman be all right after somebody Larry's size gets through with them, Conner thought. "She was a mighty handsome woman," he said, shaking his head.

Roger looked at Conner. The older man's body seemed to sag within his overalls and his face was masked with concern. Roger expressed what Conner hesitated to say.

"You think that waitress could've been Katie, don't you?" Roger asked.

Conner nodded.

"So, you agree with me that Katie's in trouble."

"If I knew where Larry was, I'd feel a lot better," Conner said.

Roger considered Conner's words for a few moments.

"I mean to find Larry before she gets back into town tomorrow," he said. "Pretty sure where he's been hiding. Found some tire tracks leadin' into one of the old fields up off the bench. Him, me and John hunt back there; it's wooly. Been in that old church south of the pit, too. I found some of his gear. Clothes, food, his rifle, and a bunch of shells. He's left 'em there for some reason, but I 'magine he'll be back to pick 'em up sometime soon."

"Why don't we go there right now and wait him out?" Conner asked.

"Because you'd go and get yourself killed, that's why," Roger said. "I've got a plan, don't you worry 'bout that. I need to talk to that engineer by himself when he comes back tomorrow afternoon with Katie."

In the dim light of the cabin, Conner studied the young man's face. After a few moments Conner spoke, his pointed index finger punctuating his words.

"Okay," Conner said. "I'll try to keep Katie corralled for a bit while you talk to Don. I'm trusting you on this, Roger," he added. "Better no harm come to that boy."

"Not from my direction, anyway" Roger said grimly.

"You settin' a trap, then?" Conner asked.

"Yep," Roger said. "The chickens have come home to roost, dammit."

"You ain't aimin' to shoot Larry, are ya?" Conner asked.

"Not unless I have to," Roger said, smiling. *I'm gonna use John and that engineer like damned bird dogs to flush him out*, he thought.

"You want me to get you some backup?" Conner asked.

"Nope," Roger said. "Got a couple of aces up my sleeve. I'll go into town tomorrow morning and see if anybody's heard a squeak from that rat."

"You gonna let Katie in on the plan?" Conner asked.

If she knew what I had in mind, she'd probably try to talk her boyfriend out of it, Roger thought. *I'll bring him up to speed tomorrow and see what he does. I figure if he really loves her, he'll want to go through with this.*

"Less said the better," Roger said. "No sense scarin' her."

"What do you want me to do?"

"Just go to Terre Haute with her," Roger said. "Stay up there as late as you can. Take her out to dinner or something."

"What happens when you can't find Larry or if you do, he doesn't want to come along peacefully?" Conner asked. The old man looked at the grim expression on Roger's face and realized that the miner expected to find Larry and hoped that he would offer resistance.

Both men sat in silence for several minutes, each alone with his thoughts. The night wind in the woods outside had begun to blow, and the branches of a leafless lilac bush fingered rhythmically on a side window of the cabin. When Roger got up from the sofa, it was after midnight.

"Nothin' to do now, I guess," Conner said. "It's getting late; you might as well take my bed, I ain't gonna sleep much."

"No, thanks," Roger said, "I'm goin' over to Katie's place. No tellin' what Mrs. Johnson might run into when she comes back to a dark house. I'll park out under the streetlight so's Larry can see my truck if he happens by. He won't mess with me. Come to the barber shop around noon tomorrow, and we'll see if anything's turned up. If I ain't there, call the sheriff."

Outside the wind began to howl and invisible drops of rain intermittently splattered heavily on the western windows of the cabin.

"Storm's a-comin'," Roger said.

Conner tilted his head to one side and looked up into the darkened slant of the roof, as if expecting to see a banshee perched on the rough-hewn trusses of the cabin's shadowed interior.

Ernie Milts had been in the ground for less than a week when Larry's engineered disaster rocked Daggett Mine and the surrounding communities. Windows rattled as far away as Linton and Sullivan; water well casings near Dugger cracked, and the county reverberated with rumors like aftershocks.

On the eve of Halloween, the day after the blast, talk at Wally's Barbershop in Dugger was typical of most conversations taking place the day after the incident. The locals, mostly older, retired members of the mining community, started arriving shortly before noon, filling the chairs along the wall. An inch-wide strip of masking tape traced a new diagonal crack in the large plate glass window at the front of the shop. Wally's red-and-white barbershop pole had stopped rotating inside its glass cylinder, and he was more than a little pissed about it.

"I heard tell that the hospital in Terre Haute's dedicated an entire floor to this latest bunch of Daggett victims," said the man getting his hair cut in the barber chair.

"They's even holdin' beds open, just in case they might be needed in the future," another man added from pit row.

"Old Emory Jones won't be needing one of those beds," Wally said somberly, punctuating his words with a few brisk snips of his scissors as he alternately combed and clipped his customer's thinning black hair. "The Dutchman might be making one available real soon, too," he added. Everyone reflected in silence on this almost certain fact.

Dutch was a regular at the shop, and rumor had it that he was in a bad way. He was well-liked in general, and those that didn't care much for him as a superintendent at least respected him as a miner. Now their regard only doubled as the man lay dying in a Terre Haute hospital, the apparent victim of his son's treachery.

To be sure, it seemed that the entire community was of the opinion that Larry was behind yesterday's "accident". If that weren't the case, they asked each other, why hadn't he shown up at the hospital for his old man? Larry's low-grade hostility had always been a part of local lore, but when he assaulted Don and openly bragged about it, that was the beginning of a change in the community's attitude because the locals connected both Don and Larry to Ernie's death, but in very different ways.

In the barbershop, each man's thoughts coupled Larry to the myriad of "instances" that had plagued the mine for the last few months. With Dutch in the hospital, the Master Mechanic now voiced his suspicion of Larry's responsibility in the haul truck's brake failure. Workers at the fertilizer plant were talking, too, but the men waiting to have their hair cut didn't want to discuss it openly.

Roger waited his turn in the corner of the barbershop hoping to hear of any recent sightings of his quarry. The men around him weren't sure of his connection to Larry, so they kept their opinions to themselves, supporting each other in silence. Roger sensed the group's quiet inquisition and lowered his newspaper, returning their suspicious gazes and making eye contact with each of them in turn.

Wally dropped his scissors into the green-glass jar of barbecide, picked up his powdered whisking brush and lightly dusted the neck of his client.

"All done," Wally said, pulling the white barber's smock to one side and snapping it free of loose hair. "Now, who's next?"

Roger folded his newspaper and rose from his chair.

"I'll find the sonofabitch," he said, walking toward the now empty barber's chair and taking a seat. "Anybody seen him this morning?"

There was an awkward silence.

Wally quickly tied the smock around the young man's shoulders. "What'll it be?" he asked, trying to act disarmingly.

"Lose this beard first," Roger said. "Then we'll see."

"You want it all gone?" Wally asked.

"Yep," Roger said. "Take about an inch or so off the hair, too."

The jury of customers resumed their silent deliberations concerning Larry, but now with a new twist. What was Roger up to? Wasn't he one of Larry's cohorts? And normally, he didn't care that much about his appearance. Why the sudden interest in personal grooming? The door rattled open, and Conner Owen shuffled into the shop.

"Howdy, boys," he said, taking up residence in the empty barber chair next to Roger. "What's this here shaggy dog you got in yer chair, Wally? Not enough business nowadays ... you takin' to pet groomin'?"

"Now, Conner," Wally said, a little embarrassed. "Show some hospitality. Roger might not cotton to yer sense 'a humor."

"Bullshit," Conner said. "He understands my sense of humor... don't you, boy?" He smiled at the bearded man in the barber chair and to everyone's surprise, Roger grinned back. The stern furrow in the miner's brow disappeared and his hawk-like eyes softened.

"Can I borrow yer customer for a minute?" Conner asked, looking Roger in the eyes, and nodding toward the door.

Before Wally could answer, Roger jumped out of the chair. With the white smock still attached to his neck, he followed Conner out the front door. "Be back in a minute," Roger said. "Don't nobody take my spot."

Outside on the sidewalk, Conner waited. "This outa get 'em wondering," Conner said as he and Roger walked out to the curb.

"Yeah," Roger said. "Maybe somebody'll break loose with some information, but I doubt it."

"You seen anything of our boy yet?" Conner asked.

"Nope," Roger said. "I was in my truck most of the night behind the Johnson house. Saw Dolores drop off Rose around eleven; I don't think either of 'em saw me. Went out to the bottoms before daybreak and drove the county road in front of the bench before the sun come up. Reckon he's back in the brush somewheres. I figure ta flush him out come evenin'."

"Well," Conner said. "After you get your haircut, come over to the house. We can have some grub, and Katie and Don ought to show up in a couple of hours."

Just shy of two in the afternoon, Roger pulled into Conner's drive. After a lunch of cold pork and beans and green onions – "straight from the can" – the two men settled down into chairs on opposite ends of the front porch to wait for Don and Katie. After about an hour, they heard a vehicle coming slowly down the shale road from the east. As it passed over the railroad tracks about a half a mile away, Roger could just make out a white Ford Bronco trailed by a plume of fine dust. The truck slowed to a stop just before Barren Fork, and Roger saw the couple get out and walk toward the grassy ditch on the south side of the road.

"It's them alright," Roger said, standing up and jacking the bolt action of his rifle. He caught the cartridge as it ejected vertically from the breech, dropped the bottle-shaped bullet in his shirt pocket then leaned his gun against the cabin wall. Conner snapped open the breech to his twelve-gauge double-barreled shotgun and pulled out two long, red shells, placing them carefully in a half-filled box by his rocking chair.

"Buckshot," Conner said matter-of-factly. "I can't see near as good as I used to. Them's my equalizers."

"Man," Roger chuckled, "that's one old gun ya got there."

"It's an L.C. Smith," Conner said. "Used to have two of 'em. They're twisted wire barrels, won't take a modern, smokeless shell. Too much pressure in the chamber they claim. You've got to use black powder. These here shells I got from a friend in Linton that hand-loads 'em for me."

"What happens if you shoot smokeless powder shells?"

"Well," Conner laughed, "they unravel the barrels like spaghetti; that's why I've only got one shotgun left. Liked to have killed me one time when I went coon huntin'. Me on the ground with the side of my face smokin'; coon up in the persimmon tree, laughin.'

Conner stayed seated and handed the shotgun to Roger. "Here," he said, pulling a set of keys out of his pocket. "Put both guns in the back of the Jeep before they get here. Take this box of shells, too. Ain't no sense scarin' her if we don't have to.

Roger picked up the guns and walked quickly across the footbridge, placing them behind the front seat of the Jeep a few moments before Katie and Don drove by. He crouched down and worked his way around the front bumper as the Bronco drove past and pulled into the Conner's drive. Katie was the first one out of the truck and walked quickly to the porch where Conner waited.

"How's Dutch doing?" she asked.

"Fair ta middlin'," Conner said. "Ray says the doctors think he'll come out of it okay, but he'll need an operation. Old Emory wasn't so lucky, but there's others that were very lucky," he said, leaning forward in his chair to see Roger crossing the foot bridge from the direction of Don's cabin.

At first Katie didn't recognize Roger without his beard. When she finally realized who the man was her face turned crimson.

"What's he doing here?" she asked, flashing an angry look at Roger as he climbed up onto the porch. Don moved to a position protectively beside her.

"Here to talk to your boyfriend," Roger said. "Quit givin' me the stink eye."

"Young lady, you set here a spell and keep an old man company," Conner said, indicating the empty chair in which the Roger had recently stood guard.

Roger picked up his chair and moved it closer to Conner, comically holding the legs forward like a lion tamer as he passed by Katie. Don smiled, but Katie didn't find the situation very humorous and with some hesitation, took a seat by Conner. A cold silence framed the triangle of her attention as she looked from Conner to Don's face, then to Roger and back to Conner.

"I need to unload some things out of the back of the truck," Don finally said, looking toward Roger.

"I'll help you," Roger said, and the two men climbed into the Bronco and backed out onto the road and drove next door to Don's cabin, pulling in beside Katie's Jeep. They unloaded the luggage from the Bronco and carried it into the house. Then, to Katie's surprise, Don and Roger climbed into her Jeep, started it up and pulled back onto the road, drove past her, and headed west in the general direction of the pit.

"Where in the hell are they going?" she asked, attempting to rise from her seat. She felt something restraining her and looked down to see Conner's big arm clamped across the arms of the chair. She looked at him with momentary fury.

"You think I'd let that man of yours get into trouble?" Conner asked, his face was a mixture of sternness and disappointment. "We'll see them in a bit and no worse for the wear."

Katie had a hundred angry questions to ask, but they all became a jumbled mass of sounds in her head, She sat in the heat of the moment and stewed.

"You just keep me company. Everything's gonna be alright; I'd bet my life on it," Conner said, remembering that the only gun he owned was in the back of the Jeep.

"So, we're agreed?" Roger asked, tossing the keys of his truck to Don.

"I think it's a good plan, but it seems like you're taking all the risk," Don said.

"Only fair," Roger said. "Shoulda done something long before now. Ernie would probably still be alive, and your face would look a lot better. Besides, he tried to kill me, too."

"So, the plan is for me to call Conner's and tell Katie to go on up to Terre Haute with him in my Bronco. I'll say I got called into the office for the accident investigation, but she won't believe it," Don said.

"Don't make no difference if she believes it, just as long as she gets in the truck and gets outta here tonight," Roger said. "The further away from here, the safer they'll both be."

"After calling Conner, I'll drive your truck down to the old church after dark and park around back by the barn. Meanwhile, you plan to use the Jeep to act like rolling bait, I guess."

"Yep," Roger said. "Don't 'spect he'll come out of hidin' before dark, but just in case he does, that Jeep'll be like waving a red flag in front of a bull. With my haircut and a white hard hat, it might just be enough to fool him."

"It might be better if I drive the Jeep," Don said.

"You don't know the roads, and you sure as hell don't know Larry and where he might be," Roger said.

"Still, it should be me."

"Should be me," Roger said quickly, cutting Don off in mid-sentence as he slammed the door of the Jeep. *It should be me in a lot of ways you can't understand,* he thought to himself. Roger turned the key in the ignition, then rolled down the window to spit out his chew. "I'll catch up to you at the barn if I don't catch that jerk first," he said, jamming the gearshift into first and accelerating out into the road.

Chapter Twenty-Four

All-Hallows Eve

It was the last night of October. Two men squatted inside the corner of the log barn; a shotgun and a rifle leaned against the wall. They crouched near a gas lantern; its light masked by a metal glare shield and extended their bare hands over the hot exhaust. Near the wall were high-powered flashlights for spotting deer, but the hunters chose to wait patiently in the darkness. From the road below, the headlights of an approaching truck filtered through the trees and strained through the chinkless log walls.

One of the men stood up and moved silently to the open, shadow-edged doorway. He heard the pop and metallic throw of gravel from beneath the tires as a truck passed close by, the cone from its headlights peripherally illuminating the front of the abandoned church near the road, animating window-veiled shadows within its graying walls. The truck continued slowly, its red taillights slurring the following dust, appearing to roll fire and smoke down the road and through the bordering woods. The watcher smiled at the illusion as he stepped carefully through the darkness to once again hover in the weak heat above the lantern. *It's Halloween,* he thought. D*on't let your imagination get the better of you.*

"Wasn't him, was it?" Don asked.

"Nope," Roger said. "Looked like Bedwell's truck. He lives south of here ... probably goin' into town."

"Maybe Larry's already lighted out of the county."

"Nah," Roger said. "He's still around. I know how he thinks; probably feels like he still has a score or two to settle. Besides, he left most of his stuff up in the church. He'll be back for it."

"Maybe we should've left that stuff alone," Don said. "If Larry sees that he's missing anything he'll probably figure something's up."

"Let him," Roger said grimly. "Let him think someone's lookin' over his shoulder ... it's about time he got scared for a change."

Roger and Don were waiting for John to show up. Roger had convinced John to come out with him on the pretext of doing some deer hunting this evening. Although the official hunting period wouldn't start for two weeks, since they were boys John, Roger, and Larry had generally opened the season a little early on Halloween because during this particular night, the local constabulary was always busy in town contending with kids corning cars or soaping windows. The friends had hunted along the roads south of the mine, spotting deer from their trucks with powerful high beam flashlights duct-taped beneath their rifles. But tonight, Roger was after different game, and as he had planned, there would be no law enforcement between him and his prey.

A light wind brushed the tops of the trees behind the barn and high clouds drifted silver over the full moon. A cold, knee-high fog began to form and blanket the ground.

"Shush," Roger said, cutting off the gas to the lantern. The white light hissed and faded to black. "Somebody's pullin' off the road into the church lot. Their lights are off."

Roger stepped quickly toward the wall and in one motion picked up his rifle. He had a shell in the breech, and Don's heart flickered at the sound of Roger clicking off the gun's safety. After a few anxious minutes, somebody thumped twice on the log wall outside. Involuntarily, Don quit breathing and tried to make out where Roger stood in the darkness. Then he heard the familiar click of the safety as Roger secured his rifle. Two thumps again ... and this time very near Don's head as Roger responded using the butt of his rifle. A shadow appeared in the doorway. Don took a deep breath and exhaled slowly and quietly.

"I could see your light from a mile away," Roger said. "Where the hell have you been; I expected you a half hour ago."

"Like hell, you could see me," the shadow replied. "It ain't even midnight yet."

Roger laughed. Don could tell it wasn't Larry and he was relieved.

"Who the hell is this?" John asked Roger. "I'm gettin' my flashlight."

"Leave the light off," Roger said quickly. "This is Don Rodgers ... Katie's boyfriend."

John hesitated in the half-light of the doorway. As his eyes got used to the darkness, he recognized the young engineer from the mine. *Now I'm confused*, he thought. *Is he here to bust us for hunting out of season? Just like a damn environmentalist.*

"Listen up," Roger whispered. "There was a truck hidden back in the field under a bunch of roses but it ain't there now. Followed the tracks down to the road on foot. I figure he must have left just before we got here. I parked Katie's Jeep out in front of the church. He'll be back."

"Who?"

"Larry, dammit," Roger said. "Who did you think we're waitin' for?"

"Oh, no," John said. "I don't feel like huntin' with Larry right now."

"We ain't huntin' *with* Larry tonight," Roger said. "Tonight, we're huntin' *for* Larry."

The transformers and insulators of the electrical substation marshaled on a concrete pad behind a chain link fence ten feet high. A concertina of barbed wire looped through the capped tops of metal posts that were spaced eight feet apart and deeply anchored in cement-filled holes. Located along the county road northwest of the mine office, the substation distributed wattage from the power plant in Sullivan that was enough to serve both Daggett Number Seven and a large portion of the town of Dugger.

An hour after dark, Larry pulled his truck out from its hiding place beneath the rose arbor. He drove up the county road to the substation less than two miles away. Backing up to the fence, he hooked a short length of chain to the truck's trailer hitch, wrapped the other end around the entrance and gunned the vehicle forward, separating the gate from its hinges.

Lying in the intensive care unit with an oxygen mask on his face and tubes sticking out of his arms, the mine superintendent seemed small and faded. His wife sat by the bedside stroking his short gray hair. Katie had always thought of Dutch's second wife as being young and vivacious, but in the cool, white fluorescence of the hospital room, she looked sterile and plain.

Dutch was conscious and smiled weakly when Katie moved to his bedside. She laid her fingers over his right hand and squeezed his palm lightly. Dutch responded by clasping her hand firmly but gently; then he winked at her.

"You picked a good week to take off," he rasped.

"Shush," his wife said. "The doctor told you no talkin'."

Dutch looked toward Conner before turning his attention back to Katie who still held his hand.

"I thought you were down south," Dutch said.

"I figured there might be something I could do," she replied softly.

Dutch inhaled deeply, then exhaled his words, breathy and strained. "The mine'll run itself," he said. "You take that new boyfriend of yours and stay away for a while."

"But, Dutch," Katie replied.

"I mean it," Dutch said, smiling. "Now git."

Katie accepted Dutch's words just as she would have obeyed any order that the superintendent issued from his office. It helped, she realized, if she looked at it that way. She squeezed his hand gently and left the room with Conner.

Ray Kelso was waiting in the hallway and rose from a chair near the wall.

"Hey, Katie," he said. "Howdy, Conner."

"How's the wife?" Conner asked.

"She's fine, just fine," Ray said, looking from Katie's face to Connor's. Ray had heard the rumors for years, but with the young girl standing next to the old miner, Ray knew with a blood certainty that Conner was her father.

"Oh, Ray," Katie said. "He looks awful."

"Dutch? Oh, yeah, I agree. But I just had a chat with his doctor, and it looks like he'll be all right."

"Really!" she exclaimed, astonished.

"Yeah," Ray said. "It seems like he had a pretty massive heart attack, but we got him to the hospital in time. They're gonna ream out his plumbing a little, but he should be up and around in a few weeks."

Tears formed in the girl's eyes, and she buried her face in Conner's jacket. He put his arms around her and began to stroke her hair.

"Is that true?" he asked Ray.

"Yep," Ray said. "But he won't be back to the mine. They're gonna retire him."

"Maybe that's not so bad," Conner said. "All things considered."

"Speaking of which," Ray said, looking up and down the hallway then speaking in a low voice. "Where's Don? Why don't you two get out of here."

"Don and I are headed back down to Newburgh as soon as we pick up a few things," Katie said, drying her eyes with a sleeve.

"I wouldn't tarry too long," Ray replied.

Katie drove back from Terre Haute in Don's white Bronco while Conner lounged on the passenger side. Don had suggested that they switch trucks so that the ride up to Terre Haute would be more comfortable for the old man. Don said that they only needed him for a couple of hours at the office. *He should be home by the time we get back*, she thought. *I want to leave tonight.*

She drove into town once more, stopping at her mother's house to pick up some extra clothes. The house was dark, and Rose wasn't home. While Conner waited in the Bronco with the engine running, she hurriedly packed, left a note on the kitchen table and turned the back-porch light on for when her mother returned.

It was a little after eight o'clock now, and all the town's children were running from one house to another trick-or-treating. Katie drove west along the main highway out of town then turned south onto the county road that split the Daggett mining area. Over the years, the road had been widened to nearly ninety feet in order to accommodate two opposing lanes of haul truck traffic. Running along both sides of the crowned road were eight-foot-high berms of rock and mud. These buffers were constructed and maintained by the grader as a safety measure to keep vehicles from going off into the water impoundments that mirrored the moonlight on both sides of the long, undulating road. As they passed the electrical substation, a truck pulled out from the gravel entrance and followed them down the road with its lights off.

Larry had not yet finished his sabotage of the substation when he heard a vehicle coming down the haul road from the north. He was hiding in the weeds near the entrance when Don's Bronco went by him. Recognizing the vehicle, he ran back to his truck to give chase. Larry kept his headlights off and stayed in the dust cloud behind the white company truck. He lined up the red taillights in front of him and inched the hood of his truck closer. Picking up Don's hardhat from the seat, he placed it on his head. *You sonofabitch,* he thought to himself. *I've got something that belongs to you, and you've got something that belongs to me. Time for a trade.*

Katie and Conner felt a sharp bump from behind and the Bronco began to slide sideways in the loose gravel. Reflexively, she steered in the direction of the slide and fish-tailed down the road. While she gained control of her vehicle, Conner looked out the dirty back window just as the driver turned the truck's headlights on and began to close on them again.

"You keep your eyes on the road," Conner said. "And don't stop for anything." *I can't make out who it is,* he thought, *but I got a good idea.*

She mashed the accelerator to the floor and the pursuing truck appeared to recede in the dust behind them.

Larry dropped back out of the spray of gravel and dust, then swung his truck wide to the left side of the Bronco in front of him. He shut off his headlights but increased his speed and within a quarter mile caught up to his prey, racing a parallel course just outside the periphery of the Ford's high beams. At nearly sixty miles an hour Larry's truck matched his quarry's speed. He positioned himself to intercept a left-hand turn that he anticipated the Bronco would make toward the mine office. *It was the only safe route available,* Larry thought; *he'll take it.*

"Turn left at the intersection and head for the mine office," Conner said. "Cut the angle but don't slow down. Yer doin' fine."

Reaching behind his head with his right hand, Larry carefully lifted his loaded shotgun off the gun rack hooks in the back window. Wedging the gun butt against his thigh, he flipped the safety off, angled the muzzle toward the passenger window and waited.

Reflexively, Katie kept checking her rear-view mirror every few seconds, but there was nothing but darkness behind them. As Conner had directed her to do, she didn't slow down, but kept up her speed and began a sweeping left turn onto the mine office road. Seemingly out of nowhere, a black truck appeared on her left side, forcing them to the right, and away from the direction they wanted to go. Angrily she turned the steering wheel back to her left and side-swiped their pursuer mirror-to-mirror. In the dash light of the truck's cab, Katie saw the mixture of surprise and hatred on Larry's face; then she saw the end of the gun barrel. She jerked the wheel to the left then quickly back to the right, bouncing off the black truck's side just as Larry pulled the trigger.

The gun's discharge blew out the passenger side window in Larry's truck but missed its intended target. Momentarily stunned by the explosion and startled by the unexpected presence of Katie in the Bronco, Larry took his foot off the gas for a few seconds, allowing the Bronco to escape down the old county road south of the mine. *She's headed toward the church*, he thought, down shifting the truck, and renewing the pursuit. *I'll catch her before she gets too far.*

In the compressed moments following the gunshot and a few hundred yards down the narrowing road, Conner realized they had escaped from Larry momentarily but were still in serious trouble. *Two miles ahead*, he thought, *there's a row of boulders across the road.* Intended to keep people out of the mine area, the barrier now blocked their way.

"Slow down a bit," he said, as his mind raced with options.

In her side view mirror, Katie saw the black truck approaching and stepped on the accelerator just as it came up behind them. Larry also knew about the roadblock ahead and began to toy with his victims. As both vehicles hurtled down the gravel road, he alternately smashed into the back of the Bronco, laid back for a few moments, then renewed his attack. Katie began to desperately honk the Bronco's horn. For a moment, the high wind opened a path through the clouds and Katie saw the church steeple above the trees, illuminated by a blue shaft of moonlight.

"Your seat belt fastened?" she asked Conner.

"Yep," he replied, tugging the loose end forcefully.

She tightened her own belt and waited for the anticipated impact from behind. Just before it came, she jammed on her brakes, instigating a jolting collision that pushed both vehicles off the road and into the ditch where they came to rest on their sides.

Larry was caught by surprise. His hardhat flew off his head, hit the windshield and rebounded into his already-broken nose. Katie and Conner were stunned but unhurt. She unfastened her belt and reached over to unfasten Conner's.

"Come on," she screamed. "We've got to get out of here!"

"You go," Conner said, rolling down his door window. "Run to the church, there's help there."

Katie was puzzled. She wanted to ask how Conner knew there would be help at the abandoned church. "I'm not leaving you," she said.

"I'll be along directly," he said. "Now git, and stay off the road."

She hesitated for a few seconds then wriggled over Conner and out through the passenger window. She saw that Larry was struggling to get out of his truck. For an instant, their eyes met, and she saw the bloodied, malignant hatred in his face. *What if he goes for Conner?* she thought. She looked toward the Bronco and realized that Conner was hidden by the dust-caked windows. She waited until she was sure that Larry's attention was focused squarely on her, then she ran across the road and clambered up the bank into the safety of the shadowed forest. Letting her eyes adjust for a few seconds, she began to work her way toward the church steeple, now a dark triangle silhouetted against the night sky.

Reaching the deeper gloom of the cedar grove behind the church, she stopped to catch her breath before making the short dash across the open field to the church. he crouched in the cemetery behind the rough-shuffled deck of headstones that leaned against a tree. Cold, shaking, her senses heightened, Katie searched the woods with moon-blind eyes, listening for any sound from the road. The low ground fog muffled the snap of a twig close by. She turned her head in that direction and started to move out from beneath the cedars, but in that instant, she was struck from behind and spun around. Larry's shadow loomed dizzily above her. He moved toward her, his silhouette a black hole that seemed to draw in what little light filtered through the trees. She collapsed into the ground mist and felt nothing.

The entreaties of the distant horn had reached the three men inside the log barn. They each grabbed their guns and flashlights, then stepped cautiously outside into the moonlight.

"There it is again," said John. "Comin' this way ... it's gettin' closer."

The men looked north toward the sound and saw the bounce and flash of headlights through the leafless tunnel of trees that lined the road from the mine.

"Looks and sounds like a chase," Don said.

"Two of 'em," Roger said. "Somebody's in trouble."

As soon as the words left Roger's mouth, the movement of the lights appeared to stop, and the throw of high beams angled upward into the treetops a hundred yards down the road. Half a second later, the three men heard the crash; they stood still and listened intently for a few moments.

"Reckon we should go see what happened?" John whispered excitedly.

"Quiet," Roger said.

"I'm gonna go see," John said. "Somebody might need some help."

"Wait a minute," Roger said, hurrying his thoughts. "Okay, go, but leave the rifle here. We may need it. Besides, if that's the sheriff, he might think you were poachin' or something."

"Good idea ...I'll just take my high beam," John said, leaning his gun against the log wall and moving toward the road below.

Don and Roger waited in the shadow outside the barn wall while John walked down the path leading to the road, disappearing around the front of the church. After a few minutes, an intense beam of light appeared in the distance when John turned on his spotlight and began to walk up the road toward the distant glow of the wreck. From the barn, Roger measured John's progress by the fading of his footsteps and the slow movement of his light.

"Listen," Don said, hearing the metallic creak and slam of a door. "That's not John. Somebody just got out of a truck."

"Yeah," Roger said. "Somebody else is comin' through the woods; headin' in this direction."

The two men listened intently for a few seconds. Roger was a seasoned hunter and could distinguish between the rapid flight of the prey and the intermittent and methodical movements of the predator.

"Nope; not deer. Sounds like two of 'em, though," Roger said. "Somebody's running and somebody's trackin'. Hear the stops and starts?"

Roger worked the bolt of his rifle, jacking a round into the chamber. "Here," he said, handing Conner's shotgun to Don. "You might need this."

Don took the gun but leaned it against the wall.

"I'm not here to shoot anyone," he said. "Especially if I don't know who it might be. I'll just use my flashlight. Why don't you go to the right; I'll go to the left, and we'll get between the two of them."

"Alright," Roger said. "But I'll bet whoever's doin' the chasin' probably has a rifle. Watch yer butt."

Roger checked the safety on the trigger guard of his gun to ensure it wouldn't fire. With a silent nod of acknowledgement, he moved quickly but silently out from the barn, off to Don's right and into the nearby woods, cutting a circling track that would bring him in behind the pursuer. Don began walking toward the hedgerow behind the church. In the lee of its shadows, he moved slowly in the direction of the dark block of cedars a few hundred feet away, audibly plotting a path that would intercept the sound of the fleeing person. Don was unaware of it, but he and Roger had adopted a hunting strategy that many a boy from Dugger had perfected when combing the woods and fields around the mines in search of white-tailed deer.

But the prey's pace through the woods was, of necessity, much faster than Don's rate of closure, and he heard the quickening footsteps stop somewhere in the soft darkness beneath the cedars. He stood still near the fence line; his senses inclined toward a murky spot less than fifty feet ahead. The predator's pursuit had apparently stopped as well. *I certainly won't be able to hear Roger*, he thought, *he's too stealthy*. The only sounds came from an easy wind that breathed and winnowed through the leafless treetops.

Suddenly, Don heard the muffled snap of a twig close to the ground and a moment later a short gasp, then the sound of something falling to the ground. For almost a full minute he waited. Then slowly and deliberately, Don brought his flashlight up, extending his arm toward the sound. He waited a few seconds, then flipped on the switch of the powerful spotlight.

Larry had taken off his jacket and thrown it to the ground. He could make out Katie's fallen body in the shadows of the cedar arbor, and only then after he saw the tumble of her dark hair across the flat-bleached marble of the headstone on which she sprawled. An instant of pity passed with one heartbeat. *I'll just do her on top of that tombstone,* he said to himself, and imagined how the cold, rough stone would feel against her hot, tender skin.

For a few moments, Larry allowed the vision of a violent coupling to play out in his mind, and the image aroused him completely. Unbuckling his belt, the big man had just unzipped his trousers when a beam of intense light hit him in the face.

"Let go of yourself and get your hands in the air," Don shouted, peering down the beam of light at the half-naked miner. "And don't move or I'll blow your head off!"

Larry raised his hands slowly, his pants falling loosely around his ankles. Don almost laughed at the sight until he realized it was Larry Miller that he held captive in the cross hairs of his spotlight.

"Who the hell are you?" Larry roared back, thinking that the voice behind the bright light sounded familiar. "Turn off that damn light," he said. "This ain't none of your business."

Don was about to respond when the body on the ground stirred. The engineer lowered the focal point of the beam toward the person at Larry's feet. *Must be a woman,* he thought, and Katie's face momentarily flashed behind his eyes. *But she's with Conner,* he thought. Don felt his throat begin to constrict.

At that moment, with the spotlight's attention directed away from him, Larry threw himself to one side of the cone of light and rolled a few feet into the darkness. His bare legs and buttocks were speared by countless unseen cedar needles. Half running, half-hopping, he managed to pull his pants up just before he tripped over an unseen grave marker beneath the vines. With his free arm flailing the unresisting air and one hand clutching at his trousers, Larry careened out of the cemetery, stumbled onto the steep talus slope of the water-filled airshaft, and rolled headfirst into the black water.

Don saw Larry's move - had anticipated it - but he kept his light on the figure shrouded in the ground mist. He walked quickly to the cemetery, set the spotlight against a headstone so that its beam flooded the over-hanging umbrella of cedar boughs and gently rolled the woman over onto her back. When he discovered that it was Katie, rage jack-hammered through his body. The heat rose in his forehead like a thermometer, and he could hear the blood squeeze through the constricted vessels of his eardrums. He felt dizzy and tears began to form in the corner of his eyes.

Don took the glove off his right hand and gently pressed his fingers against the woman's neck. *A strong pulse*, he said to himself, *not rapid but more like she's asleep*. At his touch, Katie fought to get to her feet, beating off the shadow's probing hands and scratching at its eyes. Don shielded the blows with his forearms and quickly restrained her wrists with his hands. She struggled within his firm grip.

"Get off me, you sonofabitch," she said coldly. "You'll have to kill me first."

"It's me, Katie," Don said. "It's me, Don."

"What?" she cried, fighting off the fog in her head, and recognizing that the disembodied voice didn't belong to Larry. Don's words seemed to come from far away. After a few anxious moments, she closed her eyes and relaxed. Don released his grip on her wrists and placed his hands on her shoulders, helping her into a sitting position.

"Take a deep breath," Don said. "Are you okay?"

"Where did you come from?" she asked, opening her eyes and throwing her arms around his neck. "Don, Don ... where did you come from?" Then looking wildly into the darkness at the edge of the light's perimeter she asked: "Where's Larry?"

Don slid one arm around her back, the other beneath her bent legs and stood up, easily lifting her from the cold ground. He left the spotlight propped against the headstone as a beacon for Roger and carried her out from the cemetery toward the church. A flashlight swung and bobbed up the driveway from the lower road: Must be John, Don thought. The beam of the searchlight flashed over them twice before shining directly into Don's eyes. Katie ducked her face into his jacket.

"Turn that damned thing away from me," Don called out, and instantly the light went out and he heard John running toward them.

"Hey," John said breathlessly. "That was Larry's truck back there. And I found Conner in your Bronco. He's okay, but I think your truck's totaled."

Don stopped walking for a moment and lowered Katie's feet to the ground. "Can you stand up?" he asked.

"Conner," Katie said, holding onto Don as she straightened up. "We need to help Conner."

"Conner's okay," John repeated. "Really. But he was asking about you. You want me to go back and tell him you're okay, too?"

"That's a good idea," Don said, throwing John the keys to Katie's Jeep. "Bring him on up to the church; we'll be inside."

"Where's Larry?" John asked.

"Yeah," Katie said worriedly. "Where's Larry."

Don turned to look back toward the light in the cedar grove.

"Don't worry about Larry," he said. "Roger'll see to him."

Larry had fallen heavily on his right shoulder before sliding into the flooded air shaft. His collarbone snapped, rendering his right arm useless, and he rolled like a log into the cold, inky water. The big man clawed at the rough-timbered sides with his left hand and managed to pull himself to the water's surface, his face barely above the slime. He floated an agonizing three feet from the top of the vertical walls.

From the darkness of his watery prison, the night sky seemed luminous and near enough to touch, but Larry was struggling to stay afloat. His pants were wetly bunched around his ankles and he slapped the water fitfully with his good hand. With each wind-milling motion of his arm, he drew luminescent air beneath the surface of the water. The frigid water cruelly extracted the living heat from deep inside his body, and he began to shiver, and not just from the cold.

Larry's fear of underground mining began to invade his thoughts. Like most people in the coal region, the big man also harbored druidic superstitions about water, spirits, and things deep in the earth that were better left unnamed and undisturbed. This shaft was now a conduit for those fears.

These facets of his character, swimming in the dark currents of his soul, began to surface as he realized the hopelessness of his situation. The icy water slowed the flow of his blood and thought processes. He imagined decades of cold winter rains leaching minute particles of human detritus from the moldering cemetery, decomposed organic matter that filtered through the pore spaces of rock and soil, accumulating in the turbid well that now entrapped him.

And he knew, with terrible certainty, that at the bottom of this precise air shaft were the flooded rooms and catacombed coal where reposed the remains of the ten men that died in the explosion of Daggett Number Three. That abysmal thought chilled him to the marrow, for he dimly remembered that Katie's father and older brother shared that watery grave.

Numb with cold and fear, Larry bobbed helplessly in the darkness, attempting to stay afloat by holding his breath, exhaling, and inhaling quickly. A small landslide of rocks skittered down the slopes, stirring his lethargy. A silent shadow floated above the pit, blue-framed by the night sky. Larry struggled to call out. The cold constriction of his chest muscles caused his voice to sound high-pitched and whining.

"Who's there," Larry squealed. Losing buoyancy from his exhalation, he dolphin-kicked his bound feet and burbled to the surface. Help me," he gasped.

"Go to hell," the shadow said.

"Roger!" Larry gasped, short of breath. "I was out lookin' for you."

"I'm sure you were," Roger replied.

"Fell in this here pit … think my shoulder's broke."

"Too damn bad."

"C'mon, man ... I'm gonna drown."

"I'magine."

Larry saw Roger's silhouette disappear over the edge of the airshaft. With all his remaining strength he kicked and clawed at the walls of his tomb.

"Get back here, you bastard!" he cried. "I'm gonna kill you! Roger! Dammit! Roger!"

Larry started to cry, but his tears were immediately diffused by the deep waters into which he sank. He was so cold that for a few moments he didn't realize that his head was underwater. He tried to kick back to the surface, but his legs didn't respond. He grasped at the splintered wooden walls with his left hand, peeling the flesh from his fingertips as he was sucked downward. When he expelled the last of his air in a muted, bubbled curse, he sank like a stone.

Larry's last thoughts were of the receding, starry square above him, the sensation of icy hands grasping his legs and the feeling of spectral tendrils spider-webbing around his body, drawing him down into darkness.

Roger waited in the field a few feet back from the steep slope of the shaft. When the sound of Larry's voice faded, he stepped to the edge of the pit and shined his spotlight into the murky water. A silver bubble of air ballooned up from below and broke the surface, sending out small waves that lapped lightly against the invisible sides of the airshaft. He turned off his flashlight and walked back toward the light in the cedar grove. *Ten men down there; and old Ezra Jeffries and Ernie Milts would make twelve. That makes Larry number thirteen*, he thought. *Unlucky for him.*

An' little Orphant Annie says when the blaze is blue,
An' the lamp-wick sputters, an' the wind goes woo-oo!
An' you hear the crickets quit, an' the moon is gray,
An' the lightnin' bugs in dew is all squenched away,
You better mind yer parunts an' yer teachers fond an' dear,
An' churish them 'at loves you, an' dry the orphant's tear.
An he'p the pore an' needy ones 'at clusters all about,
Er the Gobble-uns'll git you
Ef you
  Don't
Watch
  Out!

from Little Orphant Annie
by James Whitcomb Riley

Chapter Twenty-Five

Departure

Don drove Katie and Conner back to mine office in the Jeep while John and Roger followed in their trucks. They parked their vehicles under floodlight at the shop entrance, and Don led them up the backstairs to the engineering office.

As they passed inside, Don noticed that Roger lingered outside on the steps. The miner concentrated his gaze on the dark, cavernous shop below.

"I guess we better go inside," Don said.

Roger hesitated for a moment. "Figured it was either Larry or me that was gonna die tonight," he said.

Don put his hand on the miner's shoulder and joined his gaze into the shop area, noticing for the first time the fierce intensity in Roger's eyes. "I can't thank you enough, me and Katie," Don said. "I'm glad it wasn't you."

When he turned to face Don, Roger had a weary, sad expression, but he managed to give a weak smile. "Me, too."

In his office, Don brushed the papers from his desktop and gently guided Katie to a sitting position beside him. She smiled up at him and he felt her body relax slightly. The rest of the group remained standing.

"My Bronco's pretty much totaled," Don said. "In the morning I'll get someone from the mine to haul it back here to the office."

"What about Larry's truck?" John asked.

"Don't give a damn about Larry's truck," Roger said.

"You reckon he's still out there?" John asked. "Let's go get the bastard."

For a few moments no one said anything but looked toward Roger. As John waited, perplexed by everyone's hesitation, it was Roger who finally spoke up.

"He ain't goin' nowhere for a long time," Roger said as he moved toward the door. "I'll call the sheriff in the mornin'. C'mon, John, it's time to hit the hay."

"Let's meet at Cooper's around seven in the morning," Don said. "We'll call the sheriff after breakfast. That okay with you, Conner?"

"Sure, Don. Whatever you say."

When they reached the bottom of the stairs, Roger stopped and turned to face John.

"You reckon you can keep yer mouth shut 'til then?" Roger said.

"I 'magine. Let's go home."

An hour later at the Johnson house, Don sat at the kitchen table drinking coffee with Conner. Their talk centered on Don and Katie. Unspoken was a shared knowledge that Larry Miller would not be part of that future, so the big man's past actions and recent fate did not figure into the conversation.

"Are you sure you're alright?" Don asked. "That looked like a pretty violent accident. Aren't you shook up just a little?"

"Shook up?" Conner laughed. "Hell yes. I got no broken bones, but I bet I'll be stiff in the mornin'."

After taking a shower, Katie put on her long flannel nightgown and walked into the kitchen. "I think I'm going to stay here for the night," she said to Don. "I'm worn out and I need to pack some more things."

Don stood up from the table and bent down to kiss Katie on the cheek. "As long as you think you'll be okay," he said.

"I'll be all right," she replied.

"We'll need to use your Jeep to run down to my place," Don said, pulling on his jacket. Is that okay?"

"Of course. Now take this dear man home and put him to bed," she said, standing on her toes to kiss Conner on his cheek. I'll see you both in the morning."

Katie locked the back door after the two men left. She walked through the house checking every door and window to ensure that they were latched, then went to her mother's bedroom. She climbed atop the quilted bed and sat with her back to Rose, knees drawn up under her chin and arms around her legs. Rose took a brush from her nightstand and slowly stroked her daughter's long dark hair. After a few long minutes of uncomfortable silence, the young woman untangled her thoughts.

"Momma," she said, turning her face toward Rose. "Are you all right with me and Don?"

"Of course, I am, child," Rose said. "Of course, I am."

"But you always made such a big deal about me and Larry…"

"Shush! I don't want to hear about him no more. Let's talk about your beau. He seems like such a fine boy."

"He is momma; more than you can imagine."

"Oh, I don't know about that."

"What do you mean?"

Rose looked into the mirror on her vanity, indulging herself in a few reflective moments. Then she began to brush Katie's hair again, increasing the length of each stroke.

"Well, to tell the truth, he reminds me of a young man I once fell in love with."

"Daddy?"

"Yes," Rose replied softly. "Your Daddy."

"Oh," Katie sighed, turning her face away from her mother. Rose put down her brush and began to gently work a tangle out of her daughter's hair with a large comb.

"I know what yer thinkin'," Rose said after a few minutes. "Yer thinkin' how nice it would be to have your Daddy around right now, aren't ya?"

"Yes."

"Well, you still can, ya know."

Katie sat up straight and turned around to face her mother. "What are you talking about?" she asked.

"I need to talk to you about somethin'," Rose said, smiling sadly.

Throughout the day after Halloween, the world around Daggett Number Seven began to change. Toward late afternoon, the soft autumn sky grew dark with low winter clouds. The only light in Conner's kitchen floated through the dusty window, and the old miner looked out through the gray, his crease-etched features softened by the late sun.

"Well, we'd better get going, it's almost dark," Katie said, looking past Conner and out the window where Don was loading a suitcase into her Jeep. She picked up the old man's coffee cup, rinsed it out under the tap, and turned it upside down on the drain board. Then she walked around the darkened side of the table. From behind she draped her arms over Conner's stooped shoulders, placing her chin on top of his head and joining his gaze out the window.

"You don't need to get up," she said, patting her hands on his chest. After a little pause, she added, "He's a good man ... you said so yourself."

"So, I did," Conner sighed. "How's your mother?"

"She's fine," Katie replied, reflecting on last night's conversation with Rose. "Momma asked about you, too. Said you ought to come over for dinner tonight."

"She did, did she?" Conner asked.

"Yep, and I think you should take her up on it."

"I reckon I will, now that I don't have to look after old Don out there."

"Now, I told you we'd be back inside a week," she softly scolded. "After that, I may still need some help with old Don out there!"

"That you might," and he chuckled. "Now git, before I get all blubbery."

"I love you, Daddy!" she whispered in his ear, kissing his cheek. Then, her light steps barely discernible across the wooden floor, she ran out of the house.

Conner watched her go, her auburn hair bouncing as she danced across the wooden bridge and through the evening-wet grass. Wiping the moisture from his own eyes, he rose from the chair and walked quickly to the front door. He got to the edge of the porch just as Don backed the truck around and began to roll forward. The engineer rolled his window down, and Conner could see Katie smiling from inside the cab.

"We'll be back in a few days," Don said.

"You bring that pretty new wife of yours by so's we can talk," Conner said, leaning against the railing. He watched the truck pull out onto the gravel and stayed on the porch until he could no longer see the road dust rising above the corn.

"We're really doing this aren't we?" she asked.

"Yep," Don said, laughed, and asked: "Where to from here?"

"Anywhere you want to take me," she said, sliding across the seat. She wrapped her hands underneath his right arm and laid her head on his shoulder. "Let's just go there!"

Don downshifted as the truck hopped onto the asphalt that ribboned its way through the hills and headed south. Shifting into high gear, he settled back against the seat and pulled Katie closer to him.

There's a song that they sing when they take to the highway,
A song that they sing when they take to the sea,
A song that they sing of their home in the sky,
Maybe you can believe it, if it helps you to sleep,
But this one works just fine for me.

Goodnight, you moonlight ladies, rock-a-bye Sweet Baby James,
Deep greens and blues are the colors I choose,
Won't you let me go down in my dreams,
And rock-a-bye Sweet Baby James...

Sweet Baby James
James Taylor

Epilogue

The high wind pulled thin clouds across a moon that rose stained-glassed against leafless trees. From the shadow-webbed corner of a broken field, a few sentry stalks of corn clacked in the low, chill breeze. A light frost muted their sound and burdened the leaves of dried grass that wavered at the edge of the lightless woods.

A few yards back into the trees waited the owl, eyes closed, clutching a low branch that rose and fell with the wind. She sensed the vibrations of a dragline that worked silently less than a mile away, deep oscillations that moved across the ground, up through the tree roots and out to the branch on which she perched. The vague, white-footed outline of a field mouse whiskered a darkened trail to the edge of the open field. Leaving the warmth and safety of the burrow, it searched for a few stray grains discarded by the combine. At first the movements went unnoticed, or so it seemed. Through the muffled, distant tympany of bucket-dropped rock, the dry staccato of oak leaves as they were scattered and cartwheeled by the ground breeze, the owl sensed the heat and life of the mouse against the cold earth. Fixing lantern eyes on the forest's edge, she lifted from the limb as it swept upward and on silent wings glided unerringly through invisible branches down toward her prey, death on the wind.

The machine grumbled the rock from over the coal, boom lights ghosting its bulk and graying the woods with each swing.

Made in the USA
Columbia, SC
03 October 2024

43560875R00169